THE ONE WHO STAYED SOPHIE'S STORY

A SOPHIE STAR SERIES PREQUEL
PART ONE

L. J. WEBB

THE ONE WHO STAYED:
SOPHIE'S STORY
BY L. J. WEBB

eBook ISBN 978-1-7330939-6-5
Paperback ISBN 978-1-7330939-7-2

Library of Congress Control Number: 2021900505

The One Who Stayed: Sophie's Story

TABLE OF CONTENTS

**I can do all things through Christ who strengthens me.
Philippians 4:13 NKJV**

CHAPTER ONE

Sophie's daddy never sent her to her room before bedtime, except tonight. She was only six but savvy enough to understand that her parents weren't getting along. She was in first grade and understood what the word divorce meant. Many of her classmates live with only one of their parents or had a stepmom or stepdad.

Many nights Sophie heard her parents speak in angry whispers, thinking she couldn't hear. Their vain attempt to 'not fight in front of her , a failure at best. But tonight was different. There was no fighting, just talking in intonations that were harsh and unkind.

Sophie couldn t sleep. She had to find out what was happening. She quietly got out of bed, opening her door ever so slowly, and tiptoed down the stairs. Her thick, naturally curly dark auburn hair was in a ribbon tied at the nape of her neck. Her mommy always helped her get ready for bed. After her bath, she would find her nightgown waiting for her on the bed. Then her mother would brush her hair fifty times and tie it in a ribbon.

She went down as far as she could so she could hear them without being seen. She could smell the lingering scent of the pinewood from the fireplace even though the fire was out.

Sophie's parents were in the formal dining room, which was to her right as she came down the stairs. She sat on the third step from the bottom and listened. Her body bent down over her knees with her nightgown covering her legs, her arms wrapped around them. She heard papers rustling.

"Luke, I'm sorry. I didn't mean for it to happen this way." Clair spoke softly, sitting forward in her chair, her hand on top of the papers as she pushed them in front of him.

"Don't give me that. You knew exactly what you were doing...How could you?" Luke looked straight into her eyes, his voice harsh and accusing. "An affair with a client?! Did you even think about your husband and daughter when you were with him?!"

"Can we just be civil about this? We have to consider Sophie." Her façade of remorse was gone; her tone no longer conciliatory but demanding.

"There is no way you are taking my daughter with you." Taking up the papers and glancing at them.

"Wesley and I will be doing a lot of traveling now that I won his patent case. It wouldn't be right to drag Sophie around like that."

"You mean he doesn't want bothered with a kid." She gave no response giving credence to what he said. "I want full custody of her. You can see her whenever you want, but you will have no say in her upbringing, education, or medical treatment. Is that understood?"

"That's a bit harsh, Luke, don't you think? I am her mother!"

"You should have thought of that before you got in bed with your client. You're the one in a hurry. I'm happy to see what a court has to say."

She was silent for a long time. No doubt thinking of her options. "You promise I can see her whenever I want?"

"Look, Clair, she is always going to need you. I don't want her to grow up without her mother."

"Ok, then. When can I come to get the signed divorce papers and my things?"

"I'll leave the signed divorce papers with the modifications on the table. Come get them tomorrow when we are out of the house. But you take only your clothes, jewelry, and personal items.

2

Everything else stays here." He knew it wouldn't matter to her, but it felt like he took back a little control by saying it. The man she was leaving Luke for was now a wealthy man, primarily due to her winning his patent case. She could buy whatever she needed.

Sophie heard the chairs scrape on the hardwood floor. Soon she saw her parents come into the foyer. It took them a moment to notice her. She stood to her feet, tears trailing down her face in streams.

"Mommy, where are you going?!"

Clair ran over to her and sat on the stair where Sophie stood. "Oh, sweetheart, don't cry." She pulled on Sophie's hand to get her to sit next to her. "I'm going to be gone for a while. I've been away before. I'll just be gone longer this time. I'll talk to you every day, and we can Skype all you want. Ok?" She took a handkerchief from her purse and wiped Sophie's tears. "Please don't cry."

At that, Sophie threw her arms around her mother's neck and sobbed. "Please don't go, Mama, please...please. Why are you leaving us?"

Watching Sophie begging her mother not to leave was ripping Luke's heart out. He stepped over to her, took her tiny hands from around her mother's neck, and picked her up. Sophie's face snuggled down into his neck. She was sobbing uncontrollably.

Luke turned to Clair and said, "just go. This is too much for her."

Clair stood, tears making tracks down her perfectly applied makeup, as she watched the man she once loved take her daughter away. She stood there for a long-time, wondering if she was doing the right thing by leaving her family for a man she had only met a year ago.

It was too late now. There was no way Luke would ever take her back. She remembered when they met in college their junior year. Her best friend was so crazy about him. She never forgave Clair for accepting a date with him when he asked her out instead.

3

She should have said no; to save the friendship. But the competitive streak in her wouldn't allow it. It didn't take long for her to fall in love with him. Luke was the nicest, most considerate, and moral man she had ever met. She loved him. He was all she needed, and then when Sophie came along, they couldn't have been happier.

Clair couldn't pinpoint the moment she started feeling dissatisfied with her marriage. She longed for more stimulation. It seemed all she and Luke did was work or study for his exams.

Wesley came into her life at that vulnerable time, and things went from there. If she hadn't taken him on as a client, she would have worked through her discontentment and come out the other side, with her family in tack.

With that in mind, Clair left the house without looking back. She got in her car and convinced herself she was doing the right thing as she drove away.

Luke carried Sophie to her room. His arms wrapped tight around her. He went to the rocker he used since she was an infant. That rocker had traveled with them to every house they lived in.

He sat down and rocked her back and forth, back and forth. Softly shushing her in her ear to calm her. Her body was still racking with sobs. As her body calmed down, he thought she was asleep. He started to get up to put her to bed, but she clung to him, so he sat back down.

Sophie looked up at him, "Daddy, who's going to brush my hair at night, and put out my nightgown?" Her voice was hoarse from the sobbing.

The words were a dagger in his flesh. The lump in his throat almost too big for him to speak. "I will, sweet pea, don't you worry. I'll take care of you." Luke sat in the rocker with Sophie all night. He could hear her whimpering in her sleep.

His situation plagued him. How could he have been so blindsided? He didn't have a clue. Wesley Cornish was an

4

internationally known inventor. He asked Clair to be the lead counsel on his patent infringement case. They discussed how it would affect the family. Luke agreed to take care of the house, and Sophie. He even did some paralegal work for her so she could make a name for herself.

Right after they got married, they moved to Charlottesville, VA. Luke joined the Army as a paralegal. The Army would guarantee an income and pay for both their educations. After Clair passed the Bar, Luke started taking classes to finish his law degree. Luke passed the Bar six months ago.

Luke thought they were happy. He was. What did he miss? It was torturing him. The not knowing, the betrayal, the loss of the woman he thought he would grow old with. He tried to control his sobs; he didn't want to wake Sophie and cause her more pain. So he sat there rocking back and forth, praying to the only One who knew his future and could take the pain. Then he sang softly all the worship songs he could think of. He was grateful his parents raised him in Church. How would he survive this without Jesus to carry him?

At some point, Luke must have fallen asleep because Sophie woke him when she sat up. She placed her tiny hands on both sides of his face, like she had done since she was little, and said. "Daddy, I had a dream last night. Jesus came to see me. He held me in his arms and told me He loved me and would never leave me." She kissed his cheek. "Isn't that wonderful, Daddy?"

"Yes, sweet pea, indeed it is." Her words flooded through his body like a healing balm, and a peace came over him he couldn't explain. He knew the suffering wasn't over, but it gave him hope.

Luke was having a hard time deciding what was best for Sophie. Should he keep her routine and send her to school or acknowledge the trauma and give her some time.

After finding clothes for her to wear, he went and got showered and dressed for the day. Sophie asked, "Daddy, I need you to fix my hair."

Luke had no idea how to do the French braid Clair always did for her or even a regular braid, for that matter. A ponytail, maybe, but he figured how hard could it be? Luke sat on the bed, and she brought over her vanity stool and sat in front of him. He untied the ribbon that was holding the few strands of hair left in it after last night. Luke tried to brush through her long dark curly hair. He started to brush it, but the tangles were too much. So he grabbed a wide-tooth comb. That seemed to be doing the job. After getting it smooth, he grabbed her hair in one hand and took the scrunchy and wrapped it around the hair. He then pulled the ends in opposite directions to make it tight.

There, he thought, *all done.* Then he looked up and saw the tears reflected in Sophie's vanity mirror across from them. What he thought was perfect was a mess. It was lopsided with loose hair hanging out everywhere. Her bangs were half caught up in the ponytail and half not.

Right then, he knew. He was not sending his daughter to school looking like this. He took out the scrunchy, turned her to face him, and said.

"We're playing hooky today." Luke had already emailed his boss explaining the situation asking for a week off to get his house in order. "No school for you and no work for me." He kissed her forehead. "We're going to the zoo." At that, he brushed her hair straight, grabbed her coat, and they headed down the stairs.

After eating at Sophie's favorite Waffle House, they spent time at the zoo. They spent extra time at the monkeys and went to the observatory and watched the stars. It was a great way to forget about everything.

They ate more junk food at the zoo for Lunch, so Luke thought it would be a good idea to eat something healthier for dinner. They stopped at the Olive Garden and then headed home.

Seeing Sophie happy did wonders for him. As soon as they left the house, the heaviness lifted; as they headed back, he wondered if it would return.

Luke let go of her hand to unlock the door and opened it for her. She stepped into the foyer and froze. When he stepped in behind her, he felt the depression come back. It was there looming, heavy, so heavy you could breathe it.

Tears welled up in Sophie's eyes; she dropped her coat and wrapped her arms around his legs. "Why did she leave us, Daddy?"

At that moment, he decided he would get them out of this house as soon as he could.

Sophie was in the bathroom, brushing her teeth. Luke came in and put her nightgown on her bed. He grabbed the brush and the ribbon he had dropped on the floor that morning and waited for her. Luke made sure to brush her hair exactly fifty times. He sang her favorite Sunday School songs while she counted, and he tied the ribbon to hold it for the night.

After they knelt to say their prayers, he tucked her in, planning to sleep on the couch tonight. He couldn't stay in the bedroom without Clair. Not yet. But Sophie wouldn't let him go.

"Don't leave me, Daddy!" She cried. So he pulled the trundle from under her bed and laid down on it, not bothering to pop it up. She made sure her hand was touching him the whole night. He never moved an inch, still wearing his street clothes.

He lay there awake, deciding what to do next. The first thing he was going to do was find a Hair Salon. Someone needed to show him how to do a French braid and a ponytail on Sophie's hair. Then he would find a housekeeper and nanny for her so he could get back to work.

Only with your help Lord, will we make it through this. Please don't let this change Sophie's sweetheart. The heart you gave her. He prayed before he fell asleep

7

CHAPTER TWO

*L*uke was talking to Ms. Allison, their new housekeeper, and Sophie's nanny. Two months had passed, and it felt like there was light at the end of the tunnel. The first week after Clair left was brutal. Clair had only called to Skype with Sophie once. At first, he was angry she hadn't called. But seeing Sophie spend the entire time crying and begging her mom to come back; Luke decided it had been a blessing. He spent that night rocking her again.

Luke didn't want a repeat of the first week, with him laying a few inches off the ground on her trundle, hearing her whimper through the night.

Sophie's birthday was in two weeks, Ms. Allison was planning a birthday party. She invited all the kids in Sophie's Sunday School class. Ms. Allison knew them because she was their teacher. She asked Sophie who she wanted to invite from her first-grade class.

Luke was so thankful Ms. Allison agreed to come out of retirement to take this job. He would be lost without her. She had two grown children and four grandchildren, but none of them lived close by. This gave her a lot of flexibility in her hours, which he needed at times with his job.

They were discussing gifts for Sophie when the phone rang.

"Hello?" Luke answered, stepping away from Ms. Allison.

"Luke, it's me," Clair said.

Hearing her voice still caused him some pain. "What do you need, Clair?"

"Don't be like that, Luke. It's Sophie's birthday soon, and I wanted you to know I'm sending several packages. I would appreciate it if you would give them to her when I call on her birthday, so I can see her unwrap them."

He took a deep breath. "You're not coming to see your daughter on her birthday!?"

Clair hesitated to answer. "No, we are going to be in Japan. Wesley has an important customer there who wants a preview of his new system."

"Clair, you can't do this to her. She is expecting to see you." He took a breath to calm himself. "You haven't come back once since that night."

"Don't you dare try to guilt-trip me, Luke! I would be there if I could." He knew there was no point in arguing with her.

"Don't call between 3 and 5 pm because Sophie's having a birthday party. I won't let you upset her by telling her you're not coming." There was a pause before she spoke again.

"I want you to tell her for me. She will take it better that way."

This time he didn't try to hide how angry he was. "I am not doing your dirty work for you. You are the one who is breaking your promise, so you are the one who's going to tell her. Do you hear me?!"

"Ok, I'll tell her when I call. Stop yelling at me!"

He hung up before she could say anything else.

Sophie's birthday party was a huge success. He hadn't seen her this happy in months. Her friends laughed and played games while the parents looked on and even joined in at times.

Sophie hauled her loot upstairs. Luke and Ms. Allison were cleaning up remnants of the festivities when his cell phone rang. He saw Clair's face when he answered. He always thought she was one of the prettiest women he ever knew. Seeing her was still hard for him.

"I would like to speak to my daughter now." Clair said, "and if you would bring her gifts out for me, that would be great."

Luke didn't respond. He went to the closet to grab her gifts and put them on the living room's coffee table. Then he went to the stairs to call Sophie.

"Sophie, phone for you." He could hear her running from her room.

He handed her the phone and pointed to the living room and the presents. Her eyes got big, and she went to sit down.

She saw her mom's face on the phone and got excited.

"Mommy, hi."

"Hello, Sweetheart. How was your party?"

"It was so much fun, Mommy. I wish you could have come. Are you coming tonight?"

"Let's open your gifts. I know you're going to love them."

Sophie handed the phone to her dad so her mom could watch her opening the gifts. The first one was a pretty dress she could wear to Church, a hat, and a new pair of shoes. Sophie told her mom how cute they were. She moved on to the second gift, which was a high-end telescope. Clair could see she wasn't sure what it was.

"It's a telescope, Sophie. I know how much you love to look at the stars. Now you will be able to see them close up."

"That's wonderful, Mommy. Thank you. Are you coming tonight to watch the stars with me?"

Luke was watching. He had no idea how Sophie was going to react. Sophie took the phone from her dad.

"No sweetie, mommy can't come. I'm in Japan. I can't get a plane back in time. But I will see you real soon."

Sophie's face went blank. No expression. Finally, she spoke.

"Thank you for the wonderful gifts, Mommy." Then she got up and handed the phone back to her father. She never even said goodbye.

Luke could hear Clair holler for Sophie to come back, but it was too late. Sophie was gone. Luke turned the phone to see Clair.

"She didn't say goodbye," Clair said, crying.

"I don't know how this is all going to work out. But it's going to take a lot more effort on your part if you want to have a good relationship with your daughter." He had nothing else to say but didn't hang up on her this time. He said goodbye and went to check on Sophie.

Luke saw Sophie sitting on the edge of her bed and knelt down in front of her. He expected her to be crying, but she wasn't. She was staring at a spot on the carpet.

"Sweetheart, are you ok? You never said goodbye to your mother."

Sophie put her little hands on both sides of his face and looked in his eyes. "Daddy, you have to stop crying about mommy. She's not coming back. We'll be ok. We'll take care of each other."

"Sophie, you know your mother loves you very much."

Sophie never responded; instead, she looked away. "You know that, right?"

She looked at him again. "Not as much as you."

"Why would you say that Sophie?"

"Because you're the one who stayed."

Luke leaned back on his heels, his hands on his thighs, knowing he should have a response to that, but he didn't.

With that, she gave her dad a big hug. Then moved from in front of him and started putting her gifts away.

Luke sat there, stunned.

Luke finally finished the eleven-week course on military law, passing the exam in the top ten. He got his commission as a full-fledged Jag officer with the rank of 1st Lieutenant. As soon as he received the results, he went to administration and put in for an overseas post. The only one available was in Adana, Turkey, the Incirlik Air Base. The Army shared the base with the Air Force.

The US was teetering on the brink of breaking ties with Turkey. The President was working to mend the strained relationship. Having bases in Turkey was essential to keeping peace in that region. All the military bases in Turkey had been reduced in size due to the impending closure. Now they needed to restaff them. Turkey was back on the list of overseas bases that allowed dependent families. Luke's request for transfer was granted. With one caveat, he had to be there in two weeks. There had been a blunder in filling the Jag Unit posts there, and they needed him immediately.

Sophie had fallen asleep in the transport vehicle once they got off the plane in Adana, Turkey. The housing for military families was not on base. The Military had leased property from the Turkish government adjacent to the base.

It had been an extraordinary feat to leave Virginia in two weeks. They compensated him by promising a private, fully furnished home. He put everything from his two-story home in storage, which the Army paid for, except for Sophie's room. He had everything of hers packed and transported by the Army. It would take a month to get to their new post, but he didn't want her life disrupted more than it had already been.

He only had a few days before he had to report to his new job. He borrowed a car from the carpool until he was assigned one by his unit. He used one day to take Sophie to her new school. The office attendant allowed him to show her around. He wanted her to feel comfortable the first day of school, which started in four weeks. Then he took her to the Commissary and the PX to pick up things they needed.

Luke had to report to his new Jag Unit early the next morning. He hadn't been able to find a housekeeper or nanny for Sophie yet. His only option was to take her with him, hoping his Unit Commander would understand.

As he made it to the second floor, he saw the unit secretary sitting at a desk. The Jag Unit was laid out like a lot of large corporations. In the center were desks separated by dividers. On the perimeter were four offices, two small conference rooms, and one larger meeting room. He could see two large plasma screens through the large window.

Luke stepped up to the secretary. "Excuse me, ma'am, I'm Lieutenant Star. I'm supposed to report for duty today."

She smiled and stood, looking over at Sophie. "Yes, sir, the Colonel wants to see you immediately."

Luke wasn't sure what to do with his daughter. He looked down at Sophie, who was looking up at him. The woman came around her desk. "My name is Ruby Diaz. I'm the Unit Secretary. Let me set your daughter up in one of the council rooms until you get assigned an office." She reached out to take the briefcase in Luke's hand and with the other, extended her hand for Sophie to take.

Luke didn't hesitate. He squatted down in front of Sophie, "go with Miss Ruby, and I'll come to get you in a moment, ok?" Sophie gave her dad a hug and took Ruby's hand.

"Colonel Price is waiting," she pointed, "his office is the second down on the left."

"Thank you." Luke went to the door and knocked once.

"Enter."

Luke walked at attention to within two paces of the desk and saluted. The Colonel reciprocated the salute and said, "At ease, Lieutenant, have a seat."

"Thank you, Sir." Luke took a seat in one of the two wooden chairs that had padded seats and backs that sat opposite the Colonel's desk.

The Colonel opened a file in front of him and took a quick glance. "This is your first position as a Jag Lawyer? You were a paralegal in Virginia?"

"Yes, sir."

"Are you aware you will be the only Jag officer on site until a new Unit Commander is appointed? A new commander and another Jag officer are scheduled to arrive in two weeks. They released me before replacing me. Another snafu by the staffing department."

"Yes, sir."

"Well, luckily, we have no trials on the rotation. The one Court Martial trial is scheduled in two months. As a first year, you will only handle civil, contract, or estate law until you have a supervising Jag officer here."

"Yes, sir."

"Ruby will appropriate a vehicle for you from transportation and assign you an office. She is a great resource if you let her be. Her husband is the Military Police, First Sergeant of the Day Watch." The Colonel turned his chair so he could look out the window. "You have your pick of offices since you are the first to arrive. You will have to use the three paralegals assigned to our unit, to help you navigate until you are up to speed. You'll need them to do a lot of the legal filings until the other officers arrive."

"Thank you, sir."

"Normally, I would take the time to ask you about yourself and get to know you, but this is my last day, so there is no point." He pointed to a round table in the corner, "those are active files. Read through them as quickly as possible so I can answer any questions before I leave today at 5 pm."

"Yes, sir."

The Colonel stood and extended his hand. Luke stood and shook it. "Good luck, Lieutenant."

"Thank you, sir." Luke turned and left the room, releasing a breath. He was more nervous than he realized.

The One Who Stayed: Sophie's Story

CHAPTER THREE

*C*aptain David Scott rubbed his hand over his short black hair while looking out the window. He watched the rain trickling down; he had a lot on his mind.

The Captain's office was on the third floor of the Kelley Barracks Bldg. #3312 on the Stuttgart Army Base in Stuttgart, Germany.

Annie, where are you? I know you're out there somewhere. The plan was for us to go back to the States at the end of this tour, but I can't. I can't leave without knowing what happened to you...

Oh Lord, you have to direct me to her. Somehow. Please, Lord.

"Captain Scott...Captain."

David hadn't heard Staci, his civilian secretary. He turned to her, "I'm sorry, Staci. My mind was somewhere else."

"Duke's baseball game, sir. If you don't leave now, you'll be late."

David moved to his desk to shove in the rest of the files he needed to take home. "Yes, of course. Thank you."

David walked to the bleachers. The Base Elementary School allowed the summer sports programs the use of the facilities. The rain had stopped, and the heat was setting in; David took off his uniform jacket. Looking around, he spots his best friend, Jonathan, waving him over. As he moves closer, he hears Jonathan's youngest son, Liam, call to him.

"Unk Dade," Liam said as he reached up for David to pick him up. When he was one year old, 'Unk Dade' was as close as he could come to Uncle David. The name stuck. David reached down, lifted the little guy off his mother, Zoey's, lap, and gave him a big hug.

"How's my big man. How old are you now?"

Liam laughs, "I tree, Unk Dade. I tod yu." Liam holds up three fingers. David laughs as he sits and puts Liam on his lap. Liam inherited his mother's black hair and hazel eyes.

"Hi Zoey, have I missed anything yet?"

"No, the team's warming up." Jonathan's wife responds.

.

The smiling group ends up at the Stuttgart Base Pizza Parlor after the game.

David's son Duke and Jonathan's oldest son C J, short for Conner Jeremiah, were nine years old. They scarfed down their food, so they could play the arcade games in the corner. CJ's blond surfer looks and blue eyes came from his dad, a complete opposite to Dukes dark hair and brown eyes. David pulled out a ten-dollar bill and told Duke to share it with CJ.

"Me, me." Liam stood on his chair and hollers at his brother.

"Alright, you can come too. You can help me beat Duke on the race cars." CJ went over to grab his brother's hand and help him off the booster seat.

"Jon, I've made a decision. When we signed up on the buddy program, we agreed that we would transition out of the Army at the end of our tenth year. But I can't...I can't do it, Jon," Zoey noticed the tears welling up in David's eyes and patted his arm. "I don't expect you to re-up, but I have to. I can't leave without knowing what happened to Annie."

Jonathan looked over to his wife, she nodded. "Zoey and I have talked about it, Dave. We agree; we're not ready to go home without Anna."

David paused for a moment and smiled. "You know, the recruiting office thinks we're transitioning out. We have our ten years in, so a promotion to Major is a given. What do you say we milk this re-up for all it's worth?"

18

"It should be worth at least a major signing bonus."

"Yeah, and the post of our choice."

"What's on your mind?"

"Incirlik Air Base at Adana, Turkey. The Army and Air Force share the base. It's close to the border of Syria, where Anna disappeared; Faiz is still there. He has never stopped searching. I know he feels guilty about what happened." He pushed around some pizza crust on the paper plate in front of him. "It wasn't his fault; he did the right thing by finishing his mission. He needed to get that family to the next checkpoint. He came back to look for her as soon as he could."

Faiz worked with David's father and brother's non-profit. 'Mission of Peace.' The organization feeds the hungry all over the world. But it was also a front for the extraction of persecuted Christians. They have also been known to extract politicians — those out of favor for fighting for democracy. Faiz was supposed to come out himself on that last mission. He decided to stay after the accident to hunt for Anna.

"It's a good idea to move closer to the border. We'll find out what happened, Dave. I know we will." David nodded his head.

"I heard that the Administration made a blunder in staffing the Jag unit at Incirlik. The Commander and two of the litigators retired, and they have no one to replace them." David said, grabbing the last piece of pizza.

"That's because the US was going to pull out of Turkey," Jonathan said.

"That was the plan until our new President decided to try to mend the strained relations." David looked over to the arcade to check on the kids. "Alright then, we go in together tomorrow and play hard to get. Let's see what they will put on the table." Jonathan and David smiled and shook hands.

David and Jonathan received a myriad of bonuses and benefits for re-upping. In particular, fully furnished single-family dwellings. The one negative involved their choice of post. If they wanted Incirlik Air Base, they had to be there in two weeks.

Packing their belongings and transitioning out of the Stuttgart Base took a week. The trip hauling U-Hauls behind their SUV's took three days. It didn't leave much time for settling in.

Along with Duke and CJ, David and Jonathan had finished unloading the second U Haul of the day. They replaced some of the furnishings the Army provided with their own. They were ready to take those items back to the Housing Dept. and return the U Hauls when Zoey sent out some iced tea for them. David and Jonathan sat on the bumper of the U Haul and rested as they drank it.

"Hey, Dad," Duke said, "can CJ and I go check out the Park we saw on the way in?"

"Not yet son. I have no idea how safe it is here. Let me get some intel, and we'll all go together." David drank the last drops of his tea and handed his and Jonathan's glasses to the boys to take inside. They got in their SUV's hauling the U-Haul behind, and headed to base.

On the way out of the housing complex, David saw a Military Police vehicle making rounds. David waved him over and pulled to the curb. He and Jonathan got out of their cars to speak with the MP.

The MP opened his door and stepped out. "Yes, sir, how can I help you?"

David saw his name and rank on his uniform and said, "First Sergeant Diaz?"

"Yes, sir."

"I'm Major Scott, and this is Major Young." No salutes needed to be exchanged since the Majors were in civilian clothes. "We just moved in down the street." He turned and pointed, "my son was asking about walking to the Park. My question is, how safe is it in this housing community?"

"We do have a burglary off and on, and we deal with domestic violence, but overall, this area has little crime. We have a car on patrol through the night, and it's on our rotation during the day as well. All of our MP's live in the apartments by the Park, so that's added security. It's safe for kids to walk alone during the day. I don't recommend dependents walking anywhere by themselves after dark. No matter how safe we try to make it."

"Thank you, Sergeant Diaz. I appreciate the heads up."

"You're welcome, sir."

It had been a long day, but David knew Duke and CJ wanted to initiate the Park's basketball hoop. He called Jon, and the four of them took a basketball and walked the streets to the Park.

David had seen the layout of the housing community at the recruiter's office in Stuttgart. It was a planned suburb. In the center of it was a 5-acre Park. There was play equipment on one end and a running track that ran the entire Park's perimeter. A small, fenced dog park was on the east side, even though there was no leash law. There were two basketball courts and two fenced tennis courts in the center.

The suburb formed a squared horseshoe. The streets farthest from the Park were the biggest with the largest yards. Houses on both sides of the road were for the highest-ranking officers. Even the Army's General Hughes and the Air Force's General Turner lived on that street.

The next street in, on both sides, the houses were a little smaller but still for officers. On the street that horseshoed the Park, apartments lined the north side and duplexes lined the east and west side. The frontage road that led to the Military base ran along the south side of the Park.

The group made it to the Park at dusk. Streetlights lit it up on all sides. No one was using the basketball hoop, so Duke and CJ ran to claim it. They saw a woman sitting on a bench, a child on the slide and a man pushed a girl on a swing. David and Jonathan finally had to call an end to the basketball game. It was late, and they were all tired.

The next day was Sunday. David checked the internet for the service times at the Base Church for the different denominations. They found the service they wanted to attend and decided to have a BBQ after the service.

David and Jonathan had to report to work on Monday.

Sunday after Church service Luke brought out a box that Clair sent for Sophie.

"Sophie!" She came running in from the small back yard.

"Daddy, are we going to the PX to pick up my school supplies today?"

"In a bit. Your mother sent you a box." He pointed to it on the coffee table. She ran over to it.

"Open it, Daddy." He took out his pocketknife and cut the wrapping tape.

Sophie opened the box. It was filled with school clothes and accessories, including a backpack.

"Daddy, look at this." She was showing him one of the cute dresses. "Can I wear this one on the first day of school?"

"Of course. Whichever one you like."

Sophie hugged him. "These are from your mom, Sophie, not me."

"I know."

"You need to call her and thank her." He handed her his phone.

After the phone call, they headed to the PX to pick up her school supplies and ate at the food court.

Luke and Sophie checked out the Park after work. The unit secretary, Ruby, was at the Park. She had her daughter, Lizzy, the same age as Sophie, and a two-year-old boy named Ricky. The two girls became best friends and spent time together almost every day after that.

The One Who Stayed: Sophie's Story

CHAPTER FOUR

*J*t was the first day of school. Luke pressed the dress Sophie wanted to wear the night before and hung it on the hook behind the door. Now he was fixing her hair in a French braid, a technique he mastered a long time ago. She was all smiles as she looked at herself in the mirror.

After breakfast, they headed to the bus stop. Sophie's was the first stop. Luke was holding her hand. He bent down and said, "would you rather I drive you today, Sophie?"

"No, Daddy, I want to ride with Lizzy."

"Do you remember where your class is?"

"Yes, Daddy, you showed me when you registered me." She put her hands on both sides of his face. "Daddy, I'm a second grader now; you don't have to worry about me." He nodded and kissed her forehead.

"Look! The bus." She hollered.

He watched as she got on and waved at her.

Sophie knew exactly where she wanted to sit. Since she was the first stop, she had the choice of any seat. Sophie had thought about it all night. She stood at the front for a moment then headed to the perfect spot on the bus, the middle seat on the passenger's side. She could see what went on in front of her and could hear everything behind her. *Perfect*, she thought. She sat on the aisle seat, saving the window seat for Lizzy. Sophie set her backpack on the floor.

Sophie watched as other students got on the bus at each stop. About the fifth stop, two boys got on and sat two seats up on the driver's side. They were smiling and laughing. They said hi to everyone as they passed.

Finally, it was Lizzy's stop. She stepped on the bus behind some other kids. Her eyes big, nervous, until she saw Sophie wave at her. She sat next to her and said, "Sophie, your dress is so cute."

"Thank you, Lizzy, my mom sent it. I love your hair, did your mom do that for you."

"Yes," Lizzy answered. "Are you nervous?"

"No. Daddy took me to the school to show me where everything is. Don't worry, I'll show you." Lizzy nodded.

Luke got to work a couple of minutes late. He arranged for Sophie's nanny to meet her at the bus stop after school. Luke hired Deniz Kaya, a local college student, as a nanny and housekeeper two weeks ago. Ruby knew her previous employer and had recommended her. Luckily, she had already been vetted by the Army, which allowed her to go to work immediately. Luke liked her personality the minute he met her, and Sophie already loved her.

Luke was more nervous than Sophie. He was meeting his new Unit Commander and the other senior Jag lawyer today. He stepped off the elevator and smiled at Ruby as he headed for his office. She stopped him.

"They're not here yet." She said, referring to the Majors.

"Good, I won't let Sophie wait at the bus stop alone. I was worried I'd be late."

"Lizzy was so glad she was on the same bus as Sophie. I don't know that she would have gotten on unless she knew she was there."

Luke chatted with her for a few minutes and then headed to his office.

An hour later, Luke heard one of the paralegal's say, "Atten-Hut."

Everyone stood at attention and saluted as the Major's walked in. Luke came out of his office and did the same. Both Majors reciprocated the salute, and the new Unit Commander said, "at ease."

"Hello, I am Major Scott, your new Judge Advocate General, and this is Major Young. He is the new senior Jag officer. I will meet with each of you today so you can bring me up to speed with what you are working on. I know you are all efficient, or you wouldn't be here. I expect you to continue to do your best work in my Unit. Thank you."

Ruby walked up to him and directed him to his office with a hand motion. Before he followed her, he and Jon stepped over to Luke and shook his hand. "You must be the one who was holding down the fort for the last few weeks?"

"Yes, sir, it's a pleasure to meet you."

"Can you meet me in my office in ten minutes?"

"Yes, sir."

After a formal salute, the Major offered him a seat. "Lieutenant Star, this is your first assignment as a Jag lawyer." He was reading his file.

"Yes, sir."

"Why don't you catch me up on the cases you've been working on and what trials are on hold."

After informing the Major of everything he'd done since he arrived, the Major closed his file.

"Lieutenant, I understand you brought your daughter with you to this post."

"Yes, sir."

"And your wife is not with you?"

"No, sir. We're divorced."

"I take it you live in the housing complex next to the Base. There will be occasions we may have to work long hours if we are in the midst of a trial. How will you handle that?"

"I have hired a nanny. One of the qualifications for the job was that she could stay late if needed."

"Good. It doesn't happen that often, but it's good to be prepared."

He sat back in his chair. The sun was behind the Major, coming through the window. It was hard for Luke to look straight at him; he kept squinting. The Major noticed and got up to turn the blinds to a position that deflected the sun.

"Lieutenant Star, I will be pairing you with Major Young as his second chair. He will help you get the experience you need to start taking trial cases on your own. I will be the acting prosecutor until we get another Jag officer assigned. You and Major Young will handle the defense if a defendant doesn't hire a private attorney."

"Thank you, sir. I want to be a defense lawyer."

"As a Jag Officer, you will be called on to be defense lawyer or a prosecutor, depending on the situation."

"I understand, sir."

"That is all. You are excused."

Luke got up, saluted, and waited for the return salute before he left the office.

David went through the entire Unit, talking to everyone and getting up to date on the pending cases. By the end of the day, he was convinced he had an exceptional group of men and women working with him.

Jonathan poked his head in and asked if he was ready to head home. David waved him in.

"What do you think of the Lieutenant, Jon?"

"He's smart, respectful, willing to learn."

"There's something about him. I have no doubt he's a believer. We should try to befriend him off the job. He and his little girl are alone here."

"You know that gets a little dicey when you're his boss."

"Yeah, I get it, but it's the right thing to do. The lieutenant's file says his wife left him for another man."

"Man, that's rough."

"You should be the one to approach him first. It may not be as uncomfortable."

"Sure, no problem. Now let's get home; I want to hear how the first day of school went."

It was three months before Luke was the first chair in a trial. Major Young sat in as second since Luke hadn't quite finished his probation period. Major Scott was the prosecutor. He would generally act as the Judge for this Unit. Unfortunately, they were still short-staffed. They requested that the Air Force Military Judge Advocate General step in for now. Under Section 830a of Article 30a of the UCMJ, it was allowed. The defendant chose to not have a 5-panel member Jury but let the Judge decide his case.

The reason Private Malcom went AWOL was legitimate, but the Army may not see it that way.

Luke had come home late every day this week, and the entire weekend he worked on the case. He barely even spoke to his daughter but spent every moment going over his case.

He was heading to bed and went to check on Sophie like he did every night. This time he set on the edge of the bed. He missed spending time with her. When he sat on the bed, she woke up. "Daddy?"

29

"Yes, sweet pea."

"Are you going to win your case?"

"I'm going to try."

"You will, Daddy. I've been praying for you."

"Thank you, honey. I love you."

"I love you too, Daddy."

He kissed her forehead and tucked the covers in around her shoulders.

Sophie's dad waited with her every morning for the bus. She wanted to tell him she was seven after all and could wait by herself, but she didn't want to hurt his feelings. She hadn't told him about the new kid, Buster, on the bus, a bully who took some younger kids' lunch every day for the last week. If he did it again, she was going to do something about it.

The bus came, her dad kissed her cheek, like always, and she got on the bus; determined. The boys who usually got on before Lizzy's stop hadn't been on the bus for a week. Sophie figured their parents had taken them since they were at school every day. Today they were back. Lizzy got on at the next stop. The big mean kid got on the bus behind her. As he walked toward the back, he stopped at little Cory's bench and grabbed his backpack, looking for his lunch. The bus driver had gotten off to talk to a parent who had a question.

"Give that back to him," Sophie said, standing up with her hands in fists on her hips.

Buster came closer to her, "or what, stupid little girl?"

"Or I'll make you!" He laughed at her and shoved her to the bus's floor.

The dark-haired boy jumped from his seat and moved between them; the blond stood too. "Hey, leave her alone and give back the kid's lunch, Buster."

Buster was big for his age, but the dark-haired boy was taller. They were in the same grade. He moved closer to Buster and repeated.

"GIVE IT BACK!"

Buster didn't want to get into it with someone his own size, typical bully. He gave back the lunch and backed away. One of the third grader's backpack was in the aisle, and Buster tripped over it. Everyone laughed. Buster sat down behind the driver, embarrassed.

The bus driver got back on the bus and hollered. "Everyone sit down now!"

The boy turned to check on Sophie, who was already on her feet. Her hands fisted back on her hips.

"Are you ok?"

"I'm fine." Her rudeness surprised him. He went back to his seat. The driver waited for Sophie to sit before he moved the bus again.

"Sophie, what were you thinking? Buster wasn't going to listen to you." Lizzy said, dusting off the dirt on Sophie's backside before she sat down.

"I know, but he makes me so mad."

"You were rude to that boy." Lizzy nodded toward him, "he was only trying to help you." Sophie hung her head. She knew it, and the guilt was eating at her.

"I was so embarrassed when Buster shoved me to the floor."

"I know." Lizzy took Sophie's hand and squeezed it.

There were no more bus stops; the next stop would be the American School not located on the Base. Sophie knew she had to apologize before they got there. She got to her feet and stood by the boy. He looked up at her and smiled.

"I'm sorry. You were just trying to help me." She said with her head down.

"It's ok, Sophie, you were very brave to stand up to him."

"You know my name?'

"Everyone knows who you are. You're the girl who doesn't let anyone eat alone at lunch."

They both smiled. "My name is Duke; this is CJ," he pointed to him.

"Get back to your seat," the bus driver yelled.

Sophie sat down. She had no idea others saw that she invited anyone sitting alone to her lunch table. As Sophie saw Buster sitting alone in the first seat behind the driver. She wondered what made him so mean. But she refused to feel sorry for him.

By lunch, what happened on the bus had spread through the entire school. Duke and CJ were well-liked; their gregarious personalities drew people to them. They sat with the other popular kids in school at lunch. Some of the girls at the table had made snarky comments about Sophie and Lizzy. Snickering because they invited all the misfits to their table.

As Sophie walked by, one of the girls raised her voice so everyone could hear and said, "Hey Sophie. I heard trying to be a hero didn't work out so well for you."

To her credit, Sophie ignored her and went to her seat a few tables down. But CJ didn't like it. Glaring at the girl, he responded, "you realize she was standing up to a bully twice her size. Right?" The table went silent.

A few minutes later, Buster walked over to his regular table with his lunch. When he sat down, the others at the table got up and moved away, leaving him alone. The whole lunchroom saw what happened and snickered.

At first, Sophie was glad he was getting what he deserved, but then she saw how embarrassed and sad he was and felt terrible. She got up and went over to him. The room watched, expecting a scene.

"Buster, if you can be nice, you can come to eat with us." He didn't respond, so she turned to go back to her table. Buster said nothing but grabbed his lunch and followed her.

At CJ's table, the same girl hollered out, "Sophie has a boyfriend," in a sing-song voice.

Jonathan had enough; he picked up his tray and walked to Sophie's table. Duke followed. When they got to the table, CJ asked, "Can we join you?"

She nodded, and the other kids moved down to make room. He was sitting across from Lizzy and looked up to say hello when he noticed her eyes for the first time. They were the lightest blue he'd ever seen, like the tropical waters in the TV commercial. It was as if they looked straight through him. They were eyes he knew he'd never forget.

Luke's first trial was scheduled to last for two days. Private Malcom wanted to stay in the Army. Luke told him that because he came back voluntarily, there was a good chance they would let him stay in. Lieutenant Star explained that no matter how good his reason, the Army did not look kindly on men who went AWOL. There was a good chance he would end up in the brig and lose two-thirds of his pay for at least a month. The biggest obstacle was his Commanding Officer, who insisted on forwarding it to a General Court-Martial. It could have been handled in a Special Court-Martial. Those courts hand down lesser punishments.

The penalties in a General Court-Martial, besides jail time, are stiffer. This includes the loss of two-thirds pay for up to 12 months, a reduction in rank, and/or a dishonorable discharge. That discharge would cost him his VA benefits, his ability to get a government job, and his GI bill benefits. A dishonorable discharge on DD-214 papers could change the course of his life.

No matter how righteous his reason to go AWOL, the Army would not overlook it. If it had escalated to desertion, more than 180 days absent, it would have been worse. However, the reasons can make a difference in the disposition of the charges. And this is what they were fighting for.

Six months ago he got a letter from his new bride; a dear John letter. He heard from his best friend that her ex-fiancé had come back into the picture. The man was rich and wanted her back. But he had treated her terribly. When he got the post in Incirlik, he asked her to come with him. She told him she wanted to finish her master's degree. She was studying to be a pharmaceutical researcher.

He was only 2 years into his four-year stint, and he knew if he didn't get back to her now, he would lose her forever. He asked his Commander for emergency leave. The Commander denied the request because the Base was already running on a skeleton crew.

Private Malcom left the Base on his day off and took a plane home to convince her not to leave him. He convinced her to stay, but he felt he couldn't leave her until their marriage was on a firm footing. He made it back three months later. His Commander pushed for the maximum penalty.

When Luke got back to the office after the first day of trial, he and Major Young evaluated their defense. They were trying to determine if the Judge was receptive to it.

Ruby buzzed him. "Deniz is on the line, Lieutenant." Luke excused himself and went to his office to take the call. He was concerned something happened to Sophie.

"Hello, Deniz, is Sophie alright?"

"Yes, sir. I didn't mean to worry you; she had a bad day, and I wanted to see if it was alright to take her to the movies tonight on Base."

"As long as it's an early showing. Did Sophie say what happened?"

"Yes, but I think she should tell you."

"Alright, take what money you need out of the household kitty in the drawer."

"Thank you, sir."

He went back to work uneasy about what could have happened, but he couldn't think about it now. He had to win this trial. A young soldier's future depended on his defense.

When Luke got home that night, Deniz was giving Sophie a snack before bed.

"Daddy," Sophie jumped up and hugged him. He knelt down in front of her and said, "How are you, sweet pea."

"I'm ok."

She went back to her snack, and Luke spoke with Deniz.

"How was the show?"

"It was good. Do you want me to put Sophie to bed for you?"

"No. I'll do it. Can you stay late again tomorrow if I need you?"

"No problem, Mr. Luke." He watched her get into the car safely and went to sit with Sophie.

"How was school today?"

She didn't answer; she took her milk and swallowed the last of it. Luke took her hand and directed her to his lap, lifting her up.

"What's the matter, honey?"

"There was this big bully on the bus..." She went on to spill out what happened through lunch. He listened and gave her a hug.

"I'm so proud of you."

She looked up at him. "You are? But he ignored me and shoved me down. And to top it off, I invited him to sit with us at lunch."

"That's why I'm so proud of you. You stood up to a bully even though you knew he was bigger and could hurt you. But more than that, when he was on the other end of the bullying, you stepped in again."

"You don't think I was stupid."

"No, I think you *are* remarkable. And I bet most of the other kids think so too. You said two boys on the bus stepped up to protect you."

"Duke and CJ. I don't know their last names."

"If you see them when we're at the Park, introduce them to me. I want to thank them."

"Ok, Daddy." She hopped off his lap. He took her hand to help her get ready for bed. He set out her pj's while she brushed her teeth. Then he brushed her hair fifty times, tied it in a ribbon, said prayers with her, and tucked her in bed.

CHAPTER FIVE

*O*n the second day of court, Lieutenant Star called in character witnesses. Friends who Private Malcom confided in about his marital situation. And co-workers who confirmed his work ethic and his desire to be a career soldier.

Both sides made their closing statements, and now it was up to the Judge to decide.

The Lieutenant asked the guard to take the Private to a conference room before they took him back to the brig.

After they were seated, Private Malcom asked, "do you think I have a chance of getting out of this?"

Luke looked at him and gave him an honest answer. "Mason, I don't think you will come out of this unscathed. If your Commanding Officer hadn't been so aggressive, you would have had a better chance. Do you know what he has against you?"

"It's not me; he's like that to everyone."

"I understand his service is ending in 8 months, so that's good news because you will likely end up back in the same unit. Unless you get discharged."

"Is that what you think...that I'll be discharged?"

"No, I think the Court will be fair and see that your Commander could have handled this. But you will likely do some time and lose some pay. The good news is, if you do make the Army your career choice, you'll be discharged with your benefits in tack." He took a moment to consider his next statement.

"Look, Mason, no matter how this turns out, you need help navigating your life. Do you mind if I tell you my own experience?"

"I'd like to hear it."

Luke went on to tell him how his grandfather was saved in a foxhole on Hacksaw Ridge during WWII. A medic was treating his injuries in the field. While pouring sulfa in his wound, the young man gave him the abbreviated version of salvation. It was enough for his grandfather to ask the Lord into his heart.

When his grandfather got out of the hospital in the States, he found a Church. He spent the rest of his life serving God. Years later, he married Luke's grandmother, who was also a Christian. They raised his father in the faith, and his father raised him the same way.

"I was lucky to be raised in a Christian home. It gave me a moral compass that guided me and convicted me through all the good and bad decisions I made growing up. I married a woman who was not a Christian against the counsel of my father."

Luke told him about the divorce and how hard it was for him. He leaned forward over his forearms on the table and looked down.

"Mason, you need to know that without the Lord carrying me through that time...I don't know how I would have made it." Luke looked up at Mason again and continued. "I'll see to it you get a Bible if you like. Jesus died for *you*. He took the punishment for *your* sins. All you have to do is acknowledge your need of Him, repent of your sins, and ask Him into your heart." The room was silent for a moment, then the Private responded.

"Thank you, Lieutenant, for telling me your story, and I will read the Bible if you get it to me. My family never went to Church, but my mother tried everything to keep my brother and me out of trouble. My dad left after my younger brother was born."

"I'm sorry to hear that." He had nothing more to say. Now it was up to Mason to accept the truth or reject it. All he could do was pray that the Lord would open his mind and heart to the Gospel as he reads the Bible.

Luke stood and reached his hand out to Mason. "Tomorrow, we will get the Court's decision. We'll talk again after that."

The Private stood up, shook his hand, and nodded. Luke knocked on the door, and the guard took Mason to his cell.

The Courts were on the third floor of the same Administrative building their offices were on.

When Luke got back to the office, he asked Ruby if she would find out how he could get a Bible to his client in the brig.

Sophie and Lizzy were going through the lunch line. Lizzy nodded to one of the 'lunch ladies and said, "That's Buster's mom." Sophie looked at the lady. She was the one that kept giving them extra dessert on their trays. She smiled at her then noticed that the lady was wearing a lot of makeup. Sophie could still see a big bruise on her cheek. Sophie's smile disappeared.

Duke and CJ had been eating at Sophie's table since the bus incident. When Sophie and Lizzy sat down, she asked, "where's Buster?"

"He's over there," Duke gestured to a table across the room.

"Why isn't he eating here with us? Aren't you friends anymore?" Buster had changed a lot since that incident on the bus and made friends with Duke and CJ.

"I don't know. Buster said he wanted to eat by himself today."

"And you didn't ask him why?" Sophie shook her head and went to where Buster was sitting. She stood next to him. He didn't look up or acknowledge her, so she sat across from him.

"Buster, what's wrong?" Buster still wouldn't acknowledge her. "Buster!" She said a little too loud.

"Shhhh." He said and looked around.

"Then answer me."

"I don't feel like talking, Sophie."

"You need to tell me what's wrong, or I'll get really loud."

Buster looked at her, "Ok, ok. It's my dad. He gets mean sometimes when he's drinking. Which is all the time."

"Mean?"

"Yeah, he got mad last night and hit my mom." He panicked when he realized what he said. "You can't tell anyone, Sophie! My dad said if we told anyone, my mom would get a worse beating from him." He looked at her until she promised not to tell.

"I promise." She took a deep breath. "How often does this happen?" Buster wouldn't reply.

"Does he hit you?" Still no answer. "Will you please come eat with us, Buster?" He shook his head.

"I don't want to."

"Ok, Buster. But you need to tell someone who could help."

Buster furrowed his brow. "Sophie, no. You promised you wouldn't tell."

"I won't, but you should." She got up and went back to the table, feeling horrible about Buster's situation.

Luke got home early since the trial was over, and there was no more preparation he could do. He expected Sophie to run to greet him. Instead, she sat at the kitchen table, coloring a book. He walked in and sat next to her. Luke could smell the lasagna Deniz had in the oven.

"Hi sweet pea, how was your day?"

"Ok."

Luke looked up at Deniz. She shrugged her shoulders. He got up, and they stepped into the living room. "What's up with Sophie?"

"I don't know. She's been sad since she got off the bus. I asked her what was wrong, but she wouldn't say."

"Ok, I'll see what I can get out of her."

"Dinner is in the oven. The timer should go off in ten minutes. Is there anything else I can do for you before I go?"

"You're welcome to stay for dinner, Deniz."

"No, thank you, sir, my mother holds dinner for me every night. We eat late."

He nodded and watched her get to her car safely, then went to his room to change. The oven was dinging when he got back to the kitchen. He pulled out the casserole and set it out to cool. Deniz

40

already set the table. Luke placed the hot dish on the table, putting a hot pad under it. Then grabbed a gallon of milk.

"Sophie, put that away; it's time to eat." She ignored him.

He reached over and closed the coloring book. "Sophie."

"I'm not hungry."

"That's enough. You need to tell me what's wrong."

She looked at him and started crying, "I can't, Daddy, I promised."

Her statement frightened him. He went to her chair, squatted down, and turned her to face him. "Has someone done something to you? Hurt you?"

Her tears ran down her cheeks onto her shirt. "No, Daddy. I can't tell you because it's not my secret to tell. I promised."

"Sophie, if someone you know needs help, you have to tell."

She shook her head, "I can't, Daddy."

He pulled her close and hugged her. "Alright, sweet pea, but will you do me a favor?" She nodded.

"Tomorrow, talk to your friend again. See if you can get permission to tell me. Only me. Then I can figure out how to help, ok?"

At 9 am, they were back in Court. Everyone stood as the Judge Advocate General came in and brought the Court to order.

"You may be seated." He said. "Before I give my verdict, I would like to address the defendant." Private Malcom stood.

"Private Malcom, your defense put on a strong case. However, when you join the Army, it's not like any other commitment you make. The Army is not a democracy but defends democracy. To do that effectively, the men who join must be disciplined and follow orders. You don't get to make your own decisions as to where or when you go or stay. If this were a perfect world, we would not need armies. But this isn't a perfect world, and we are the Watchmen. We are the ones who stand on the front lines and hold back the enemy. The ones who sound the alarm. We have to be perfect, or like the 'Good Book' says, 'strive to be perfect.'

Your Commanding Officer denied your emergency leave for a good reason. By leaving, you showed you are not ready to be a Watchman. But, I do believe you have the desire to be. So in light of that, I am prepared to give you my verdict."

Lieutenant Star rose to stand with his client.

"Private First-Class Malcom, I find that you are guilty of disobeying a lawful order, and in doing so, you went AWOL. I sentence you to three months in the Stockade. In addition, you will have two-thirds of your pay docked for three months. I also order that you be demoted from E-3 to E-2." He hit his gavel on the desk but continued speaking.

"Private Malcom, I am giving you a second chance. Don't disappoint me."

"Thank you, sir. I won't let you down."

Everyone stood as the Judge left the room.

Major Young stepped over to the Lieutenant and shook his hand. "Good job, Lieutenant. I expected the punishment to be worse."

"Thank you, Major."

Luke asks the guard to give him a minute with his client.

"Private Malcom, I was hoping for a little more leniency."

"Lieutenant, all I wanted was to have another chance to stay in the Army. You got that for me, and I appreciate it." He stretched out his hand. Luke shook it and nodded. As the guard was leading him out, he turned and said, "Thank you for the Bible; I stayed up all night reading it." That's all he said, and then he was gone.

Luke wasn't sure how he should feel. There was no chance Malcom would get off 'scot-free', but he was hoping for less time in the Stockade. Luke gathered his things and headed back to the office. He was glad to have his first trial under his belt.

When he got off the elevator, Ruby told him Major Scott wanted to see him. He put his briefcase in his office and knocked once on the Major's door.

"Enter."

Luke walked at attention to within two steps of the Major's desk and saluted. After the Major reciprocated, he motioned for him to sit.

"I'd like you to evaluate your performance in the court, Lieutenant."

"Evaluate?"

"Yes, how do you think you did?"

"Sir, I knew the Judge wouldn't summarily dismiss the charges. He was guilty, and his only defense was his reason for leaving. All we could hope for was leniency. Detailing the circumstances surrounding the Private's AWOL was our only hope. I planned my defense with that goal in mind. I know the verdict could have been worse. What he wanted was to stay in the Army, so on that front, he got what he wanted."

The Major was tapping his pen on the blotter in front of him. "I see. So you felt your defense was appropriate and successful."

"I don't know that I would say successful but appropriate."

"Alright, Lieutenant. I would agree with your assessment."

"Thank you, sir." He started to get up.

"One more thing."

"Yes, sir."

"The papers came through for your promotion to Captain. I have them on my desk to sign. You have done good work here, Lieutenant, keep it up." With that, he signed the papers and gave them to Luke. "You can pick up your new insignias at the PX."

Luke had a smile on his face and said, "Thank you, sir, I will."

"You're excused." Luke stood, saluted, and left the room.

Luke stopped by the PX to pick up his new brass and headed home. He was still concerned about Sophie's secret. As he walked in the door, Sophie ran up to him and hugged him.

"Daddy, did you win your case?"

"We did good, sweet pea; we did good." She clapped her hands for him.

"I want to show you something; come sit down with me."

They sat on the couch in the living room, and he pulled out the Captain bars from his pocket.

"What is it, Daddy?"

"It's my new brass. I got a promotion today. I'm a Captain now." Sophie jumped up and took the bars to show them to Deniz.

"Look Deniz, my daddy's a Captain now. Isn't that wonderful?"

"Yes, it is."

Deniz moved into the living room from the kitchen where she had started dinner.

"Mr. Luke, congratulations!"

"Thank you, Deniz. Have you started dinner yet?"

"I was just getting to it when you walked in."

"Good, I want to take Sophie out for dinner to celebrate." Sophie jumped up and down.

"Yeah."

"Ok, Mr. Luke, I'll put the food back in the refrigerator."

After Deniz left, it didn't take long for Luke and Sophie to change, although he did take time to redo her hair.

At Shari's Restaurant, after dinner, he finally asked, "Sophie, did you talk to your friend today? Did you get permission to tell me the secret?"

She nodded, "he told me I could tell *only* you. But you have to promise not to tell anyone, Daddy."

"Sophie, I can't promise that. If your friend needs help, I can't hear it and forget it."

"But Daddy..."

"You'll have to trust me to do the right thing, Sophie."

"Ok." Sophie was ready to pass this burden on to someone else.

"Remember when I told you about the incident with the bully on the bus?" He nodded. "After that, Buster tried to be nicer. He would sit at our table and made some friends. Then yesterday, he sat by himself at lunch, so I went to ask why..." She looked down at her melting ice cream on the table. "He was so sad, Daddy.' Sophie looked back up. "He said his dad gets real mean when he drinks and hits his mother."

"Does he hit Buster too?"

"I asked, but he wouldn't answer."

When he heard this, he was outraged. But he couldn't let Sophie see his reaction. He needed time to think, to handle this right.

After he put Sophie to bed, he sat at the kitchen table with a cup of coffee. He picked up the phone and dialed.

"Manny?"

"Luke, how did your trial go today." Luke and Manny had become friends. They spent time playing basketball in the park while the girls played on the swings.

"It went as well as I could have expected. Thanks for asking. My promotion came in too."

"Congratulations." Luke could hear him holler to Ruby.

"Luke got his promotion." He heard Ruby's voice in the background. "Congratulations, Luke."

He smiled, "thanks, guys."

"What's up?"

"I've got something I need to talk through with someone. Can you come over?"

"Of course, I'll be there in a minute."

Luke handed Manny a cup of coffee as he sat down across from him at the table in the kitchen. Luke sat forward, his hands on his coffee cup.

"There is a friend of Sophie's who may be being abused by his father. I know for sure his mother is because the boy told Sophie." Manny furrowed his eyebrows, concerned.

"How much can you tell me."

"I know his name, but he's afraid that if his dad finds out he told, things could get worse."

"Well, that's a valid concern. Who is it?"

"I don't know his last name, but his first name is Buster."

Manny thought for a moment. "Yeah, I know who that is. They live on the third floor of my apartment complex. The dad's a big guy. One you'd expect to see in a plaid shirt with the sleeves cut off when he's out of uniform."

Luke drank his coffee, waiting to see if Manny would go on. He didn't. "What can we do without putting the boy in harm's way."

"Not much. All I can do is approach the man since there is no one pressing charges. But he'll know someone talked."

"We have to do something. Abuse only gets worse, whether anyone tells or not."

"You're right, now that I know I have to do what I can."

"Do you handle a lot of domestic abuse cases?"

"That's the wrong question. If you ask me if there are a lot of domestic violence cases on Base, my answer is yes. But we seldom get called in." He was turning his coffee cup in circles. "Military life is stressful; on everyone. Soldiers and dependents move away from their extended families, their support systems. All their emotional and financial help, even a helpful break from the kids, are thousands of miles away. On top of that, the base pay for enlisted men is low until they are eligible for promotion, creating more stress.

46

Most abusers don't think of themselves that way. But there is a fragile line between anger and violence. Most men come up to the line at some point in their life. That's when you find out what you're made of. Having self-control, and discipline constrains most men. Others with convictions may be able to keep themselves from crossing that line. Christ is the one I trust to keep me on the right side of it.

If the abused turns in their spouse to their Commander, there is a risk the abuser will end up in the Stockade. Likely he will lose a rank, which means a pay cut. Thus more stress. The spouse can't just hop a bus to a relative's house for the evening. What are they to do?"

"Aren't there support groups to handle these things?"

"It's only been in recent years that these issues have been addressed in the military. The problem is the spouses don't trust the counselors. If anything they say gets into the files, it can hinder promotions and pay. It's a catch 22."

"Wow. What will you do?"

"I'll go by his work tomorrow, see if I can talk some sense into him. We'll have to pray that works."

Luke had refilled Manny's coffee, and they sat and talked about other things for a while.

After Manny left, he checked on Sophie before he went to his room. He stood over her and wondered how anyone could hurt their child. No matter how upset he got, it never crossed his mind to hurt his wife or daughter. It was unimaginable to him. He tucked the covers over her shoulders and kissed her forehead.

Sergeant Diaz parked his marked car in front of the bay door at the transportation garage. He spotted Corporal Herschel Krause working on the engine of an RMMV Survivor R.

Manny walked up to him and said, "Corporal Krause?" The Corporal straightened up; he was at least 6'2". He had blond, curly hair, cut short, and was large and muscular.

"Yes?"

Manny nodded his head in the direction of his vehicle. "Can we speak for a moment?"

"Sure." They moved outside. "What can I do for you? Your vehicle need work?" He appeared relaxed.

"No. I have heard some very disturbing things about you, Corporal." The Corporal wiped his greasy hands on a shop rag that was hanging out of his back pocket. Then he leaned his backside on the car.

"Like what?"

"Like you get physical with your family."

"Has someone pressed charges?"

"That's not a denial, Corporal."

"There's nothing to deny until there are some charges, Sergeant."

"That's still not an answer." The Sergeant said.

Corporal Krause stood straight. "I don't respond to rumors. Why don't you come back when someone makes a formal complaint?" He turned to go back to the garage. Sergeant Diaz put his hand out to stop him.

He got within two inches of his face. "You listen to me! If I hear any more about you abusing your family, I'll be back. And I won't be alone."

The Corporal snickered. "You do that."

Sergeant Diaz watched as the Corporal walked back to the vehicle he was working on. Manny got back in his car, convinced now that what Luke told him was true.

Luke was in his office when Major Young came in. "Congratulations, Captain."

Luke stood, "thank you, sir." Major Young sat on one of the two chairs on this side of the desk.

"Would you and Sophie come over to my house Sunday after Church for a celebration? I'll BBQ."

"That's very generous, sir."

"Come over about noon. We go to the 10 am Church service on Base. That will give us time to get things in order. You know where I live?"

"Yes, sir. Your address is on the office contact list." The Major stood to leave.

"Great. My wife will be pleased. She loves to entertain."

"Thank you, sir."

The One Who Stayed: Sophie's Story

CHAPTER SIX

*B*y the time Herschel got home; he was fuming. The more he thought about the Sergeant interrogating him, the more upset he got. When he walked in the door, Amy was putting dinner in the oven. She turned to him and said, "Hello, Hersch, how was your day?" He threw his uniform jacket and hat on the coffee table and got to within inches of her face.

"Who have you been talking to?"

"What?"

"You heard me. Who have you told about our personal life?"

"No one, I swear." At this point, she saw trouble coming. Buster heard the yelling and came out of his room and stood in the corner of the kitchen.

Herschel pushed Amy against the wall. "How many times do I have to tell you that what happens in this apartment is our business. What do I have to do to get that to sink into that hard head of yours?" He kept poking her forehead with his finger.

"Stop it, Herschel." She tried to move around him. He grabbed her and shoved her against the wall again.

"You don't tell me what to do."

"Dad, stop. Leave her alone." Buster said. His dad started toward him. His mother maneuvered around him to stand in front of Buster.

"Don't touch him."

That was the last thing she said before he started punching. Buster tried to wrap his arm around his dad's elbow to stop him from hitting his mother. His dad threw him off, hitting him in the process. When Herschel stopped beating her, he stood up, breathing hard. He walked away, leaving his wife unconscious on

51

the floor. Buster knelt by his mom and held her hand, sobbing. Herschel came back with some rope and pushed Buster away, telling him to go to his room. He grabbed his wife under her arms and dragged her into Buster's room, tying her arms to the headboard. Then he locked her and Buster in the room.

Herschel had put a deadbolt on Buster's door that required a key on both sides. He would lock Buster in there for hours, even a full day, when he punished him. His father also nailed shut the window that led to the fire escaped.

Two weeks ago, Herschel put the same kind of deadbolt on the front door. When he locked it, there was no way out of the apartment without the key.

Saturday, Herschel brought home some tools to fix the kitchen sink. When he left to buy a new faucet, Buster grabbed a hammer and used the claw side to take the nails out of his bedroom window. Then he put the hammer back exactly as he found it.

Buster heard the door unlock a few hours later. Herschel saw Amy was conscious, "I know you squirrel cash away from the grocery money I give you. Where is it?"

"I don't know what you're talking about." He wrapped his big hand around her neck. Buster jumped on his back to try to stop him. Herschel knocked him off. He walked over to Buster with his hand lifted to hit him when Amy yelled.

"It's in the freezer, in the Fish Sticks box." He left the room to check. They heard him open the freezer and throw things on the floor.

After he found what he wanted, they heard him say, "nice." He came back.

"I'm going to play poker with my buddies." He moved closer to her. "You better be in the same spot when I get back." Then he turned to Buster. "If you untie her. I'll beat her, and then I'll beat you. Do you hear me?" Buster nodded his head.

Ruby opened the door and welcomed Luke and Sophie. "Manny is changing his clothes. He'll be right out."

"Thank you, Ruby." Sophie gave her dad a big hug and kiss.

Sophie whispered in his ear, "don't forget to ask the Major about Lizzy coming to the BBQ." Then she ran off with Lizzy to her bedroom.

"Want some coffee?"

"Sure.

Manny came out almost immediately in his blue jeans and T-shirt. "Hey, Luke."

"Hi, Manny." Ruby poured a cup of coffee for him too.

Little Ricky ran up to Luke. "Hi." Luke lifted him and put him on his lap.

"How are you, my man?" He lifted his hand so Ricky would hi-five it, which he did. Then Ricky squirmed down and went to his daddy and hugged him. After that, he ran off. No doubt to bother the girls.

"Manny, did you talk to Buster's father?"

Ruby sat down to listen to the answer.

"I did. For all the good it did." He told them what happen, "I've interviewed a lot of stone-cold men. I have to say he had the coldest demeanor of any of them. I have no doubt he's abusing his family. But there is nothing I can do unless someone presses charges." The room went silent for a moment.

"You said he lives in this complex?"

"Yes, upstairs about two apartments down across the hall."

Lizzy came running in right then, Sophie and Ricky in tow.

"Daddy, can Sophie and I go to the Park until dinner?" Manny looked at Ruby; she nodded her head.

"Sure. We'll watch you guys from the living room."

Ruby refilled their cups of coffee, and they all moved into the living room. Luke looked out the window and saw the girls run to the swings. Ricky stared out the window, crying because he couldn't go with them.

"I'll take you after dinner, son," Manny told him as he patted him on the head. There weren't many people in the Park this time of day, but he saw two boys playing basketball.

Luke sat with Manny on the couch that looked out the window. Ruby sat on an overstuffed chair to the side.

"So, there's no way you could hear anything going on in his apartment?"

"No. But I can unofficially ask the neighbors if they have heard anything."

When his dad left, Buster went to untie his mother.

"No, Buster. If he finds me untied, he will hurt you." He saw tears running down the side of her face mingled with blood, fall onto his bedsheets.

Buster got one of his white t-shirts from his dresser and poured some water from the bottle by his bed on it. He tried to wipe the blood from her face. His heart broken that he couldn't stop his father from beating her.

It was 2 am when he heard his dad come back into the room. He pretended he was asleep on the floor, lying on his sleeping bag.

Herschel moved to the bed where Amy was tied, "you still awake?"

"Herschel you have to untie me."

"You see, here you go telling me what to do again." He squeezed her cheeks hard with his right hand. "You're so stupid. I'm going to have to give you lessons on how to be a good wife." He stumbled to sit on the edge of the bed. "You are not leaving this house again until you can keep something in that ignorant brain of yours."

"You're drunk. Please untie me; I need to go to the bathroom." He sat there for a few moments, then untied her. He took her by the arm and lifted her off the bed, walking her to the bathroom.

"Can I have some privacy?"

"No." when she finished, he tied her back up, locked the door, and passed out on his bed.

Sophie and Lizzy woke up to the smell of waffles. They jumped out of bed and followed their nose, still in their pj's, their hair askew.

Ruby couldn't resist taking a picture of the two on her cell phone and sent it via text to Luke. They plopped themselves in chairs at the kitchen table. Ricky was already there in a booster seat, drinking orange juice.

After breakfast, Ruby sent the girls to their room to get dressed for the day. Sophie went into the bathroom to wash her face and brush her teeth, noticing how awful her hair was in the mirror. She still got a little homesick when she was away from her dad at bedtime. He always brushed her hair and put it in a ribbon.

Ruby came into Amy's room after dressing Ricky to see how they were doing. She offered to help when she saw the result of them trying to fix each other's hair. The girls wanted matching ponytails. Ruby did her magic then put matching barrettes in their hair.

They had to wait for Lizzy's dad to get home before they went to the Mall to ice-skate. So they got permission to say hi to one of their school friends in the complex. The girls walked up the stairs to the third floor and knocked on the door.

"Yeah?" The huge man who answered said.

"Hi, we would like to say hi to Buster," Sophie said.

"He's got chores to do; get out of here." He slammed the door in their face.

The mean man frightened the girls so much they ran down the stairs and went outside. They stopped running when they got to the side of the building. Lizzy put her hands on her knees and tried to catch her breath. Sophie leaned against the building.

Luke couldn't remember the last time he woke up to an empty house. Sophie usually woke him up on the weekend. With no one to wake him, he slept until 10 am. Before showering, he made himself scrambled eggs and toast.

He sat at the table alone; he hated the feeling. Luke and Clair had decided not to have children right away when they first got married. They both wanted careers. But then Sophie showed up unscripted. From the moment he held her, he could not imagine life without her. He thanked God for her every day.

After getting dressed, he decided to go to the gym on Base. A couple of the guys at the office said the equipment was top notch. He remembered to call Major Young before he left the house.

"Hello?"

"Major Young?"

"Yes."

"Sir, this is Captain Star."

"Yes, of course, Captain. How are you this morning? My wife is looking forward to meeting you and your daughter tomorrow."

"Thank you, sir..."

"Please call me Jon."

"Yes, sir, thank you. I had a question. I would usually never impose like this. But my daughter wanted to know if her friend Lizzy could come with us tomorrow. She's First Sergeant Diaz's daughter. The MP day watch Sergeant."

"Hold on a second." Luke could hear him walk somewhere; he couldn't hear what was said. The Major came back and picked up the phone. "Captain, my wife insists you invite the whole family."

"Are you sure?"

"Yes, she hasn't had an opportunity to meet many people in the housing project and would love to meet them."

"Thank you, sir. I'll pass on the invitation." They said their goodbyes, and he headed to the gym. On the way, he used his car's Bluetooth to call Manny and told him about the invitation. Manny said he'd get back to him after he talked to Ruby.

"Lizzy, we have to go back."

"No, that man is scary."

"That's why we have to go back. When Buster's dad opened the door, I could see the dining room table. Somebody knocked over a chair, and I saw broken plates on the floor. It looked like there was a fight."

"Maybe it was an accident." Lizzy stood up straight.

"Lizzy, the day you pointed out Buster's mother, I saw a bruise on her face."

"I didn't see it."

"She tried to cover it with lots of makeup. But I could still see it. When I went to ask Buster why he wouldn't eat with us that day, he told me he was upset because his dad hit his mom. Then he swore me to secrecy.'

"He told you that?"

"Yes, and I think his father hits him too." Sophie looked around and saw the fire escape. It was like the one on the other side of the building that went by Lizzy's bedroom.

She pointed to it. "We can go up the fire escape and look in. Maybe that's Buster's room." Lizzy shook her head.

"Sophie, if he sees us, he could come after us."

"He won't see us; we'll be quiet." They walked over to the ladder. They couldn't reach the spring-loaded bottom rungs. Sophie cupped her hands to give Lizzy a boost. She grabbed onto the last rung; the cold metal caused goosebumps on her arms. The ladder came down.

The girls hurried up the stairs as quietly as they could and reached the third-floor landing. They moved over to the window. It was Buster's room. The blinds weren't closed; they could see in.

57

There was nothing on the walls. All she could see was a bed and a dresser, so different from her and Lizzy's rooms. They could see Buster leaning against the wall with his legs bent and his head resting on his knees. Lizzy pointed to the bed. They saw a woman tied to the brass tubes that made up the headboard.

Sophie tapped lightly with the tip of her finger on the glass. She had to do it again before Buster looked up. He went to the window, pulled up the blinds, and opened the window as quietly as he could.

"What are you doing here? You have to go. If my dad sees you, there'll be big trouble."

Sophie squeezed past him and crawled in the window. Lizzy stayed on the landing. "Buster, you have to come with us." She whispered.

I can't; I won't leave my mom." The voices woke his mother. She couldn't move enough to see who was there.

She whispered, "who are you talking to?"

He moved over to his mother; Sophie followed. "It's Sophie, Mom."

Amy's battered face made Sophie shutter.

Lizzy quietly moved to the other window to see if she could see where Buster's dad was. She saw him grab his keys and go out the door, but he didn't shut the door all the way. She went back to Buster's room.

"Your dad just left Buster, but he didn't close the door all the way."

"He must be getting something from his truck. Sophie, you have to take Buster somewhere safe. Then call the police," Amy said.

"I won't leave you, Mom." Buster moved closer to her.

"Mrs. Krause, we won't leave you here." Sophie went to the top of the bed to untie her. Amy knew Buster wouldn't leave without her; there wasn't time to argue. If Herschel caught them, she had no idea what he would do.

"Alright, we need to be very quiet." Amy grimaced when she tried to move her arms. They were stiff from being in an unnatural position for so many hours; her right arm felt like it was out of the socket.

They climbed onto the fire escape and moved as quickly as possible down the stairs. When they hit the bottom ladder, their weight made it drop.

"Hurry," Sophie said. "We can go up the fire escape on the other side to Lizzy's house. That way, we won't run into your dad. Lizzy's dad is an MP."

When they got to Lizzy's bedroom window, it was locked. Lizzy knocked on it, but no one heard. A few seconds later, Ricky came into the bedroom to get one of Lizzy's stuffed animals he liked. She knocked on the window again; he looked up and smiled. "Sissy."

"Ricky, you need to go get mommy to open the window, ok?" He ran off, and a few seconds later, Ruby came.

"Lizzy, what's going on." Lizzy tried to explain as each one crawled through the window into the apartment. When Ruby saw the state that Buster's mother was in, she went to help her and led her into a chair at the kitchen table. Then Ruby fetched the First Aid kit to tend her wounds.

"Mrs. Krause, my name is Ruby; please tell me what happened." Amy told her everything. Ruby could see the relief in her face at telling someone what was going on in her home. The kids were all standing around listening. Ruby stopped her long enough to ask them to go to the den and watch TV. Buster wouldn't move away from his mom. She told him she was ok now. Amy waited to hear the TV turn on before speaking again. Amy finished telling all that was going on in her home. Ruby said, "Manny will be here soon. He will arrest your husband and put him in jail."

"NO! No." She lowered her voice. "I don't want him in jail. I just want to call my parents. They will get us airline tickets so we can get away from him. I'll divorce Herschel when we are safely back in the States."

"You can't let him get away with this. If for no other reason, then that he needs help with his anger."

"I don't care what happens to him, but if he gets out of jail before I get out of here. I'm dead." Ruby saw her wringing her hands, stressing about it.

"Ok, that has to be your decision. But if that's the case, you need to stay here until you are on a plane." Amy grabbed her hand, then grimaced at the pain in her shoulder.

"Thank you; I couldn't leave before because I had nowhere to hide. I ran once when we were stationed in Japan, but I had to go back because I had no place to go. My folks were on a cruise, and I couldn't get ahold of them." She lowered her head and let go of Ruby's hand; tears started down her cheek. "I paid the price for that."

"Mrs. Krause, would you like to clean up. You can take a shower if you wish. My clothes may be a little big for you, but if you like, I'll get some for you."

"Please call me Amy... and yes." She stopped Ruby when she started to go. "Could Buster get something to eat? We were locked in the room for a long time. He hasn't eaten since lunch yesterday."

"Of course."

After setting Amy up in the bathroom, she poked her head in the den and asked Buster if he would like some waffles and strawberries. He didn't say anything but nodded his head. Ricky jumped up.

"Waffles."

"You already ate, Ricky." His little face was crestfallen. She gave in.

"Ok, you can have a waffle." He lit up.

Herschel came back from his car and closed the door behind him. He didn't lock the deadbolt. He had no intention of letting his family out of Buster's room any time soon.

Herschel made himself a BLT and grabbed a beer. As he ate, he planned how he intended to handle his wife. Since he would be doing all the shopping now, he wouldn't have to give her any money. That way, she couldn't steal from him anymore. He planned on calling the school Monday morning to say Amy quit to home school Buster. That would take care of two birds with one stone.

Herschel put his dish in the sink. Her first lesson would be to make sure she had this home immaculate at all times. He would have her scrubbing the floors with a toothbrush on her hands and knees. He laughed to himself. He would keep her so busy she would be too tired to sass him. He walked by Buster's room and headed to the shower. He would have to let them out soon so they could go to the bathroom. He had no intention of feeding them till he was good and ready.

Herschel finally went to the bedroom door and unlocked it. When he saw they were gone, he panicked. He ran to the open window and crawled out onto the fire escape to see if they were in sight. He didn't see them. *Where could they have gone?* As he crawled back into the apartment, he saw a barrette lying on the metal landing. "Those bratty girls were wearing these. I know one of them is the daughter of the MP who harassed me yesterday." He said out loud.

Herschel ran downstairs to the mailboxes to see what apartment they were in; 218. He rushed to the second floor and found the apartment.

Buster finished his waffle without saying a word. Ruby knew he was traumatized by his mother's beating. Amy came out from the bathroom, dressed, and sat by her son. She ran her hand over his head and kissed his cheek. "We'll be ok, son. We're safe now. We're going to grandma's house in Tennessee." He hugged her tight and cried.

A knock came on the door. Ruby went to the door and looked through the peephole. Her eyes got big, and she ran to Amy and put her finger to her lips, then motioned to follow her to Lizzy's room. Then she went back to the door.

"Who is it?"

"You have my wife and son in there. I want to talk to them."

"I don't know what you're talking about." She got the attention of the girls and Ricky in the den and hurried them into the bedroom. She whispered, "go out the fire escape..." She was interrupted by loud banging on the door.

"Amy, come out here now! Do you hear me?"

Ruby handed Lizzy her phone "call your dad tell him we need help." Ruby helped them get out the window. "Hide in the bushes by the front door until help gets here."

The group started down the fire escape when Lizzy noticed her mother wasn't coming. She went back, "Mom, come on."

"No, I'm going to stall him." When Sophie saw that Ruby was staying, she crawled back into the apartment. Lizzy grabbed her arm to stop her.

"Come on, Sophie."

"No, Lizzy, you need to go take care of Ricky and call your dad. I'm going to stay and see if I can help your mom." Lizzy hesitated but left.

The banging on the door got louder. "Listen, I don't know who you are or who you're looking for, but if you don't go away, I'm calling the police," Ruby yelled through the door.

Sophie watched the last person get off the fire escape and then went into the kitchen. It got really quiet, and Ruby thought Buster's dad gave up and left.

Ruby went to look through the peephole to make sure he was gone when the door came crashing in. She didn't have time to get out of the way and ended up on the floor. She was scrambling to get up. In a blink, Herschel was standing over her. He reached down and pulled her up.

"Where is my wife?"

"I don't know who you're talking about." He shoved her against the wall hard.

"I won't ask you again."

"You can go see for yourself. There is no one here." He turned to go check out the rooms. Ruby was waiting for him to get far enough away for her to run out the door. She didn't know Sophie was still there.

Herschel stopped and reached back to grab her arm and take her with him. Sophie hid behind the counter as he went by and checked out the house.

"See, there is no one here." He stopped to think for a moment letting go of her and rubbing his hands over his face.

Then he noticed Amy's clothes folded on the bathroom sink. "She was here. Those are her clothes. You lied to me." He pushed her against the wall and put his big hand around her neck.

"Where are they? Where did you hide them?

The One Who Stayed: Sophie's Story

CHAPTER SEVEN

*L*izzy called her dad once they hid in the bushes. She was shaking and had to dial twice to get the right number. Ricky was crying. Amy was trying to calm him down so he wouldn't give away their location.

Manny never got a chance to say hello. Immediately he heard his daughters' voice.

"Daddy, come quick. Buster's dad is beating at our door. Daddy, we need you," she said, crying.

"Calm down, Lizzy. Tell me what's happening." As Lizzy was talking, he put on his lights and sirens and headed to his apartment. When she hung up, he got on his radio to call out for any MP's in the address's vicinity to answer a call of an assault.

"This is car 21; I'm in the housing complex. Isn't that your apartment?"

"Yes, hurry. I'm five minutes out," Manny said.

"I can be there in three."

"This is car 6; I can be there in three, too."

"Hurry, please." Then he signed off and called Luke. Manny was weaving in and out of traffic, going at speeds that were not safe for anyone.

Luke answered, "Manny, hi. Did you talk to your wife?"

"Luke, listen. Corporal Krause is beating down the door at my house. Get there as soon as you can. Are you home?"

"No, I'm on Base, but I'll be there as quick as I can." He didn't bother to ask any questions. Whatever was going on was urgent; that's all he needed to know. He had gotten out of the gym's shower when the phone rang. He finished getting dressed in a hurry.

Ruby was turning red, grabbing his hands, trying to get them loose from her neck. He was too strong. Sophie was afraid he was killing her. She grabbed the broom that was leaning against the wall. Ruby was cleaning before all this happened. She snuck up behind Herschel and started hitting him on the head as hard as she could with the broom handle.

The first hit stunned him for a second, then came a second hit. Herschel turned to see who was hitting him. He let loose of Ruby to grab the broom handle from Sophie and pushed her away. Ruby fell to the ground, gasping for air.

Herschel headed over to Sophie, "this is your fault. You are the one who helped them escape. I saw your barrette on the landing. Where are they?" Sophie was crawling backward, trying to get away. She never said a word.

Herschel reached down to pick her up when Ruby jumped on his back and started pulling his hair.

"Run, Sophie. RUN!" Sophie got to her feet, but Herschel had ahold of her shirt. Ruby pulled harder on his hair. He let go of Sophie, took ahold of Ruby's arms, and threw her over the top of him.

There were only a few people in the Park. Duke and CJ were playing basketball when they heard sirens. They moved over to the edge of the Park to see what was happening. That's when they saw Buster, his mother, Lizzy, and a little boy come out of the bushes. The group moved over to the steps of the apartment entrance and sat down. The boys ran across the street.

"Lizzy, what's going on. Are you alright?" CJ asked. Ricky was screaming now, and she was trying to calm him. CJ picked up Ricky and started whispering in his ear, soothing him, and patting his back.

Duke was talking to Buster, trying to find out what was going on. A police car came screeching to a stop at a diagonal, blocking the street, sirens blaring. The MP got out of the car, running right past the group on the stairs.

Ruby was lying on the ground, stunned. Herschel was able to grab Sophie before she got to the door. He picked her up and threw her across the room like she was a gym ball. She hit her head on the edge of the kitchen table and hit the ground, unconscious.

Herschel moved back to Ruby, who was still lying on the ground. He straddled her and put his hands around her neck. Herschel was no longer asking questions. He was in a rage and out of control.

The MP came barreling in and tackled Herschel knocking him off of Amy, onto the floor. Herschel was twice the MP's size. They wrestled; the MP got back on his feet. Herschel stood landing a solid jab into the MP s jaw and knocked him back down. The MP got up and tackled him again. Another MP came in, and between the two of them, they managed to subdue Herschel. They were struggling to get the big man's hands behind his back.

Manny and Luke screeched to a stop at the same time in front of the apartment. They got up the stairs as they were putting the cuffs on Corporal Krause.

Manny saw his wife lying on the ground and ran to her. "Call an ambulance." He ordered.

"Sophie, where's Sophie." Ruby's voice was hoarse from being choked.

Luke heard her say that and looked for his daughter. She was unconscious under the window by a chair. He ran to her; his heart strained to keep beating.

"Sophie?" He was afraid to move her, but he checked her pulse.

Manny came up next to him. He checked her out and saw a bump on the side of her head. He pointed it out to Luke.

"She must have hit her head, Luke. There's an ambulance coming." Manny tried to direct Ruby to the couch, but she staggered over to where Sophie laid instead.

She placed her hand on Sophie's leg and started praying for her, tears running down her face. Ruby put her hand on Luke's forearm.

"She saved my life, Luke." He didn't respond; he was too focused on praying for his daughter.

By the time the ambulance got there, three other cruisers had pulled up. Sophie regained consciousness as the EMT's walked in the door. One went to check out Ruby; the other went to Sophie.

When she opened her eyes, she saw her dad's face looking down on her, holding her hand. "Daddy, I knew you'd come save me." He didn't have time to tell her, she and Ruby saved each other; the EMT moved him aside to get to Sophie. She grabbed his hand tighter, "Daddy?"

"I'm right here, sweet pea. Let him check you out." She let go of his hand.

Manny was giving orders to his men. "Coulter, I need you to take Corporal Krause to the station and put him in one of the cells until I can interrogate him." Coulter grabbed Herschel's arm and directed him out of the apartment.

Private Phillips, I need you to memorialize the crime scene. Get photos, fingerprints, any evidence the Jag can use to prosecute Corporal Krause." His apartment looked like a war zone. "Do you have your CSI kit in your cruiser?"

"Yes, sir." With that, the Private ran down to get it. Manny called out to him. "Find a way to secure the door when you leave." The MP nodded his response.

The EMT's were taking Sophie out on a gurney. Luke followed but stopped to talk to Manny.

"I'm going in the ambulance. Can you have someone move my SUV? It's in the middle of the street." He handed Manny the keys.

68

"Of course, Luke. I'll see you at the Hospital."

When Luke got downstairs, he moved to where an MP was talking to Mrs. Krause. A crowd was growing outside, wondering what was happening. The police had cordoned off the area with Police tape. He hugged Lizzy and Ricky, then asked if they were alright. CJ had put Ricky down but was holding his hand. Duke was standing next to Buster. He thanked them for helping.

"What's wrong with Sophie? Why is she in the ambulance?' Lizzy asked, worried.

"She bumped her head. They're just going to check her out at the Hospital."

"Is my mom ok? That man was beating on our door." She pointed to the man the MP put in the back of a Police cruiser. Luke realized none of them had any idea what happened in the apartment.

"Your dad is bringing her down now." One of the EMT's hollered at him that they were ready to go. Luke kissed Lizzy's forehead, patted Ricky on the head, and got in the back of the ambulance.

Manny and Ruby came down in the elevator. He was supporting her with his arm around her waist. She was still weak from the skirmish with a man that outweighed and outsized her many times over.

Lizzy and Ricky ran to her the minute she stepped out the front doors of the building.

"Mommy, are you hurt? They took Sophie to the Hospital." Lizzy was crying. Ruby knelt in front of the kids and hugged them close.

Amy turned from the MP that was still writing down her statement and went over to Ruby.

"Ruby, are you alright? I'm so sorry I got you involved with this. It was my problem, not yours." Ruby stood up and hugged Amy, "you're wrong. It's important to reach out when you need help. I'm glad you trusted me."

Manny waved the MP over. "Take Mrs. Krause and Buster to the Hospital to be checked out. After everyone is checked out, you can finish taking statements. I'm taking my wife and kids with me to the Hospital now."

The MP nodded and directed Amy and Buster to his cruiser, helping them get in the back seat.

As Manny and his family headed to his marked police SUV, Lizzy pointed out Duke and CJ. "They helped us, Daddy."

Manny walked up to them. "My daughter said you helped. Thank you." Then he helped his family get into the vehicle. Ricky was hanging onto his mother as if his life depended on it. Manny had to loosen his hand from her to get him in a booster seat. All the police vehicles kept a booster seat with their supplies in the back.

When most of the emergency vehicles left, so did the looky-loos. Duke and CJ retrieved their basketball at the hoops and headed home to tell their dads what happened.

David hadn't gotten home yet. His meeting with the General took longer than he expected. The General had some concerns about the new policies he wanted to enact. The General asked David to review them to make sure they weren't in conflict with other procedures.

At the Base Hospital, everyone was in an emergency room. Amy had a dislocated shoulder, some loose teeth, a cracked rib, and a small crack in her jaw. They decided to keep her overnight.

Ruby had bruises on her neck and body, but they released her. Sophie had a concussion and bruises. Since she had been unconscious, they decided to keep her overnight.

Buster had some deep bruises but otherwise he was unharmed; the doctor released him.

Two MP's at the Hospital were taking statements.

Manny and Lizzy went to find out what room Sophie was in.

Sophie was awake in a hospital bed set at a 45-degree angle. Lizzy ran over to her and sat on the edge of the bed, leaning down to hug her. "Sophie, does your head hurt?"

"Yeah, but they gave me some medicine for it."

"Can I stay here with you?" Lizzy asked Sophie but was looking at her dad.

Manny was standing by Luke. "It's up to her father."

Luke knew it would make Sophie feel so much better with her here. "Of course she can stay." Sophie immediately scooted over. Lizzy took off her shoes and laid next to her.

"Manny, what on earth happened?"

"I don't have the whole story yet, but it sounds like the girls found Amy tied up in her apartment and got her out. When Krause found out, he came after them. Ruby sent them all out the fire escape. She planned on stalling Krause. She didn't know Sophie stayed behind to help..." Manny looked over at Sophie. "Ruby said Sophie went after Krause with the broom handle when he was choking her. Sophie saved her life, Luke."

"She thinks I saved them. When she woke up and saw me, she said, '*I knew you would save me*'." He lowered his head, "I need to tell her it wasn't me."

"It won't matter to her. You will always be her hero." Manny patted him on the back. "I'll get a couple of pairs of pj's for the girls when I take Ruby and Ricky home and come back.

"Thanks, Manny." Luke knew the trauma would catch up to Sophie at some point. He would help her deal with it. But right now, she seemed to be handling it well.

Manny went back downstairs after kissing both girls on the forehead.

Jonathan walked into the emergency waiting room. Once Duke and CJ told him and Zoey what happened, Jonathan grabbed his keys to head to the Hospital.

He saw one MP taking a statement from a woman who looked like she'd been in a fight. She was holding a little boy in her lap. He recognized Buster, who was also speaking with an MP. Buster had been to his house many times since he became friends with

71

Duke and CJ. He walked over to him. Buster stopped talking to the MP and stood to hug Jonathan.

"Are you alright, Buster?" He turned to the MP, "what happened here?"

"Sir, are you related to him?"

"No, I'm a Jag officer. My name is Major Young."

"I'm afraid you'll have to talk to First Sergeant Diaz, sir. He'll be right back."

Jonathan sat next to Buster to wait for the Sergeant.

David came rushing into the emergency waiting room. He saw Jonathan sitting with Buster. He sat next to him and asked, "What happened? I called Duke to say I was coming home when he told me you were at the Hospital."

Jonathan was about to tell David what little he knew when Sergeant Diaz came off the elevator. David recognized the Sergeant from the day he first moved to Incirlik Air Base. David stepped up to him and introduced himself. "First Sergeant Diaz, I'm Major Scott, Commander of the Army Jag Unit. Can you tell me what happened?"

"I recognize you, sir." He stretched his hand out to him. David shook it. Jonathan stepped up next to David. Sergeant Diaz explained to both Majors as much as he knew about what happened.

"They are keeping Mrs. Krause and Sophie overnight," Diaz said.

"What about Buster? Does he need a place to stay?" Jonathan asked.

"He can stay with us unless he would feel more comfortable with one of you," Manny said.

Jonathan walked over to Buster and sat down next to him. "Buster, the doctors want to keep your mother overnight. Sergeant Diaz said you could stay with him, or if you'd like, you are welcome to stay with me."

"With CJ and Duke?" Jonathan looked to David, he nodded.

"Yes, you, CJ, and Duke will all be together at my house."

"Can I say goodnight to my mom, so she knows where I'm going?"

"Yes, I'll get permission, then we can go to your house to get some of your clothes."

"NO! I don't want to go back there." He stood up, panicked. Jonathan took his arm and eased him back down.

"Buster, your dad is in jail; he's not there."

"I don't care; I'm not going back!" Jonathan patted him on the shoulder.

"That's fine. You can wear CJ's clothes." Jonathan stepped back to David and Sergeant Diaz.

"Buster wants to see his mom before he comes home with me."

The Sergeant pointed out the receptionist and told Jonathan to get the room number from her.

The only ones left in the Hospital waiting room were the Diaz family.

"I told Lizzy she could spend the night here with Sophie. I'll come back with pj's and toothbrushes after I take you two home."

Ricky had fallen asleep on Ruby's lap while sitting in the padded wooden chairs. She took a moment and laid her head on Manny's chest. He held her and stroked her hair.

"Manny, I have never been so scared. I know Sophie must be traumatized." He lifted her chin and kissed her tenderly.

"You are the bravest woman I've ever known. Putting yourself between him and his wife and son."

"Sophie is the brave one, she saved my life, Manny." She laid her head back on his chest.

"Thank God, she stayed behind."

On the way home, Ruby told Manny that David wants to pay for Mrs. Krause and Buster's tickets to go back to the US.

"He asked me to find out what day and flight she wants and let him know."

"That's very generous of him." Manny commented.

The nurse came in every two hours to check on Sophie. Luke pushed back the recliner into a laying position and rested his eyes. He couldn't sleep; he was to upset. Since Luke was a teenager, he battled anger. His father shared with him what the Lord taught him when he was dealing with the same issue.

Anger is a human emotion. The Bible says, 'Fools vent their anger, but the wise quietly hold it back'. Prov. 29:11 (NLT). Sin comes in when you pass that invisible line from controlled righteous anger to an uncontrollable rage that takes over. If you aren't controlling your emotions, that means someone or something else is. And make no mistake, his father said, you know when you're getting ready to cross that line.

Although Luke could never explain it to anyone else, he understood what his father was telling him.

He did not want the devil to control his life in any area, so he worked hard never to cross that line. Until recently, the only time he let his anger get away from him was when he was a teenager. Luke saw some boys bullying a little kid. He beat up on the bully. It took two adults to pull him off. He ended up spending a week in juvey for that. It was a lesson he wouldn't soon forget. Since the night Clair asked for a divorce, when it came to her, he found himself not even trying to control it. Although, he never even thought of doing her any physical harm. His anger toward her was evident in the way he spoke with her.

When Luke looked over at his sweet daughter in a hospital bed, his mind was running rampant. The same anger he thought he had overcome as a teen was back. He knew if he had been there when the fight was happening, Krause would be in the Hospital and not his daughter. But Krause would be in ICU. He had to pray most of the night to get his thoughts under control. He didn't want to be in that state of mind when his little girl woke up.

CHAPTER EIGHT

*W*hen the nurse came in at 5 am, Luke moved to sit on the doctor's stool next to the bed. He put his head over the railing to look at Sophie.

"Hi, sweet pea."

"Daddy, that lady keeps waking me up."

"She's doing her job. She has to make sure you're alright."

"I'm alright until she wakes me up." The scowl she had on her face was familiar to him. He'd seen it many times when he asked her to do something she didn't want to do. "I didn't get to go ice-skating." They were whispering so they wouldn't wake up Lizzy, who was asleep next to her.

"I know, honey, we'll reschedule it."

"What about the BBQ? Can we still go to that?"

"Major Young called and rescheduled it for next week." He saw her disappointment. "But he said he wanted Lizzy's whole family to come with us." Her eyes lit up, and a smile came to her face.

"Really?"

"Yes…Does your head hurt?"

"A little."

"Do you want the nurse to get you some more medicine?"

"No. If you get me some Twizzlers, I think that will take care of it." Luke tried hard not to laugh, but he failed. Sophie didn't see what was so amusing.

"Alright, honey, but I can't get them till we get out of the hospital." He took her hand, "you were very brave, helping Ms. Ruby. I know you think I saved you, but I didn't get there until i﹁

was over. But Jesus was there with you every minute taking care of you."

"I know He was, Daddy. He is always with me. But you were there when I opened my eyes." She put her little hand on his cheek. "You're always there too, Daddy."

"I love you."

"I love you too, Daddy."

Can you go back to sleep?"

"I think so."

Luke sat watching her until she fell back to sleep, then he went back to the recliner. He must have fallen asleep because he didn't hear Manny come in hours later.

Manny touched his shoulder and spoke quietly, "Luke."

Luke opened his eyes and set the recliner up, "Manny, is everything ok?" He was groggy.

"Yeah, I came to pick up Mrs. Krause and check on you guys." He sent down a small duffel with clean clothes in it for the girls.

"Sophie's fine, a little annoyed; the nurse wakes her up every two hours."

Manny laughed, "I can appreciate that."

"She should get released today. Is it alright if Lizzy stays with her tonight at my house?" Luke stood and moved closer to the door.

"Sure."

"I don't think I'm going to send her to school Monday. I'll see if Deniz can stay with her. Have you interrogated Corporal Krause yet?" Luke asked.

"No. As soon as Herschel got in his cell, he asked for his phone call and hired a private attorney."

"He won't get bail, will he?"

"That's not up to me, but we have fingerprints, blood, and witnesses, so I don't see him getting out. But you know the law better than I do."

"Yeah, I don't think he'll be getting out."

Manny went over and lightly kissed his little girl on the forehead and stroked her hair. Then he did the same to Sophie.

"Ok, Luke, call me when you get back home." Luke nodded.

The next week a lot happened. The long-awaited new Jag officer requested months ago finally arrived. Major Scott assigned Captain Maya Patel to the prosecution in the Krause case. He was afraid a claim of conflict of interest would arise if one of them handled it.

Captain Patel offered a plea deal. Corporal Krause's private attorney suggested he take it. The evidence against him was strong, and if he ended up in court, he would most likely get a more severe sentence.

Herschel Krause pled guilty to three counts of felony assault in the third degree. And two counts of child abuse. The plea agreement offered was 22 months in the stockade in Virginia. When they released him, he would get a dishonorable discharge. Instead of docked pay, he had to sign his entire paycheck over to his wife. His attorney countered asking that two hundred dollars a month go to Herschel's prison Commissary account. This agreement would be in effect until the divorce was final. A Civilian Court would decide on spousal and child support.

Major Scott needed to sign off on the mutually agreed upon plea. He felt it was too lenient. But decided not to undermine his new Jag officer, and Amy Krause had told him she would not testify in court. She was afraid if she did, no matter where she went, Herschel would find her when he got out.

Amy spent the week packing her and Herschel's possessions. None of the furniture belonged to them, so there wasn't much to pack but their personal items. She packed Buster's toys, video games, and books, making sure not to leave anything. Ruby came up every night after work to help her. The Army agreed to transport her belongings back to her mom's address in the States. They also agreed to hold Herschel's things in storage until he gets out of prison.

While helping Amy pack, Ruby was able to talk to her about Jesus. Amy was responsive and promised to find a Church when she got back home.

Buster refused to go back into the apartment; he spent the week with Duke and CJ at Zoey Young's insistence.

The BBQ at the Young house happened as rescheduled the next Sunday after Church. Amy and Buster said their goodbyes to everyone. The only thing Amy hated leaving behind was Buster's friends. They had been good for him.

Luke finally connected Duke and CJ to David and Jonathan. He didn't realize they were his colleague's children. The BBQ was great and sealed a friendship among the group that would last the rest of their lives.

David kept his promise to pay for Amy and Buster's tickets back to the States. Unknown to anyone else, he also gave her one thousand dollars to help her get settled.

Major Scott was working in his office when his secure cell rang. He kept this cell on his person at all times. It was the one used to stay in contact with his father's Mission of Peace non-profit organization. The Organization feeds the poor all around the world. The more clandestine work of the Organization was smuggling. They smuggle Christians out of Countries in danger of persecution for their faith. They also smuggle Bibles to underground Churches that request it.

David tried texting Faiz in Syria when they first got to Incirlik but had not heard back. He feared the worse, that Faiz had been arrested.

"David, it's me, Faiz."

"Faiz, I thought your cover was blown."

"No, I was out of range chasing a lead." David stood up; he didn't want to get too excited. All the leads on Anna so far had gone nowhere. He took a deep breath and looked out the window.

"What lead?" David asked. Faiz's position as Sergeant Major in the Intel division gave him inside information. His unit was part of the Political Security Directorate in Syria. All calls of suspicious activity ended on his desk. He filed all arrest warrants. Anyone accused of being dissidents, which included Christians, fell in his jurisdiction. He would help 'Mission of Peace' extract the Christians in danger of imprisonment or worse.

"Some rumors have reached me about a foreign woman being seen in a rural area north of here."

"What kind of rumors?"

"It's being said that she is tending to people in the neighboring small villages. They refer to her as Mumarada."

"Nurse." A bolt shot through him. "It's her, Faiz. It's Anna." Anna is a nurse practitioner.

"Maybe." Faiz paused. "I tried to track down anyone who had any firsthand knowledge. Everyone I talked to led me to someone else who heard the same thing. I could find no one who actually saw her themselves, or new where she was."

"I can be there in a couple of days; I'll help you look for her."

David, Jonathan, and Jared, David's brother, spent a month searching the area where she went missing. They came using papers saying they were emergency aid workers.

"No, David. You Can't. Things are too dangerous here now. The Military is looking for anyone crossing the border illegally."

"I don't care, Faiz. If there's a chance it's her I have to come."

Faiz was quiet for a long time.

"Faiz?"

"If you come, you'll likely get us both arrested. Then there will be no one here to look for Anna. Let me follow this up. I promise you I will track down every piece of intel I get."

David sat in his chair and leaned back. He knew Faiz was right. "Faiz...do you think she's still alive?"

"I don't know, David, but I won't leave here until I know for sure."

"Thank you. Please call or text me whenever it's safe to do so. I will keep praying for your safety."

"Thank you, my friend."

David hung up. He swiveled his chair around to look through the window. He didn't know how many more times he could stand up under the disappointment of a lead going nowhere. His mind went back to the day Faiz called to tell him his wife was missing.

Anna wasn't supposed to be on that mission. But David and Jared got called into an emergency extraction in Iran, and Jonathan was ill. Anna had worked extractions without him before, and he trusted Faiz to get her out safely. She carried the forged passports in with her for the family they were smuggling out.

There was only a small window of time to get the family to the rendezvous point. The forecast said to expect strong winds. Sandstorms in Syria were dangerous, but the forecast also said it was four hours out. That would give them time to get the family to the border. Then they could wait the sandstorm out there. They carried respiratory masks with them in case they got caught in it. Sandstorms could be worse than a blizzard in Colorado. They were on the last leg of the trip, also the most dangerous, because of the narrow winding road up the mountain.

They could see the storm off on the horizon. It was early; the sand was beginning to make visibility difficult. The vehicle could be disabled by it. But, the group was close to the destination, so they pressed on.

Faiz couldn't see the truck coming straight at him on his side of the road until it was too late. He tried to avoid a head-on collision and swerved to the right. The Van careened down a slope and landed on its side at the edge of the river. Anna was thrown out of the vehicle. The family in the back had a few injuries, including one broken arm. Faiz searched for Anna but couldn't find her.

The protocol for off-script incidents like these was in the mission handbook. It gave guidelines for when things go awry in an extraction. The priority was to get the family out at all costs. So that's what Faiz did. He led the family on foot the last three miles. They walked through the sandstorm using his compass and the respirators. When he passed them safely on to the next guide, he went back and searched for Anna.

The sandstorm lasted twelve hours; he searched through all twelve hours of it and two days after. Anna was gone. The only logical conclusion was she was thrown into the river, and it carried her downstream.

Anna has been missing for almost eight months.

Major Young was speaking on the phone with a Lieutenant at the Procurement department. The procurement officer had a question about a contract with one of the PX vendors. When Jonathan saw his friend's face, he politely excused himself from the conversation, insisting he would call him back shortly.

David stood at the open door, hesitating to come in. Jonathan got up and went to him. He put his hand on David's shoulder.

"David, what is it?" David walked over to the window. Jonathan followed after closing the door. He knew this was going to be a personal conversation.

"David?"

"I got a call back from Faiz."

"And?"

"The last week, he's been following a lead about a foreign white woman. The rumor is she is tending to the sick in the rural area to the north of the accident. Another rumor said they referred to her as Mumarada."

"Nurse," Jonathan whispered.

"He wasn't able to track down anyone who knew firsthand information." David moved over to one of the chairs in front of Jonathan's desk and sat down.

Jonathan stood over him, "so when do we leave?"

"We don't."

"What do you mean, we don't?" Jonathan sat down next to him, confused.

"Faiz insisted it was too dangerous. He's afraid we will blow his cover and get us all killed." David bent over with his forearms on his thighs. He covered his face with his hands.

"I'm afraid to get my hopes up again, Jon. But I trust the Lord she's still alive."

Jonathan laid his hand on David's back, "can I pray for you?"

"Yes, please. I need your prayers."

Luke got back from an interview with an enlisted man in the brig for unauthorized use of Alcohol, commonly known as drunk. The man asked to speak to a Jag officer. He wanted to see if he could fight the charge. After hearing the facts, Luke told the man it was unlikely. It was more likely than not that he would get a reprimand and a five-day rip without pay. Luke told him the penalties get progressively worse. He could end up with a dishonorable discharge if he continues to get drunk at work.

He walked to Major Young's office door to knock. He wanted to invite him to lunch. Before he knocked, he heard Jonathan and David praying. He stepped away and went to his office. He prayed quietly for whatever the need might be.

A few minutes later, David and Jonathan left the office and headed to the elevators.

The holidays were rapidly approaching. The group, as they affectionately referred to themselves, decided to eat Thanksgiving dinner together.

There were lots of events planned on base for Christmas. The Church they attended announced they were putting on a Christmas play. Duke and CJ volunteered to be Wise Men, and

Sophie and Lizzy asked to be Angels. Practice started the week after Thanksgiving.

Luke realized he hadn't thought ahead when he left Virginia. He had left all his Christmas decorations and their Christmas tree in storage. Today, he and Sophie were going to the PX to pick up all the decorations they needed. They would decorate the weekend after Thanksgiving.

Thanksgiving dinner couldn't have been more perfect. Zoey set a beautiful table with Ruby's help and the food was abundant. Everyone contributed. Luke noticed an expensive camera set up on a tripod close by. He could hear its shutter close off and on. It had a remote timer that David set to take pictures every few minutes.

Jonathan noticed Luke looking it over.

"David brings it to events he thinks Anna will want to see when she gets back."

Luke nodded; he knew a little about what happened to David's wife. He decided he would ask when the time was right; now wasn't that time. Luke remembered the wall of memories his mom maintained at home. He had spent many hours as a child looking at all the family pictures. Some included family or friends that had died years before he was born. He especially liked the many photos that included him. Luke decided to do that for Sophie.

"Do you think I could get a copy of those pictures?"

"Don't worry, he always puts the pictures on a flash drive and gives them to us. I'm sure he'll do the same for you."

Putting up Christmas decorations with Sophie was fun. He didn't have a fancy camera, but Luke took lots of pictures with his cell phone. He lifted Sophie on his shoulders to put the Angel on the top of the tree.

They finally rescheduled the trip to the Mall. The group decided that the adults would trade off watching the kids at the ice-skating rink, and the rest would shop.

They asked if Deniz wanted to earn extra money by watching Liam and Ricky for the day at Zoey's house. She jumped at the opportunity. Her family was Christian. Although Turkey claims to be a secular country, allowing all religions to practice their faith. In truth, they are a Muslim country. It is not uncommon that a Christian is imprisoned for their faith. Some were murdered; the perpetrator able to skirt prosecution. Deniz's family goes to an underground Church. They celebrate Christmas but only inside their home, privately. She was grateful for extra money to buy some small gifts for her siblings.

The group sat together at the Christmas play the Sunday before Christmas. A moment of sadness passed over Luke. He wished Sophie had her mother to see her perform. Clair was missing so many precious moments in her daughter's life. Luke shrugged off the thought; it was her choice.

The group agreed to have a traveling party on Christmas Eve. There would be food served at each house, and that family would hand out the gifts they had bought for the others. They had agreed not to exceed the preset price on gifts. It became evident early on that no one honored that commitment.

They ended at Luke's house. He served Root Beer Floats, hot chocolate with marshmallows, coffee, and Sparkling Cider. He also had a variety of desserts he bought from the Commissary Bakery. By the look of it, everyone was having a wonderful time, including him. It was the first Christmas without Clair, and he worried it would be hard on Sophie. Everyone opened their gifts. The night ended after David read the story of Jesus's birth and sang Christmas carols.

When everyone was gone, Sophie hugged her father and said, "Oh, Daddy, isn't this the best Christmas?" She kissed his cheek, "I love you, Daddy."

"He lifted her into his arms and twirled her around. "Yes, it is, sweet pea." She laughed then he set her down.

"What are we doing tomorrow?"

"Let's see what the day brings. Why don't you take the gifts your friends bought you to your room and get ready for bed?"

He waited for her to come out of the bathroom in the new pj's Ruby bought her to match Lizzy's. Before she crawled into bed, he brushed her hair exactly fifty times, gathered it up, and put it in a ribbon. After praying, he tucked her into bed and kissed her forehead.

The One Who Stayed: Sophie's Story

CHAPTER NINE

*L*uke never told Sophie that Clair called and said she was coming to see her on Christmas day. He was afraid Clair would back out, and he had no intention of seeing Sophie disappointed again. Luke had just put the last gifts under the tree. He always hid some to put out after midnight, gifts from Santa.

Luke turned out all the lights, leaving only the tree lights on. He grabbed a cup of hot chocolate and sat in his recliner, thanking the Lord for all He had done for them this year.

He heard the scuffling noise of little feet. Then he saw Sophie loaded down with wrapped gifts. She carefully placed them under the tree, then stepped back. She clapped her hands softly, and admired her work, never noticing him in the dark. Ruby and Zoey must have helped her shop and wrap the gifts.

Sophie went to bed well past her bedtime, but she was still up early to check out what Santa brought. He heard her whooping and hollering. Luke knew it would only be seconds before she would be running in and jump on his bed to get him up.

Sophie drug her father out to the tree to show him all the gifts. To his surprise, there were gifts he hadn't seen the night before. Only one person had a key to his home, and it wasn't Santa; it was Manny. He wanted someone he trusted to be able to enter in an emergency. It had to be him, but there was no way Sophie would let him take time to find out before they opened the presents.

Luke's mystery gift was an expensive camera with accessories Including a tripod and remote control. Sophie's mystery present was a laptop that had extensive parental controls. The computer had age-appropriate games and educational Apps loaded on it.

After they opened gifts, Sophie helped Luke make waffles, Sophie's favorite for breakfast. They finished cleaning up when the doorbell rang.

Sophie jumped down from the stool she used to help wash dishes and said, "I'll get it."

Luke followed behind her. When Sophie opened the door, she screamed, "Mommy!" Sophie grabbed her hand and pulled her into the house, hugging her. Luke took the box of gifts from the town car driver standing behind her and thanked him.

Clair looked around the entryway and into the living room. "This is nice, Luke."

"Thanks, Clair. Let me take your coat."

"Come see our tree, Mommy." She led Clair to it.

"I put the Angel on top, all by myself."

"All by yourself. That's amazing, sweetie."

"Well, Daddy put me on his shoulders. But I placed it on top myself."

"I would have loved to see that" Clair laughed.

"I took a selfie; I'll send it to you," Luke said. He stood back and let Sophie enjoy her mother. Clair sat down on the couch.

"Clair, would you like some coffee?" Luke asked.

"That would be nice, thank you."

"Sophie, open the gifts I brought you." Sophie dragged the box from the entryway and sat on the floor in front of her.

Luke sat across the room and watched Sophie open one expensive gift after another. Sophie was happy, but it was hard for Luke. Clair's betrayal still stabbed him in his gut, and although he didn't love her anymore, there were still some feelings.

"Sophie, I understand there is a Mall in town that has an ice-skating rink. Would you like to go? Then we could shop for a while and go to lunch."

Sophie jumped up and clapped her hands. She hugged her mom and said, "yes, Mommy, that will be so much fun. I got ice skates for Christmas." She turned to her dad. "Can I go, Daddy?"

"Of course you can. Go get ready."

"Mommy, you have to come help me get ready. You can put my hair in a French braid." That stung Luke's heart. Fixing her hair had become their thing in the last year. It looked like Sophie had forgiven everything. That all the pain Clair caused never happened.

Luke felt guilty for how he was feeling. Of course, he wanted his daughter to have a good relationship with her mother.

Sophie and Clair came back out twenty minutes later, looking beautiful. Sophie could see that her dad was sad. When she hugged him goodbye, she whispered, "I won't go if it makes you feel bad, Daddy."

He whispered back, "of course you're going to go, and you are going to have a wonderful time. I love you." His answer must have satisfied her because she kissed his cheek and skipped out the door. The town car was outside waiting for them. Clair must have hired it for the day.

Luke got dressed and went to a hardware store in Adana. The PX on base wasn't open on Christmas, and he wanted to pick up picture frames for the memory wall. Then he called Manny to find out where the mysterious gifts came from.

"All I can tell you is the gifts were in a box with a note saying they were for you."

"Where did the box come from?"

Manny laughed, "haven't you ever heard the saying 'don't look a gift horse in the mouth'? Especially at Christmas."

"Yeah, I guess it's the lawyer in me that questions everything."

"Clair showed up today."

"Really?"

"She took Sophie to the Mall. I hate to admit it, but I'm having a hard time with it. Clair ignores her daughter for almost a year.

Then when she shows up, Sophie acts like there was no abandonment, no betrayal. All is forgiven."

"Man, I'm sorry, and I certainly can't tell you how to feel. It's amazing how forgiving children are; I see it all the time. Even abused children will cling to the parent that abuses them. I don't understand why, but they will work twice as hard to get the abuser's approval. I'm not saying Clair is an abuser. It just goes to show how much children yearn to be loved and accepted by their parents when they are young. As they get older, anger and resentment tend to set in."

"I don't want Sophie to hate her mom or resent her; she needs her. It's me. I'm having a hard time letting go of my resentment and anger at Clair."

"Why don't you come over, and we can play hoops at the park for a while."

"No, I'm not taking you away from your family on Christmas Day. I'll talk to you later."

"Alright, but if you change your mind, let me know."

"Thank you, Manny. And I'll get to the bottom of those mystery gifts, sooner or later." Manny laughed and hung up.

Several hours later, Sophie comes bounding in, arms overburdened with packages. Clair was a few steps behind. "Daddy, we had so much fun." She turned to her mother, "didn't we, Mommy?"

"Yes, we did, sweetheart. Now go put your packages in your room."

Sophie went to her room, struggling with all the bags.

Clair stepped closer to Luke and spoke softly. "Luke, I intended to stay a few days, but Wesley called and said some things have come up; he needs me back right away."

"What!" Luke realized he was too loud and lowered his voice.

"Are you kidding me? Your daughter needs you, too. You can't just drop in for a few hours when you haven't seen her for almost a year."

"Luke, stop. I already feel bad enough. Wesley is working on an important new project; he needs me to help him finish it."

"Is it more important than your daughter, Clair?"

Sophie came back out of her room. "Mommy, we can watch Scrooge tonight. Daddy will make popcorn." She looked at her dad, "won't you, Daddy."

Clair knelt in front of her. "That sounds like great fun, Sophie, and I planned on staying a few days, but somethings come up. I have to leave."

Sophie's expression went blank; she didn't say a word.

"You understand, don't you, sweetheart. It's work. But I will make it up to you next time." Clair hugged Sophie for a long time and kissed both her cheeks. Then she stood. Mouthed *'I'm sorry.'* to Luke and left.

Luke had no idea how Sophie would react to this. He remembered how she had clung to her mother, sobbing, begging her to stay when Clair first left them. But there was none of that; Sophie didn't cry or beg. There was no response, no tears, nothing. She just turned around and walked back to her bedroom.

Luke gave her a minute, then followed her. "Are you alright, Sophie?"

She was folding her new blue jeans to put in her drawer. "I'm fine, Daddy."

"Come here, sweet pea, talk to me." He sat on the edge of her bed and patted the spot next to him. Sophie passed by all her new dolls and grabbed her old favorite and sat on the bed next to him.

"I'm sorry she couldn't stay longer, but at least you got to see her, and you said you had a great time."

"We did."

"Are you upset that mommy left?" Sophie was looking down at her doll, holding it tight to her chest.

"A little."

Luke wanted her to express how she was feeling so he could comfort her. "What's on your mind, sweetheart?"

"It's kind 'a like when your best friend lets you hold her new, beautiful doll. It's exciting and fun for a moment, but you know you have to give it back. It's not yours. Your special doll is waiting for you on your bed. She's always waiting whenever you want to play with her. She turned her head to look at him, do you see?"

Luke lifted her onto his lap and wrapped his arms around her. He held her and her doll close for a long time. "I do see, honey. I do...I love you."

Northern Syria: Mumarada

She opened her eyes, desperately trying to cling to the dream she had, but it flitted away like all the others. Is anyone looking for me, worried about me? Is there someone out there who loves me; misses me? What was I doing in that van? Maybe it's better I don't remember. She had wondered those same questions for the ten months she'd been here.

She had no idea how or why she came to Syria. She only knew what people told her. Ten months ago, a man and his wife found her by the edge of a river in a sandstorm. They were on their way back from an underground Church service. They told her there was a crashed van about 25 yards from where they found her. It appeared she'd been thrown out of the van into the bushes at the edge of the water. Her body sank into the bushes and hid her. The man, whose name was Nabil Maleh, told her the bushes protected her from the sand that would have torn her skin—and filtered enough air for her to breathe. Nabil said as he and his wife, Rima, were passing by, when they saw a blue glow coming from the bush. He thought a flashlight had been thrown from the wrecked van. When he went to retrieve it, he found her. They took her to

92

their home before the worst of the sandstorm hit. They tended her wounds, the worst being a large cut and a bump on the side of her head. Rima crudely stitched the cut to stop the bleeding. She woke up two days later with no memory. Based on the fact there was a wrecked van close by. She assumed her head hit something on the van when she propelled out.

The next week, when Nabil and Rima went to their Church service, they looked for the van. They hoped to find something with her name on it. Or some personal items, but the van was gone. There were men there searching the area, but they had no idea if they were friends or foes, so they stayed clear.

Her mind held onto a few critical things; her love for God and her training as a physician's assistant. She knew that procedural or muscle memory functions often remained in cases of amnesia. In her case, there was no injury to that part of her brain.

When she stitched up a neighbor Nabil brought to her who had cut himself while butchering a lamb; word got out she was a nurse. The sick and injured in the surrounding area started coming for help. There were few medical services available in the remote regions of Syria. Nabil bought basic medical supplies from the underground so she could treat them. Mumarada (nurse), as they began to call her, made the patients promise not to tell. But word got around, and more came. She was afraid for Nabil and Rima. If word got to the wrong people, that they harbored an undocumented alien; they could go to prison.

Incirlik Air Base

It was the last day of school for the summer break, and they were having a 'Field Day'. They set up an obstacle course, relay races, and other activities, providing a sack lunch. The parents brought baked goods. The school released early; 1:30 pm.

All the Jag Unit except two of the now six paralegals had children in the American School. Major Scott made a deal with the two paralegals. If they held down the fort so the others could take a two-hour lunch break, they could leave two hours early on Friday. It was a good deal.

They made it to the School about 11:30 am. Luke and Ruby watched as Sophie and Lizzy ran the obstacle course. David, Jonathan, and Zoey were watching the relays. Zoey picked up Ricky at preschool for Ruby so she wouldn't have to be late.

Ruby called Manny to see if he was going to make it. "Hello?"

"Manny, can you get here to watch?"

"Sorry honey, I got a call to pick up two enlisted men. They got in a fight at CikCik Ali in Adana. Two enlisted men came in, already soused and started a ruckus."

"This early in the day?" Ruby asked.

"It was a carryover from last night. Anyway, Sergeant Demir called; he's holding them for me."

"We'll be here until 1:30 if you can make it."

"Thanks, hon, I'll try." Manny signed off.

As a courtesy, the Turkish Polis would contact the MP's if there was a disturbance that involved an enlisted man. As long as they paid for the damages, the Turks allowed the Americans to handle their own problems. It could get dicey if it were anything more serious. Sometimes they had to go through political channels to get their men back.

When Field Day ended, Luke took Sophie home, where Deniz was waiting for her. He was almost back to the office when his cell rang. He put it on Bluetooth and said, "Hello?"

"Luke, I'm so glad I caught you."

"Hello, Clair."

"Luke, I want Sophie to visit me at our home in Paris for two weeks this summer."

"Two weeks? You haven't had her for more than a few hours in over a year." Luke retorted.

"You told me I could see her whenever I wanted when we signed the divorce papers."

"I did, but you have chosen not to."

"Well, I am choosing *too* now," Clair barked.

Luke rubbed his hand down his face to calm himself.

"Look Clair, that's a long time. Let me talk to Sophie about it. If she wants to go, when would you want her."

"Next week, School is already out, isn't it?"

"Yes, today was the last day. If we do this, I have some stipulations."

"Of course you do." Clair let out a disgusted sigh.

"I'll escort her to your doorstep in Paris. But you have to escort her back at the end of two weeks. I don't want her on a plane alone." He was pulling into his parking spot as they spoke.

"That's reasonable. Thank you, Luke. Call me as soon as you talk to her."

Luke took a moment to think about it. He was not crazy about her being so far away for that length of time. But Clair was her mother, and as far as Luke knew, Wesley was a decent man. If Sophie wanted to go, he would let her.

When Luke got home, Sophie came to hug him and say hello.

Deniz pulled a casserole she had made out of the oven and set it on top of the stove. The table was set for dinner.

"Hello, Mr. Luke. Dinner is ready." He handed her an envelope with her pay for the week.

"It smells great, Deniz. Thank you."

Deniz gathered her things, hugged Sophie, and Luke watched her get into her car safely.

Sophie was sitting at the table, "Daddy, I'm so glad you came to Field Day."

He moved the casserole to the table and grabbed a spoon to put some on her plate. "I wouldn't have missed it." He kissed the top of her head and sat down.

When they finished eating, Sophie asked for ice cream. Luke nodded, and Sophie got up and grabbed it from the freezer, then took two spoons from the drawer. They always shared it right out of the carton. Clair would have never approved of it. But it was a tradition for them now.

"Sophie, your mother called today." Sophie smiled.

"She did?"

"Yes, and she would very much like you to come stay at her house in Paris for two weeks." Luke wasn't sure what the look on Sophie's face meant. "Would you like to do that?"

"Will you come with me?"

"I will fly over there with you, but I wouldn't stay at your mom's with you," Luke said, trying not to let his trepidation about it spill over to her.

"Do I have to?"

"No, sweetheart, you don't *have* to."

"Who will be here for you if I go?" Sophie's brows furrowed, worried about him being alone.

"You don't have to worry about me. I can visit my friends. I'll be fine."

"Will you miss me, Daddy?"

Luke took her hand and pulled her over to him. "Of course, I will miss you terribly. But you have a mother and a father, and right now, your mother wants to see you. It's up to you, sweet pea, whatever you decide."

"When would I go?"

"Next week," Luke said. Sophie's eyes got big. "You can think about it, ok?" Sophie nodded.

After cleaning the kitchen, Luke put on a movie they wanted to watch and made popcorn. She had never been away for two weeks. It was going to be harder for him than for her.

CHAPTER TEN

*L*uke had never been to Paris. They grabbed a cab outside the airport and headed to the address Clair gave him by the Eiffel tower. The building was older, built in the 1930s, but kept in excellent condition. The doorman asked which apartment he was visiting and took Sophie's Suitcase. He said he would bring it up in a few minutes. He walked them to the elevator and used a security key to punch in the floor to the two-story penthouse.

There were only two apartments on that floor; he knocked on the condo number she gave him. When the housekeeper opened the door, they stepped into an opulent foyer. It had 10-foot ceilings with decorative crown molding. The housekeeper directed them to a formal living room, a large room with long, narrow windows across the wall that looked out onto the street with the Eiffel Tower in the background. Two of the windows opened like French doors onto a small terrace, only wide enough for a little rod iron table and two chairs. The ceiling medallion had a chandelier hanging from the middle, and they walked on floors made of marble. The European furnishing fit the rest of the decor.

Luke could tell Sophie was getting nervous. She wouldn't let go of his hand and was squeezing it tightly. Luke slipped the backpack off Sophie's shoulder and onto the floor. They sat on one of the white Valentina loveseats the housekeeper directed them to and waited.

"Daddy, what if I don't want to stay?" Sophie asked, looking up at him like a doe in the headlights.

He let go of her hand and wrapped his arm around her shoulder. "Sweetheart listen to me. Your mother wants to spend time with you. She loves you. But if you get afraid or want to come home, call me. I will come get you."

Sophie nodded as her mother rushed into the room, followed by a Maltese clipping along behind her. Sophie's eyes lit up when she saw the dog. Clair hugged and kissed Sophie. Then she acknowledged Luke and thanked him for bringing her.

"May I hold him, Mommy?" Sophie asked, looking at the dog.

"Of course, darling, his name is Beau." Sophie bent down to pick him up.

"Look, Daddy isn't he cute?"

Luke pets the dog, "Yes, he is, Sweet Pea."

Leaving Sophie was hard. He hadn't been away from her since the divorce. She clung to him when he said goodbye, finally letting go when her mother spoke to her.

After escorting Sophie to her mother's, he decided to use his three days off to enjoy the city.

Luke decided to go up the Eiffel Tower. First, he dropped his duffel off at his hotel room since he was only a few blocks away. He would have liked to take Sophie but felt it would be unfair since Clair wanted to show her the city.

At the Eiffel Tower, Luke walked the stairs instead of using the elevator. He used the telescopes to look at the city. After that, he decided to walk to the River Seine on the Rue de Rivoli. All sorts of vendors lined the Riverside of the street. Scenes of Paris or sketches of tourists done in charcoal were the favorite of the ones buying. He strolled along, looking at all the vendors' products. He intended to come back at the end of the day to buy a few paintings he liked. He didn't want to pack bundles this early in the day.

It was almost 2 pm when he decided to stop at one of the many restaurants on the other side of the street for lunch. He took a seat outside and watched people until a waiter came and gave him a menu. He didn't think to ask for one in English and stared at it, trying to decipher what the words meant.

A woman sitting a few tables over asked if he needed help.

"Yes, I guess I should have asked for one in English." Luke laughed at himself. She walked to his table, pointed at things on the menu, and told him what they were. Once he decided what he wanted, she called the waiter over and ordered for him in French.

"You speak the language very well, are you French?"

"No, I was born in Washington State. My father taught French and Spanish at the University of Washington in Seattle. I guess it was inevitable that I would take up the languages."

"Are you waiting for someone?" Luke asked.

"No, I'm on a two-day layover. I always end up doing the touristy things when I'm here. I love it." She said.

"I guess I should be polite and introduce myself before I ask if you would like to join me? My name is Luke Star."

"Hello, Luke Star, my name is Marcella Beauchene." She extended her hand to him. Luke decided to kiss it like the French rather than shake it. She laughed.

"Your parents are French?"

"My father. My mother is from Italy." She said, walking back to her table to retrieve her sweater and a small umbrella that fit in her shoulder bag.

"Are you expecting rain?" Luke asked, looking at the blue sky.

"In Paris, you must always expect rain."

Luke enjoyed his lunch with Marcella. He found out she was a stewardess on the airline carrier he and Sophie came to Paris on. He wasn't sure if she would think him a predator if he asked if she would like to spend the day with him touring the city. He decided to ask, deciding it was worth the possible embarrassment of rejection if she said no.

"Marcella, if you don't have plans for the day, would you like to do the American tourist thing with me?" Luke asked.

"I think that would be fun. Yes." Luke insisted on paying for her lunch. She grabbed her sweater and umbrella, and Luke put a generous tip on the table.

Luke and Marcella spent the day walking the streets of Paris. They visited the Louvre, Notre Dame Cathedral, and a million little shops and bakeries. At 7 pm, they ended up at the Champs Elysees Avenue, at the Arc de Triomphe, and decided to eat at a nice restaurant. They spotted one that had glass-enclosed seating extended onto the sidewalk.

During the meal, he finally had a moment to admire the woman seated across from him. Earlier in the day, the wind came up, and she gathered her thick, long, cinnamon hair and put it in a ponytail. After arriving at the restaurant, she let it cascade over her shoulders again. Her brown eyes and flawless skin complimented her naturally tan complexion.

Marcella caught him staring, "is something wrong?" She asked.

"Just admiring the scenery," Luke said.

Marcella burst out laughing, "did you really just say that?"

Luke laughed at her response. "Yes, as a matter of fact, I did." They both laughed until people started staring at them.

It was 9 pm when they finished dinner. Luke didn't want the night to end. He suggested a final escapade. If they walked fast, they could make it to where the boats dock on the Seine for the next ride. They practically jogged to the boat launch and made it. They sat in the glass-enclosed seating on the boat since there was a chill in the air.

On the return trip, the Eiffel Tower lit up, and they could see the light show. When they got back to the boat launch, he held out his hand to help her off the boat.

"Thank you for entertaining me all day, Luke. I enjoyed your company." Marcella said, putting her arms into her sweater that was over her arm.

"Thank you for playing tourist with me. How far away is your hotel? Do I need to get you a cab?"

"No, it's only a few blocks down."

Luke held out his crooked elbow for her, "then let me escort you, *me lady.*"

Marcella laughed and put her arm in his as they walked along the street. They inhaled all the wonderful smells of the restaurants they passed. Luke hated to say good night to her. Even though this wasn't a date, it felt like it to him.

"Marci, would you like to have breakfast with me in the morning? Unless you already have plans." He realized she might have a boyfriend. Although the way she received his attention today, he didn't think so.

"Don't you have anything better to do than entertain me?"

"Actually, no." Luke smiled. She laughed at his response.

"Alright, I know a wonderful bakery where we can eat. Meet me in the lobby here at 9 am. Will that work for you?"

"I'm at your disposal, ma'am."

Marcella pushed his shoulder playfully and shook her head. He watched as she walked to the elevator.

His hotel was about half a mile away, but he decided not to take a cab and enjoy the scenery and the people on the streets.

Luke woke up excited to meet Marci for breakfast. He got to her hotel forty-five minutes early and sat in the lobby to wait.

Marcella walked into the lobby expecting to sit and wait but saw Luke sitting on one of the settees.

"Well, hello, Mr. Star." She said in a flirty voice.

"*Me lady,*" Luke bowed and did a flourish with his arm.

He put out his crooked elbow, and she slipped her arm into his. Then they were off to the Bakery.

After a long day of site seeing, shopping, and food, Marcella said, "I'm afraid I will have to call it a night, Luke. I have an early flight in the morning."

"I understand. I want to say I have enjoyed your company. If you ever find yourself with a layover in Adana, call me. I'll show you around." After trading email addresses and cell numbers, he walked her to her hotel.

Luke went back to where the street artists were the first day. He had his eye on a few pieces he wanted to bring home. Then headed back to the hotel; he wanted to talk to Sophie one more time before leaving tomorrow morning.

Sophie was having fun with her mom; it was almost like old times. They went site seeing and shopping. Sophie's new favorite food was crepes filled with chocolate, sold by vendors on the streets. The smell came from every direction.

Sophie met Mr. Wes, her new stepfather, for the first time. Although he treated her well and spoke kindly to her, he was very emotionally distant. Not at all like her loving and warm father.

Sophie heard the landline in the house ring. A maid came to her and said her father was on the phone for her.

"Hello, Daddy?" Sophie said, taking the cordless phone.

"Sophie, Sweetheart, how are you? Are you having fun?"

When she heard her father's voice, she got homesick for him; her voice wobbled. "Daddy, I miss you."

"Oh, Sophie, I miss you too. Are you having fun?" He asked again.

Sophie came out of her melancholy quickly when she started talking about all they had done.

"Daddy, we had so much fun, we went to this tall steel thing and went up an elevator. There were big binoculars there you could look through and see for a long way. Then we took a boat ride in the river. They have a big river right down in the middle of the city."

"They do? Right downtown?" He smiled.

"Yes, it's called the Sin, and we rode on a boat made of windows." Luke laughed at her pronunciation of the Seine.

"That's wonderful."

"I have a new favorite food now, Daddy. I like crepes with chocolate in them."

"Oh, I do too. Maybe we can learn to make crepes when you come home. Sophie, I'm leaving Paris tomorrow, but I want you to have lots of fun with your mother. Will you call me once in a while?"

"You're leaving?" Knowing he was close by was her security blanket. "Do you have to go, Daddy?"

"I do, sweetheart, but I'm just a phone call away. If you need me."

"What if I want to come home?" Luke could hear how nervous she was.

"Listen, Sophie. I want you to have this time with your mother. She loves you and wants to spend time with you, and you're having a great time. Enjoy yourself. If something changes, call me, and we can talk about it, ok?"

They said goodbye, and she threw kisses over the phone.

Sophie held on to the phone, looking at it. She knew her father wanted her to stay, but she was already so homesick. Luckily, her mother came into the room right then, or she would have started crying.

Luke headed to the Charles-de-Gaulle International Airport. He sent a goodbye text to Marcella, knowing she wouldn't see it until she landed at her next stop. He didn't call Sophie for fear it would upset her too much. Manny was picking him up at the Adana Sakirpasa Airport. It was a seven-hour flight, so he bought a few things to read at the airport, but his mind kept going to Marcella. Luke noticed she was much taller than Clair. Catching himself, Luke wondered when he would stop comparing everyone he met to Clair.

It was only Wednesday, and Luke hated going home to an empty house. Ruby had invited him to eat dinner with them tonight, and he accepted the invitation.

As he walked in the door, his landline was ringing. He closed the door and set his briefcase down, rushing to get the phone.

"Hello?"

"Daddy, you have to come to get me." Sophie was crying. Luke was panicked, worried about what was going on, with him so far away.

"What's happened, Sophie?"

"I want to come home, Daddy."

"Tell me why, honey. You were having such fun with your mother."

"I'm all alone? Mommy's at work all day, and every night she's out with Mr. Wes."

"Your mother would never leave you all alone, honey. "

"Ms. Ava and Beau are here with me.

"Ms. Ava?"

"Mommy says she's her maid."

"Where's mommy?"

"She's with Mr. Wes at a dinner party. I asked if I could go, but she said it was for adults only."

"Daddy, you said I could come home if I wanted to."

"Yes, I did. Let me call your mother. Why don't you and Beau watch a movie, and I will call you back."

"You promised, Daddy."

"I know honey, let me call you back."

Luke was so angry he had to calm himself before he called Clair.

Clair was at a fancy restaurant in Paris with her husband. They were entertaining clients that were interested in outright purchasing his newest invention. The sale would net them millions of dollars. Her phone rang, and Wes gave her a stern look. He told her to turn it off, but she refused in case Sophie needed her. She stood and moved away from the table. She grabbed her napkin as it was sliding off her lap.

"Hello?"

"Clair, Sophie called me. She wants me to come get her. She says you left her all alone." Luke knew the minute he spoke; his anger spilled through.

"Hold on, Luke. First of all, she is not alone; she has Ava with her. Second, you go to work every day along with thousands of other parents. So don't try to guilt me."

"That's all true, but when I go to work, she's not miles away from anyone she knows. And you were the one who insisted on having her for two weeks. If you only wanted her for the weekend, we could have worked that out. "

"I didn't intend to work this week, but these new clients came to town, and it's an important deal, Luke."

"More important than a relationship with your daughter? Because that is what's at stake here. Clair, you haven't spent much time with her since you left. There was a time there was nothing more important to you than Sophie. If you don't make this right with her, she may never want to spend time with you again. I want this to work; she needs you in her life." Clair said nothing. Luke thought she hung up. He was about to hang up when she spoke.

"You're right."

"What?"

"I said you're right. Sophie needs to be my priority when she comes. There is nothing more important than my daughter. I need to make this right with her."

"I told her I would call her back. I can give you an hour, Clair. But if she still wants to come home, I'm coming to get her."

"Alright."

Clair hung up the phone and looked over at the table. She took a deep breath and felt the tears running down her perfectly applied makeup. She dabbed her eyes with the napkin, hoping her mascara wasn't running down her face.

Clair didn't know how Wesley was going to handle what she was about to do. She stepped over to him and whispered in his ear. He stood up and excused himself from the table. They stepped away from their guests.

"What is it, Clair?"

"I have to leave."

"What? You can't leave! You know how important these clients are." He placed his hands on her arms.

"I never should have left Sophie alone these last few days. She called Luke and wants to go home."

"This is why I told you I didn't want to have children," Wesley said.

"And we agreed on that. But I have a daughter, and I told you she was part of the package. When I have her, you are going to have to handle business on your own. I'm going home; if you don't like it, you can stay in a hotel for the rest of her stay." Clair said. He lowered his head for a moment.

Wesley nodded and said, "I'm sorry, Clair, your right. I've been selfish, not wanting to make room for her in our lives. You go home and take care of your daughter; I'll make your excuses at the table. Have the town car take you home. I'll take a cab." He took her napkin and wiped some mascara from her face, kissed her cheek, and went back to the table.

Clair rushed out of the restaurant. All the way home, she thought of how she could convince Sophie to give her another chance in the next 45 minutes.

After his conversation with Clair, Luke sat for a moment, trying to collect himself. He hadn't expected Clair to try to make things right. Luke went to his room to change. He would wait out the hour he promised Clair before calling Sophie back. There was still plenty of time before he had to leave for dinner at Ruby's. He considered canceling. But he needed to talk to Manny about the anger that so quickly took him over.

CHAPTER ELEVEN

*T*he door to the penthouse opened. Beau heard and jumped out of Sophie's arms to greet Clair. Sophie was sitting cross-legged on the floor in the TV room watching 'Little Orphan Annie'".

Clair walked into the room with Beau padding along behind. She walked to where Sophie was sitting and knelt beside her. Beau climbed back on Sophie's lap.

"Sophie." Sophie ignored her, keeping her eyes on the TV.

Clair touched her shoulder, "Sophie, please talk to me."

Keeping her eyes forward, she said, "Daddy's coming to get me."

"That's what I want to talk to you about. Please look at me."

Sophie turned to her. "I am sorry I left you alone these last few days. It isn't that I don't want to spend time with you. We have these new...that's not important. What I meant to say is, I'm sorry. I want you to stay. I want to spend this time with you. I love you."

Sophie didn't respond. She could see her mother felt terrible, but she was so homesick. Sophie missed her dad, her friends. She didn't realize how hard it would be to be away from them for so long.

Sophie broke down, crying, "Mommy, you left me all alone."

Clair grabbed Sophie and held her tight, rocking her, "I didn't...I should never have done that. I'm sorry." She pulled back so she could see her daughter's face. "I am so sorry. Please stay and let me make it up to you. I told Wesley I wasn't working for the rest of your stay." Sophie moved out of her mom's hug.

"Really?"

"Yes, I told him I wanted to spend every minute with you."

"But Daddy's coming for me."

"If you want to stay, we can call him. Do you want to stay, Sophie?" She nodded her head.

"Ok, let's give him a call."

Luke had gotten a cup of coffee and sat at the table, waiting to call Sophie back. His phone rang.

"Daddy, It's me."

"Are you alright, sweet pea?"

"Yes, Daddy, mommy came home. She wants me to stay."

"Do you want to?" It was quiet on the line for a few seconds.

"Would it be alright if I decided I wanted to stay?"

"Of course. If that's what you want. Is it?"

"Mommy said she is taking a vacation from work to be with me."

"She did? That's wonderful. But is this what you want?"

"Uh-huh, I want to stay. Will it hurt your feelings, Daddy?"

"You spending time with your mother will never hurt my feelings. I want you to enjoy yourself. And I will call you every day to make sure you're ok." Luke said.

Knowing her father would call her every day and check on her gave Sophie the security she needed.

"Ok, Daddy, I want you to call me every day."

"I love you, Sophie. Can I talk to your mother for a minute?"

"I love you too, Daddy." Sophie handed the phone to her mother, "Daddy wants to talk to you."

"Luke, can you hang on a minute?" Clair put the phone away from her mouth and spoke to Sophie. "Did you eat dinner?" Sophie nodded. "Then let's go to that little Italian Ice shop down the street for dessert," Clair said. Sophie smiled.

"Can Beau come?"

"Sure, go get his leash and get a sweater. I'll be right with you." Sophie got up and left the room. Clair put the phone to her ear.

"Luke, thank you."

Luke had planned on telling her she better straighten up, but he thought better of it and said goodbye.

After a good meal, Ruby went to give the kids baths and read to them. She knew Luke needed to talk to Manny.

Luke told Manny all that happened since he got home from work and how angry he was. "Manny, I need help. I am carrying such resentment toward Clair, and I find myself letting anger take control of me. My greatest fear is if I don't get ahold of myself, I will show this behavior to Sophie."

"God gave us emotions when He created us. He didn't want us to be robots. Emotions are meant to be a good thing. They only become bad when we let our flesh take control. Even anger has a purpose; it causes us to do something about the wrongs that need to be righted in this world. Anger should be directed at sin, not people." Manny got up to retrieve his Bible from the living room. "Let's see what the Bible says. In Ephesians 4:26 it says, 'Be angry, and do not sin; do not let the sun go down on your wrath.'"

"I'm not sure how to be angry and not sin," Luke responded.

"It's saying that there are times to be angry, but you can't harbor it, feed it because it will lead to sin. You have to control it. It goes on to say, 'or give place to the devil'. If you let your flesh get out of control, it leaves room for the devil to get a foothold in your life." Manny said.

"That's what I'm feeling. Like I have let my anger and resentment get out of my control." He lowered his head, "I don't want that. My relationship with Jesus is more important to me than allowing my flesh to rule my emotions." Luke confessed.

"We all have things we have to overcome to stay right with God and not cross over into sin. When I first met Ruby, I would get jealous whenever she would talk to a male friend. It started getting bigger and bigger in me. I knew it wasn't right. She wasn't flirting with these guys.

I had a good Christian friend who helped me realize it was my insecurities that made me so jealous. I felt she was out of my league, and she would compare me to other men. He prayed with me about it for months. During that time, the Lord opened my eyes to the realization that I am a child of the King. If I didn't start changing how I thought of myself and let my insecurities rule my emotions, I would lose her. I still fall short, but with Him, I can get there. I can become the man God intended me to be when he created me in my mother's womb. My love for God's Word started then. It began to take a more important place in my life. Everything I need to know about who I am in Christ and who I should be is in this Book." He held up his Bible.

"Thanks for sharing that with me. Knowing you overcame lets me know I can too. Will you pray with me that God helps me overcome this? I don't want to carry this anger and resentment any longer."

"Yes, and if you want, we can ask David and Jonathan to pray about this too. There is strength in numbers, and I do believe God brought us all together to help each other grow," Manny said.

"You're right. I've been embarrassed to bring it up, but that's my pride. Look where that's got me. I need all your prayers."

When Luke got home that night, he felt so much better. Manny prayed with him and gave him some scripture to memorize. He knew with God all things are possible.

Northern Syria

About sixteen months after she woke up in the Maleh's home, a group of men barged in. They were carrying an injured man.

A big man went to the kitchen table and, with one swipe, wiped off everything on it and had the wounded man placed on it. Mumarada (nurse), as Nabil and his wife Rima referred to her, knew what to do. She ordered the men to assist her while the big man translated. Mumarada took out the bullet and sewed up his leg with V 36 nylon sewing thread. Rima used it to make a few dollars repairing upholstery.

Rima had taught Mumarada some Arabic in the months she was there, but she could not speak or read it. She understood some of what was being said by the men.

The big man spoke to her host family and wanted to know who she was and where she came from. Nabil told them how he came to bring her to his home.

It was apparent the men were soldiers. Not ones on the new President's list of loyal soldiers, or they would have been able to go to a hospital in town for treatment. The man she was working on appeared to be a Major. From what she understood, they were being hunted. She recognized the name of those hunting them, 'The Political Security Directorate', the President's personal Army.

They wanted to move him, but Mumarada explained that he would die if they did. The Major needed time for his wound to stop bleeding.

"Then you must come with us to make sure he lives." The big man said. He was the only one who spoke English.

His brass indicated he was a Lieutenant. He told her they were FSA Soldiers now out of favor in their country.

Nabil came over to her, "you do not have to go. They won't make you. They were once the most elite divisions in the Army. The new President has labeled them terrorists."

"Why," Mumarada asked.

"They were trained by the Turk's once our allies, now an enemy. The new regime feels the FSA will be loyal to the Turks instead of their own country. It's not true. But no matter how many times they swore their allegiance, the President refused to believe them. They are not bad men. Just men without a country." Nabil took her hand, "you can stay with us as long as you need to. It is up to you."

Mumarada moved over to her patient; he was unconscious. She felt a stir in her spirit to go with the soldiers.

"Ok. I will go with you." She said to the Lieutenant, but we must prepare a safe way to transport him."

Nabil spoke with the men, and together they made a stretcher to carry the Major. Mumarada asked Rima for items she could use to dress his wound. She was able to come up with enough to last a few days.

Rima handed Mumarada her Bible. It was written in Arabic and was Rima's most prized possession. Mumarada would have refused, knowing what a great sacrifice it was, but Rima insisted. Mumarada held it to her chest and thanked her, then hid it with the few clothes Rima made her during her stay.

The small band of men and Mumarada had been walking for several hours. Mumarada asked to stop so she could tend the Major. All the movement had caused his wound to continue to bleed. The men carefully brushed aside rocks to make a comfortable place to lay the stretcher. It was apparent the men cared for their leader.

Mumarada lifted the blanket Rima gave to cover him. She had cut off the pants leg so she could get to the injury back at the house. She unwrapped the soiled bandage. As she rewrapped his wound, the Major started to stir.

The first thing the Major felt when his senses came back was the pain. He moaned as Mumarada wrapped his leg. Then he was distracted by the bright light that was coming through his eyelids. It was more brilliant than the Sun but didn't burn.

The Major slowly opened his eyes. What he saw caused him to gasp. A man over seven feet tall, with long hair and built like a warrior, looked down at him from behind the woman. He thought his clothes might be white, but they shimmered like the Sun reflecting off diamonds. It made it hard to tell. The reflection from his clothes blurred his facial features. His one hand was on the hilt

114

of his sheathed sword, on his belt. His other hand was on the shoulder of the woman who was tending his leg. The implication was clear; his mission was to protect her.

When the Major was finally able to speak, he pointed to the man and said, "Malak haris'.

The Lieutenant did not see what the Major saw. He assumed he was referring to the nurse, so from that point, they all referred to her as Malak (Angel).

The Major started talking in Arabic, too fast for Malak to understand. She looked to the Lieutenant who spoke English for the interpretation.

The Lieutenant said the Major was delirious and was talking about a Guardian Angel.

Malak checked his temperature to make sure he wasn't getting an infection. She gave him some water to drink and wet a cloth to put on his head.

The Lieutenant told her they had to keep moving. They were still hours from their camp, and men were looking for them.

Malak stood from the rock she was sitting on and checked on her patient one more time. When she touched him, he opened his eyes. She thought it strange that he never looked at her but past her. She looked around to see what he was looking at.

She covered him up again and made sure the pillow Rima gave him was securely under his head. Then she gave the 'ok' to move him.

When she tried to stand so they could go, he grabbed her wrist and pointed behind her, "Malak haris." She nodded, even though she had no idea what he was pointing at.

When the men lifted him, the movement made him groan. She had nothing for the pain and asked the Lieutenant, "do you have any medical supplies at your camp?"

"Yes, we have supplies."

"Do you have any pain medication?"

115

"We do, but I doubt he will take it. There is a limited supply and would not want to take it from his men if they need it."

Incirlik Air Base

Major Scott was spending most of his time presiding over Summary Court Martials. The Jag Unit was busier now that the Base had started restaffing all the Base's departments.

David worked on writing his verdict on the last Court Martial to put in the file when his secure cell rang.

"Hello?"

"David, it's Faiz. I have some news."

"What is it, Faiz?"

"A call was directed to me from an informant; this informant said he was heading up into the hill country to take care of a sick relative when he passed by the home of Nabil Maleh. He had suspected the man was an underground Christian for a long time but had no proof."

"I don't understand, Faiz."

"Give me a minute to get there. When this man passed by Maleh's home, he saw a woman who was not his wife. She was getting eggs out of the hen house. When she stepped out of the structure, a wind came up and blew off her head covering. She was a foreign woman with blond hair."

"Is that all he knew?"

"Yes, and the other problem is that the news is months old. The informant's family had no phone, so he couldn't call until he came home. But I decided to follow up anyway."

"I take it, it wasn't Anna, or you would have led with that."

"I'm not so sure. I went to visit, but the Maleh's were too afraid to talk to me. I looked around. I didn't see anything that indicated another person was living there. But I had a strong sense that they were not telling me everything. I'm going to go back again in a few weeks, see if I can gain their trust. It's a good lead, David."

"You think so?"

"Yes, they were hiding something."

"Thanks for letting me know, Faiz. I wish you would let me and Jonathan help look. But I understand your concern."

"It is better this way. That is why I called. I want you to know I'm following every lead."

"Thank you, Faiz. I owe you so much."

"You owe me nothing, my friend. I'll keep you informed."

David paused, watched a leaf dancing in a gust of wind, and took a deep breath. *Lord, please help me.*

Luke had gone into Jonathan's office to get his opinion about an enlisted man who wanted to know if filing bankruptcy would affect his security clearance. Jonathan was in the middle of a sentence when he saw David at his office door. He seldom closed his door.

Luke turned and then stood at attention.

"At ease," David said, deciding it was time to tell Luke about his situation. "Am I interrupting something?"

"No, sir. Captain Star was asking my opinion about something. Please come in." They were all still standing.

"I can leave, sir," Luke said.

David hesitated for a moment. "No, Captain. I want you to hear this." He closed the door, stepped over to take a seat, sat and motioned the others to do the same.

"How can I help you, sir," Jonathan said.

David turned to Luke and said, "I have never told you what happened to my wife. I don't talk about it much, it's too painful, but as my Christian brothers, I need your prayers."

"What's happened, Dave?" Jonathan asked.

David started at the beginning and told his story to Luke. Then he said, "Faiz just called with another lead."

"Is it viable?" Jonathan asked.

"He thinks so. I need your prayers. Every time I hear from him, I get my hopes up just to have them crushed again. I don't

117

know how long I can stay sane on this roller coaster ride." He bowed his head. Jonathan moved from behind his desk and put his hand on David's shoulder.

"We will help carry you," he nodded toward Luke. "Can we pray for you?" David nodded.

Jonathan and Luke laid hands on David and prayed for strength and that this new lead would bring them closer to finding Anna. When they finished praying, David felt better; knowing his friends were there to help carry this burden.

CHAPTER TWELVE

*L*uke kept his promise to call Sophie every day. She told him all the fun things they were doing.

"Even Mr. Wes came with us to the Opera at the Palais Garnier. And Saturday we're taking a car to drive into the countryside, and we're going to have a picnic." Her exuberance stalled for a moment. "Daddy, I wish you were here with us."

"I do too, sweet pea, but this is time for you to be with your mother. I miss you, but I want you to have a good time. Are you doing ok now?"

"Yes, I still get homesick at night when you're not there. But I'm ok. I love you, Daddy."

"I love you too. I'll call you tomorrow."

They hung up, and he went back to work.

Paris, France

Clair and Sophie were in her bedroom packing. Clair's two weeks with Sophie were over. She was going to miss her. Sophie needed an extra suitcase for all the presents she insisted on buying for her friends. Clair didn't mind spending the money. She wanted Sophie to be generous and think of others.

Clair had promised to fly back with Sophie and deliver her to Luke, but Wesley felt it a waste of her time. They were still negotiating the sale of his newest invention. Clair spending the last two weeks with Sophie had slowed them down. Clair was the chief counsel for their corporation. She had better ways to spend her time than seven hours each way on a plane. She reluctantly agreed with him, although she knew it would cause a big fight when Luke found out.

After breakfast, Clair road with Sophie in the town car to the airport. Clair was allowed to escort Sophie through the security checkpoint to the terminal gate. Sophie was a minor and had to be accompanied.

Before they got to the check-in counter, they stopped at a little store. Clair bought snacks and a Paris Color book with colored pencils for Sophie's trip. When they found her gate, they sat down.

"Daddy said you were going to go on the plane with me." Clair could see she was nervous about being on the plane alone.

"Oh, sweetheart, I wish I could, but I have to work. A nice stewardess will take you to your seat and make sure you are well taken care of."

"But you made a promise to daddy." Sophie's eyes were starting to tear up.

"I don't want you to leave upset with me, Sophie. But I can't go with you. We had a great time, didn't we?" Sophie nodded her head. "I love you so much, sweetie. We can do this again soon; would you like that?"

"Yes." Sophie hugged her mom. Clair kissed her cheeks and told her again how much she loved her. Her own eyes started to water as the stewardess came to take Sophie on board. As a minor, traveling alone, she had pre-boarding privileges.

Sophie looked back at her mother with tears streaming down her cheeks. It took everything in Clair not to break down. She should have gone on the plane with her, but it was too late now.

Clair sat facing the window to watch the plane take off. She dialed Luke; she might as well get it over with.

Luke woke up excited to have his little girl back today. Last night he cleaned her room. He dusted and vacuumed and washed the sheets on her bed and the trundle. This morning he lined up all her dolls and stuffed animals on her bed the way she liked it.

He stepped in front of the memory wall he had finished this week. The wall was almost full; he would have to start on the other side soon. Sophie spent a lot of time looking at those pictures. She would ask to hear stories about relatives she'd never met. Luke would ask her to tell the story of photos that had her in them. She liked reliving the time spent with her friends.

Luke still had to go to the Commissary to get groceries. He had eaten out most of the time Sophie was gone. Then Luke intended to go to the PX to pick up balloons and flowers for her. He was changing to leave when the phone rang.

"Hello?"

"Luke, I wanted to tell you that Sophie is on her way."

"What do you mean *Sophie* is on her way? You were supposed to escort her to my door. What did you do, Clair?!"

"Calm down. I took two weeks off in the middle of important negotiations to spend time with Sophie. But it's a waste of my time to spend 14 hours on a plane."

"Is that you talking or Wesley?" Luke felt his anger rising in his chest, getting out of control. But at that moment, he didn't care or even try to control it. He was furious with her. And the fact that she let Wesley decide what was best for his daughter was too much. It brought up all the resentment he had been harboring for over a year.

"I agreed with him. Wesley bought her a non-stop flight in first class. He paid extra to have a flight attendant take care of her and deliver her into your hands."

"Clair, she just turned eight, and you sent her alone on a seven-hour flight? She won't have a shoulder to rest her head on when she sleeps or anyone to talk to. And you know Sophie is a worrier. She will fixate on the fact she won't know how to find me." The depth and intensity of the anger toward Clair was beginning to frighten him.

"The flight attendant will make sure she gets to you."

"Yes, but Sophie will worry herself sick about it. Why would you break our agreement? I would have come for her if I had to."

"Luke, I understand you're upset, but she will be fine. You need to understand that we will have different opinions on how to handle our daughter."

"Clair, if anything happens to her…"

"Stop! Nothing is going to happen to her. She is fine."

"Give me her flight information." He started to say more but shut his mouth.

After Clair gave him the information, he hung up on her. He ran his hands down his face and walked out into his back yard. He reached his hand to heaven and prayed.

Lord, you have to help me. I can't live with this anger and resentment. It's like acid to my spirit, eating me up inside. I don't want it; I recognize it's out of control. Lord, I repent for allowing this in my life. Please, Jesus, I want to lay it at the foot of the Cross. Cleanse me with your blood and deliver me. He fell to his knees on the grass, his head to the ground. He stretched his arms in front of him, palms down on the ground, and wept until his lungs ached.

He didn't know how much time had passed, but he sat up and raised his hands to his Father in heaven and started worshiping Him. A sensation of warm thick honey pouring over him began at his fingertips. Then slowly covered his head and body clear to the tips of his toes. He started thanking God for his great mercy. When he finally stood, he was a new man; he'd never be the same again. God had delivered him.

The flight attendant took Sophie's hand and headed for the jetway that led to the plane. She turned, tears streaming down her cheeks, to look at her mother standing there watching her go. Sophie felt so alone.

The Lady took her to the first seat in first class and placed her backpack under her seat.

"Hi, my name is Marci; what's yours?"

"Sophie."

"Sophie, if you need anything, all you have to do is get my attention, alright?" Sophie nodded.

Sophie watched all the pretty ladies dressed in nice clothes boarding the plane. Sophie was looking for kids her age. A little girl walked in, holding her mother's hand. Sophie smiled and waved at her as she passed. The girl smiled back. She watched as they sat four rows behind her on the other side. A few other children came in but were either older or younger. One little boy being carried by his father spotted Sophie and smiled at her. He opened and closed his little hand, trying to wave. When the parade of people ended, she watched as the passengers settled in. She noticed some passengers struggled to put carry-ons in the overhead compartments.

The plane took off, and the attendants showed everyone the proper use of masks and seat belts. Sophie stopped Marci as she walked by.

"Miss Marci, can you see if that little girl," she pointed to her, "can come color with me?"

"I will ask, but she only speaks German; she may not understand you."

"That's ok." Sophie leaned over the armrest, knees under her, to watched as the attendant spoke with the mother. The mother looked over to Sophie and nodded her head. The little girl came to sit with her.

The two girls managed to communicate with a few universal words and hand motions. Sophie took out her new color book of Paris and colored pencils. She took out a page then handed it to her friend, who did the same. They colored for a long time then looked at the comic books Sophie brought with her. The other passengers could hear the girls giggling and enjoying each other.

When it was time to serve dinner, Marci came over to Sophie.

"I'm sorry, but your friend will have to go back to her seat now."

The girls hugged and said goodbye. Marci put dinner on her retractable table and moved on to the other passengers.

Sophie ate her dinner, then laid down across the seats and fell asleep. She woke up crying. Marci sat down beside her.

"What's the matter, honey?"

"I had a bad dream that my dad didn't know where I was. He couldn't find me. I'm all alone. My mother was supposed to take me home."

Marci pulled her close and hugged her. "Don't you worry, I won't leave you until you are in your daddy's arms."

Sophie gave a sad smile. "You promise?"

Marci took a napkin from her apron and dabbed Sophie's eyes. "Yes, I promise."

Luke got to the airport an hour early, his hands full of balloons and flowers. He checked the large screen to find the terminal where Sophie's plane would land and if it were on time. Luke moved to the waiting area on the east side of the security checkpoint. He figured the passenger from that gate were likely to come through that side.

The plane landed, and all the passengers got off before Marci took Sophie by the hand and walked her out. When they stepped off the jetway to the gate, Sophie looked around.

"Daddy's not here. He doesn't know where I am." Sophie panicked.

Marci squatted down in front of her. "No, Sophie, he knows where you are. The Airport Security makes everyone wait on the other side."

Luke watched as a caravan of people started coming past the security point. He stopped a man in a US Air Force Uniform and asked what flight he came in on. It was Sophie's. He kept watching as the line thinned out, and only stragglers were still coming through.

Luke strained to see around the check station and saw a woman holding hands with a little girl. He could spot Sophie anywhere. With a big smile on his face, he waited for her to notice him.

It only took a few seconds for her to see him. He heard her yell, "Daddy." She let go of the flight attendant and ran to him. He got down on one knee and opened his arms for her. Sophie wrapped her arms around his neck. He lifted her and swung her around in a circle, causing the flowers and balloons to tangle.

"Daddy, I missed you so much." She kissed his cheek.

"I missed you more." He managed to untangle the flowers and balloons and handed them to her. "These are for you."

"Oh, Daddy, they are so pretty." Then Sophie whispered in his ear. "Can I give them to my friend? She took care of me."

"If you like." He finally looked over to the woman who had walked with Sophie. "Marci?"

Sophie handed her the flowers. Marci bent down and kissed her cheek. "Thank you, Sophie, you are delightful."

When she straightened back up, she responded to Luke. "Is this your little girl?" They moved deeper into the waiting area so others could get by them.

"Yes," Luke said while stroking Sophie's hair.

"She is such a sweet, lovely girl, Luke."

"Yes, she is." He said, looking down at her.

"Do you have a long layover?"

"No, I only have a short break before I have a turnaround flight."

"Remember my offer. If you ever have an extended layover, call me. I will come and keep you company."

Marci smiled, "I'd like that."

They said goodbye and headed to the baggage claim.

"Daddy, how do you know Ms. Marci?"

"I met her after I dropped you off at your mother's."

"Oh. Marci's really pretty. Isn't she Daddy?"

"Yes, she is."

The carousel just started turning when they got down to the baggage claim.

"I have two suitcases. Mommy had to buy me another one to bring back the presents I bought."

"Ok, point them out to me." Sophie was still holding the balloons.

"There." She pointed.

Luke grabbed them off the carousel and rolled them across the hall to where the carts were.

"Can I put the dollar in, Daddy?" He handed her the dollar. Then went to the end and pulled off a cart when the arm released. He set both suitcases on it, and Sophie tossed her backpack on top. Luke tied the balloons to the side of the cart.

"Can I ride the rails?" Sophie had her unique definition of what 'riding the rails' was. She thought it meant putting her feet on the bottom bar of the cart and placing her hands on the handlebar.

"Sure." Luke enclosed her by putting his hands on either side of her. Then he pushed the cart and headed to his car.

Sophie talked a mile a minute about her trip, but Luke's mind was on something else. He thought of Marci and how grateful he was that he had met her. Luke knew he wasn't ready for a relationship yet. But she had made him realize there was still the possibility of romance for him after the divorce. She had jump-started his heart.

As Luke and Sophie pulled into the driveway, Sophie asked, "Can Lizzy spend the night tonight?"

"We'll have to ask Aunt Ruby first. As soon as we get your things in the house, we have to go to Uncle Jonathan's. He is setting up a BBQ to celebrate."

"Really?" Sophie got excited. Duke and CJ had always called each other's parents, Aunt, and Uncle. Sophie and Lizzy picked up on it, and now they all referred to each other's parents that way.

"Yes, they are so happy you're home."

Sophie hurried into the house to change. Luke brought in her suitcases.

"Daddy, I want to bring their gifts." She opened the case with the wrapped gifts in it and pulled them out.

Luke went to get some shopping bags with handles to carry them.

Sophie gave her dad his gifts first to open. The shirt and wallet were expensive. He knew Clair must have spent a decent amount of money on them. He was sure the other gifts would be equally expensive. Sophie put on her new shirt over a new pair of jeans with embroidering on the back pocket. The shirt was lavender and sparkled with beads forming the Eiffel Tower.

"Isn't this pretty, Daddy?" She modeled it for him. "I got a pink one for Lizzy. I like the pink best, but I wanted Lizzy to have it because it's her favorite color."

"That is very considerate of you. Now let's put these in the bags, so we don't keep everyone waiting."

Luke pulled into Jonathan's driveway to Sophie's squeal and laughter. She pointed to a huge sign outside that said, "WELCOME HOME SOPHIE". The balloons around it were moving with the wind. Sophie was bouncing in her seat.

"Look, Daddy, it's for me. It has my name."

"Yes, it is. I told you everyone missed you." He put the car in park. Sophie undid her seatbelt and jumped out first.

Lizzy was looking out the window and screamed. "Sophie," as she ran out the door, leaving it open, and swallowed her friend in a big hug. The girls were giggling.

The house emptied onto the yard as they went to greet Sophie. She got hugs and kisses from everyone.

Jonathan saw Luke getting some bags out of the back of his SUV. "Let me help you with that." He grabbed one of the bags.

"Jonathan, thank you for doing all this," he swiped his hand around the yard at the decorations. "It means so much to her." Luke got a little choked up.

"Hey, everyone chipped in, and the boys and Lizzy put up the sign and balloons. We are all family, Luke." Jonathan added.

During the BBQ in the backyard, Sophie passed out all the gifts. Zoey and Ruby loved their silk scarfs from Paris. The men roared with laughter over the caricature sketches, making fun of each other. Sophie had an artist make it from a picture she carried of the four men. They had their arms around each other, smiling for the camera. Each one over-exaggerated the man who received that sketch. So all the pictures were different. Duke and CJ got a nice long sleeve Polo shirt with Paris embroidered on it and the newest X Men movable action figures. Lizzy squealed with delight at the new pink shirt that matched Sophie's and her pink wallet. Ricky and Liam got extra-large size Legos that could build the Eiffel Tower.

The BBQ was great, like always, and the kids were so happy to be together again. Lizzy got permission to spend the night with Sophie, so the two girls were talking and giggling in the back seat.

When they got home, Sophie and Lizzy went to the memory wall to look at the new pictures.

"Daddy, you have to put up pictures of my party tonight," she said.

"No problem. We have lots to choose from."

Luke put away the leftovers Zoey sent home with him. He knew the girls would keep busy until bedtime talking, so he did some work he brought home with him.

Luke was a little disappointed that the summer had slipped by so fast. He had wanted to take Sophie somewhere on vacation, but it didn't work out. Instead, he paid Deniz extra to allow Lizzy to stay with Sophie during the days. Deniz had a college class at 2 pm, so she picked up Duke and CJ and took them to the REC Center on Base. The Center had activities for the High School teens from 9 am to 12:30 pm. From 1:30 until 5 pm, the Elementary age children had use of the facilities.

Everyone was happy with that and had a great summer. Duke and CJ kept an eye on Sophie and Lizzy, which made Luke much more comfortable.

There was a box on the porch the next morning when he headed for work. He knew it was school clothes from Clair for Sophie. He had never asked for child support, even though she offered. He knew if Sophie needed something that he couldn't take care of himself, she would help. And Clair kept Sophie in clothes, including PJ's and underwear, all year long.

That night after Deniz went home with the perfume, Sophie brought her from Paris. Luke finished making the dinner Deniz started and then brought out the box from Clair.

Sophie loved all the nice clothes her mom had sent. She had told her mother that she gave some of her new clothes to Lizzy. So this time there was a bundle of new clothes with a note on them, 'for Lizzy'.

"Look, Daddy, these are for Lizzy." Sophie was more excited about that than her own clothes. "She sent an extra backpack too.'

Sophie lifted the two and said, "oh, Daddy, isn't this the cutest. I'm going to give it to Lizzy."

"But Sophie, if you like it the best, why don't you keep it," Luke said, feeling a little ashamed of himself.

"Because Daddy, it will make me happier seeing her wear it than if I keep it for myself. Can we go to her house so I can give them to her?"

"Sure, let me call and make sure it's ok."

Sophie picked a few more things from her pile of new clothes and put them in Lizzy's pile.

Luke couldn't remember ever being so giving and selfless in his own life. He prayed she would never change; that kind of giving heart only comes from the Lord.

CHAPTER THIRTEEN

Sophie didn't feel well but didn't want to miss school, so she didn't tell her dad. He would have made her stay home, and that was too boring.

Sophie felt better once she got to school. But by the last class of the day, she started having a headache and a stomachache. Sophie walked with Lizzy out to the bus when her stomach started turning. She felt like she would throw up, so she pushed her things on Lizzy and said she had to go to the bathroom.

The bus pulled up, and Lizzy let everyone get on ahead of her. She stood there by the bus door and watched for Sophie to come back out the doors. The substitute bus driver was staring at her.

"Hey, you need to get on the bus now. It's time to go."

"But Sophie isn't here."

"I'm sorry, but we can't wait for her. If I'm five minutes late, parents will start calling transportation, and I'll get in trouble."

"I can't leave without her."

"If you don't get on, I'll have to leave you." Lizzy stood there, not sure what to do. She couldn't leave her best friend, she backed away, and the driver closed the door and drove off.

Lizzy tried to get into the school; the door was locked. She banged on it, but everyone in the office was already gone. If there were any teachers there, they were too far away to hear.

Sophie made it into one of the stalls before she started throwing up. Every time she thought there was nothing left to throw up, she threw up again. Sophie didn't remember eating this much. Finally, she started throwing up bile.

I have to get to the bus before it leaves me. Sophie thought as she went to the sink and rinsed out her mouth. She took some paper towels to dry her hands and face and put some more in her pocket.

She felt better now as she walked out the front doors pushing the standard panic bars. The bus was gone. *It left without me!* She did a 360° turn, looking for anyone still there. That's when she saw Lizzy sitting on a bench.

"Lizzy." She looked up when Sophie called her name.

"Sophie, I was so worried about you. I tried to look for you, but the door was locked." Lizzy hugged her friend and handed back her backpack.

"Why aren't you on the bus?" Sophie asked, putting her backpack over her shoulders.

"He wouldn't wait, and I couldn't go without you."

"Thank you, Lizzy." She hugged her friend again. She went to the school doors to see if they could get in and find a phone to call her dad. But the door had locked itself after Sophie walked out.

"I guess we'll have to walk. We know the bus route." Sophie tried not to let Lizzy know how sick and worried she was.

"Ok," Lizzy agreed.

Duke and CJ were busy talking with their friends. The new Fantastic Four movie was supposed to come out soon. They relived some of the best fight scenes from the last film when the bus started moving. They had traveled a few miles when CJ noticed the girls weren't in their seats.

"Duke, where are Lizzy and Sophie?"

"I don't know; Lizzy was at the end of the line when we got on."

CJ half stood in his seat. "Does anyone know why Lizzy and Sophie aren't on the bus?"

A little hand went up in front. CJ recognized him, "Tyler, what do you know?"

"Sophie was sick. She ran back into the school. Lizzy wouldn't get on without her, and the bus driver said he couldn't wait."

Duke got up and went to the bus driver. CJ went after him.

"You two have to sit down." The bus driver said.

"You left Sophie and Lizzy at school. How are they supposed to get home?" Duke said, reaching out his hand to steady himself on the bus's door lever.

"I'm sure someone in the office will call their parents."

"What if there's no one in the office. The office closes right after school." Duke said.

"I'm sorry, but I can't make the rest of the children late; their parents will be worried. It's policy." The driver said.

"Then let us off. We'll go back and check." CJ said and headed back to get their backpacks.

"I can't do that. Now you need to sit down. Or I'll have to pull over."

Duke wouldn't move. CJ came back with their backpacks as the bus driver pulled over. "You have to get in your seats!"

Duke took hold of the lever that opened the door and pushed it before the driver could stop him. Duke and CJ jumped off the bus and started back toward the school. They heard the doors close behind them as the bus left.

A cold wind started up, and a chill went through Sophie's body. She didn't have on her heavy coat or her gloves. She reset her barrettes to catch the loose strands blowing in her face.

Lizzy noticed her rubbing her hands on her coat sleeves. She took off her gloves and offered them to her friend. Sophie refused.

"No sense in both of us being cold." Sophie said.

Lizzy handed one of the gloves to her, "this way, we'll both be half warm." Lizzy smiled. Sophie took the glove and put it on her right hand.

Sophie started feeling like she would throw up again. She moved to the grass under a tree and threw up. Her face was white as a ghost.

"Sophie, are you alright?" She took Sophie's backpack and stroked her hair like her mom always did when she was sick.

"I'm not feeling good." She took a paper towel from her pocket and wiped her face.

"Can you walk?" Lizzy asked.

"I think so; I feel better after I throw up."

"But you're not throwing anything up; it's only water," Lizzy said.

"I'll be ok." Sophie started walking again but let Lizzy carry her backpack for her.

Sophie knew where they were. She could see the 12-foot cyclone fencing that surrounded the cities tennis courts. They were for public use, donated to the park by a rich tennis player. They were still about four miles from home.

As they got to the fence, a tall thin, scary-looking man was standing there. The only thing separating them was the fence. He started saying things to them in Turkish while walking alongside them. They couldn't understand what he was saying, but his tone was creepy, and it sounded nasty. Lizzy started crying.

Duke and CJ started jogging back to the school. Duke sped up; he felt an urgency to find them. CJ kept up. As they got closer to the tennis courts, they saw two girls in the distance. A man was on the other side of the fence. When they were close enough, CJ could see Lizzy was afraid. Then they saw Sophie move to the grass and bend over.

They ran as fast as they could to get to them. CJ jumped on the fence, shaking it, and hollering, scaring the man off. Duke went to Sophie; she was still throwing up bile.

"Sophie, are you ok? Can you walk?" He had his hand on her back.

134

"I don't know…I'm so sick." She started coughing and sat on the grass.

Duke went over to CJ and Lizzy. "She's too sick to walk. CJ, carry my backpack, and I'll piggyback her."

CJ helped Sophie onto Dukes back. Then he took their backpacks and grabbed Lizzy's hand. Duke and CJ took turns carrying her. After a few blocks, Sophie's hand started to slip from around Duke's neck.

"Hold on, Sophie, we'll get you some help." Duke stopped. "CJ, she's slipping. Can you help me push her up higher on my back?" CJ dropped the backpacks he was carrying and helped Duke readjust Sophie.

At this rate, it was going to take a long time to get home.

Deniz was at the bus stop waiting for Sophie. When the bus passed her by, she ran to the next stop, after it. When he opened the door, she asked where Sophie was.

"I don't know. She didn't get on the bus." The driver said.

"Is Lizzy here?"

"No, she wouldn't get on without her."

"What about CJ and Duke?" Deniz asked. She knew they could tell her what was going on.

"They got off the bus when they saw the two little girls weren't on."

"And you just left those kids to fend for themselves?!" Deniz asked.

"Listen, young lady. I have a schedule I have to keep." The driver said. The parents were gathering by the stop listening to the conversation.

"You could have called someone," Deniz said.

"That's the school's job. You need to move so these children can get off the bus.

Deniz stared at him but moved. She ran to her car; she knew the bus route and figured that was the way the kids would walk.

135

She could hear the parents behind her upset at what the bus driver had done. No doubt he would get written up for this.

Duke had switched back with CJ. They were both getting tired, but Sophie was getting worse, and there was no way she could walk.

Lizzy was looking down the road and saw a car that looked familiar. "That's Deniz's car." She yelled, pulling on CJ so he would look. Duke put Sophie down, and they waved to get her attention.

Deniz saw them. She waited for some cars to pass, then she made an illegal U-turn and pulled the car up next to them.

Deniz hopped out of the car, "are you guys alright?"

"Sophie's real sick. That's why she missed the bus." Duke said. Deniz went to Sophie to check on her; her skin was hot and clammy. Deniz decided to take her to the hospital on Base.

"I'm going to give you guys a ride home and take her to the hospital." Lizzy asked if she could go to the hospital with Sophie. They all climbed in. Deniz called Luke on the phone he supplied for her in case of emergencies.

The first few months of school had passed by quickly. Luke noticed Sophie wasn't her bouncy self this morning. He decided he would check her temperature when she got home. He only had a few more files to go through, then he could leave.

Luke couldn't help but chuckle out loud when he thought of her first day of third grade. He had ahold of Sophie's hand, waiting for the bus when he asked her if she was nervous about having new teachers.

"No, Daddy, but we have to talk." Luke squatted down to be face to face.

"What is it, sweet pea?"

"That, Daddy. That was my nickname when I was little. I'm in third grade after all. I need a more grown-up nickname." It was so hard for him not to laugh out loud. But he contained himself.

He put his finger up to his chin and closed his eyes like he was thinking hard. When he opened his eyes, he said, "what about pumpkin?"

Sophie put her hands on her hips and scowled. "Do I look like a pumpkin, Daddy?" This time he couldn't hold it; he laughed. Sophie was not amused.

Luke put his finger to his chin again and closed his eyes. He opened them and said, "what about princess?"

She imitated him and put her finger on her chin and closed her eyes, lifting her head a little. Then her eyes popped open, "I like it."

"Ok, princess, it is. Deal." He stood and put out his hand to shake hers as the bus pulled up.

Sophie shook it and said, "Deal." Then headed to the bus. Luke hollered after her.

"Have a good day, princess." She turned to him and smiled.

His phone rang, bringing him back to the moment.

"Hello?"

"Mr. Luke, Sophie is really sick. I'm taking her to the hospital." Deniz was using her earbuds on the way to drop off the boys.

"What happened?" Luke asked as he grabbed his briefcase to meet her there.

"I'm not sure. All I know is Sophie missed the bus. Lizzy wouldn't get on without her. When Duke and CJ saw they weren't on the bus, they got off. I was at our bus stop when it drove right past me. I chased it to the next stop. That's when the bus driver told me she wasn't on the bus." She paused as she slowed to turn into the housing complex. "The boys had been carrying her piggyback when I found them."

"I'll meet you there." He went to Ruby to tell her where he was going and got on the elevator.

Luke parked and was standing in front of the emergency room doors when Deniz pulled up. Sophie had laid her head on Lizzy's lap, eyes closed.

Luke opened the back door. He reached in and scooted her closer to him so he could lift her out of the car. Then he ran into the hospital with her. She was lethargic. Luke felt her hot skin when her face touched his.

Sophie stirred long enough to realize who was carrying her, "Daddy." She said, then laid her head back on his shoulder.

Hearing her say his name ripped at his heart. He should have made sure she wasn't sick this morning. This was his fault.

As Luke was heading in the door, Manny pulled up behind Deniz in his marked police car.

"Deniz, what happened?" Ruby had called him.

"Sophie's really sick, Mr. Diaz." Lizzy heard her dad's voice and opened the back door.

"Daddy," she cried. "Sophie is so sick." She wrapped her arms around his waist. He lifted her.

"I know, sweetheart. But the doctor will take care of her."

"Mr. Diaz, should I wait?" Deniz asked. She didn't know if she would be in the way.

"If you want to. But I can call you as soon as I know anything if you'd like." She thought about it and decided that would be better.

"Yes, thank you." She gave him her number.

The receptionist took Luke's information and asked him to wait until a nurse called for them. He saw Manny come in just as the nurse ushered Sophie and Luke to an exam room. She took off her coat, shoes, and one mitten. Then took her vitals and placed an oxygen reader on her finger.

Luke sat next to her until the doctor walked in. The doctor introduced himself as Captain Nguyen, shook Luke's hand, and moved to Sophie's bedside. He checked her ears, nose, and throat,

138

then asked. "What are her symptoms?" The more information he had, the better he could diagnose her.

"All I know is she started throwing up at school," Luke said.

The doctor ordered a chest x-ray and a throat swab. He turned to the nurse, "what's her temperature?"

"104," she replied.

"It could be the flu, but I want to make sure." The doctor said. "I'll be back as soon as I get the results." He turned to the nurse. "Get some intravenous fluids going. She is dehydrated." He nodded to Luke then left the room. The nurse took over from there.

Luke went to the waiting room when they took Sophie for an x-ray. He knew Manny would be waiting.

When he walked through the door, he saw Lizzy and Manny sitting in padded, wooden chairs. The same ones they sat in not too long ago. Luke walked over to them. Manny and Lizzy met him halfway when they saw him come through the doors.

"What's going on, Luke?" Manny asked.

"They're taking an x-ray now. They have fluids going in her arm, and they tested for strep."

"Is Sophie going to be alright, Uncle Luke?"

Luke knelt on one knee in front of her and put his hands on her arms. "She will be. The doctor is taking care of her. Thanks for staying with her. You are a good friend."

"I'm her best friend," she gave a sad smile.

"Yes, you are." He took the single mitten from his pocket. "Is this yours?"

"Yes. Her hands were cold, so I shared my mittens with her. I offered her both, but she wouldn't take them."

Luke stood up, and they moved over to the chairs. Manny told him that David, Jonathan, and Zoey called, wanting to know if there was something they could do.

"Can you call them back and thank them for me. Please ask them to pray for her, ok." Manny nodded. "There is no sense in you and Lizzy waiting. I'll call you as soon as I know anything."

"Are you sure, Luke? We don't mind waiting." Manny said.

Luke put his hand on Manny's shoulder. "I'm sure. I know your only a phone call away if I need you." With that, Luke got up and went back through the doors.

Luke finally helped Sophie into her pajamas at 11 pm. The doctor said she had the stomach flu and Bronchitis. He gave her a strong dose of antibiotics intravenously. He said they could leave after the fluid bag was empty. But he needed to bring her back to the nurse's station the next day for more fluids and antibiotics. The rest of the antibiotic regimen she could take orally. The doctor suggested Luke pick up some acetaminophen and Pedialyte. He didn't think she would be able to keep food down for a few days. He told him to give her lots of liquids.

When he finally tucked her in her own bed and prayed with her. He headed to his room to change. He intended to sleep on the trundle in case she had trouble breathing through the night. He was at the door when Sophie's week voice said, "Daddy, you didn't brush my hair."

He grabbed the brush and the ribbon off her vanity and told her to lie on her tummy so he could brush it. He sang to her and brushed it exactly fifty times, then tied the ribbon on. By the time he finished, she was sound asleep.

Luke was able to work from home on the days he didn't have to meet with a client or be in court. Deniz agreed to take her classes virtually on the days he couldn't be there.

By the seventh day, Sophie was begging to go back to school. She finished the antibiotic regimen for the Bronchitis; the fever and cough were gone. And it looked like the stomach flu ran its course. So two days later, Luke was back outside, holding her hand, waiting for the bus.

David was heading out the door; his dream still lingering with him. He dreamt he, Duke, CJ, and Anna, were back at Disneyland riding the same rapid water ride they did three years ago. Only this time, Duke and CJ were older; Anna laughed as the boys whooped and hollered. He was sitting across from her in unbelief. Even in his dream, David knew this couldn't be happening. It was a happy dream; he hated to wake up from it. He wouldn't have thought twice about it if it were a memory, but this felt like a promise. He shook himself and locked the door behind him.

It had been months since David heard from Faiz. The lead about Nabil Maleh was solid, but he wouldn't talk to Faiz.

David was driving on Base when his cell rang.

"Hello?"

"David, Faiz here. I have some news."

"Faiz, I've worried about you," David said.

"Thank you for that. Keep praying. I told you about my last visit to the Maleh home. They were reluctant to speak. I've been going back as often as I could, without the uniform, trying to gain their trust. It took a while, but yesterday, they told me what they knew."

"Was it Anna, Faiz?"

"Yes."

"Are you telling me it was Anna at their home?" David was shaken by the news. He pulled his car over so he wouldn't cause an accident.

"Yes," Faiz paused. "Nabil told me she treated many of his neighbors who could not go to the hospital. He said she would talk to them about Jesus. Many became believers."

"Where is she now?"

Faiz told him everything that Nabil told him.

"So he saw us looking for Anna after the accident but didn't tell us?"

"Yes, he didn't know if we intended her harm, so he stayed away," Faiz explained.

"Now she's with a band of FSA fighters?" David asked.

"Yes, she went with them to nurse the Major's wound...we just missed her, David." Faiz's voice was crestfallen.

"So how do we find her now?"

Faiz was silent on the other end. David thought they lost their connection. "Faiz?"

"David, the Kurds are fighting the Turks on the border. The safety zone is breaking down. That FSA company, if it's still a company, is hiding right in the middle of it."

"Why are the FSA out of favor with the new Administration."

"Because the Turks trained them when they were allies with Syria. The President has ordered them on the terrorist list because he wants to avoid a potential coup. The FSA has always been the people's army, and the people would back them."

"Are the Kurds against them too?" David asked.

"No, they will leave them alone. The Major might be trying to cross over into Turkey and join the man who trained them. He's now a General in the Turkish Army. I think he hopes the General will let them attach to his troops. He has the authority to allow it as a joint Military training exercise. That way, they would be safe until the political climate in Syria changes."

"How will they treat Anna?" David was almost afraid to ask.

"She's a nurse; they need her. I don't think the Major will let anything happen to her. But if they get caught in the middle of a skirmish, things could get dangerous."

"Faiz, I'm coming down. I don't care how dangerous it is. I need to find her."

"David, listen to me. Wait until I find them. I need to have a reason to get away from the office. As soon as I can come up with a legitimate reason, I will hunt for her."

David rubbed his hand over his face. "Alright, I'll wait. But Faiz, please get to her before anything happens. This is the closest we've ever been. I can't lose her now."

"Alright, David, keep praying."

"And Faiz."

"Yes."

"Once you find her, you need to come out. You should have been out of there long ago."

"I will, David."

David's hands were wrapped tight on the steering wheel; they started sweating. When Faiz hung up, David leaned his head on his hand and prayed. *We're so close, Lord. Please send your Angel's to protect her and bring her back to me.*

David drove to work. He needed to tell Jonathan and Luke what Faiz told him.

The One Who Stayed: Sophie's Story

CHAPTER FOURTEEN

$\mathcal{T}$he office was getting ready to head out to the last day of school's Field Day. The few who didn't have children stayed to allow the others to go. Major Young had a court date, so he couldn't make it this year.

With school out, Luke was dreading a call from Clair wanting Sophie for two weeks. He knew it was good for her, but Luke spent those two weeks worrying and missing her.

That evening the call came. "Hello?"

"Hello, Luke, Wesley and I are in Milan for the month and would like Sophie to join us."

"For a month?"

"No, we have business to do, but I'm taking off two weeks to spend with my daughter." Luke was glad she brought that up because he planned to if she didn't.

"I'll ask her if she would like to go."

"Luke, there's asking, and then there's discouraging."

"Clair, I wouldn't do that. If she wants to go, I want her to have the experience. But this time, you pick her up here, and I'll bring her home."

"That's fair."

"When do you want her."

"As soon as possible."

"Alright, I'll call you back."

As he headed to Sophie's room, he felt light; there was no anger, no resentment. It was so different than before. He thanked

145

the Lord for his deliverance. He stood at her door, watching her put up the medals from the field day on her vanity mirror. He'd have to get hooks so she could put them on the wall. It took a minute for her to see him.

"Look, Daddy, my medals."

"I see, princess. You did a good job." He walked to her bed and sat on the edge, patting the spot next to him.

"Come talk to me for a minute."

Sophie smiled and sat next to him.

"Your mom called. She and Wesley are in Italy and want you with them for two weeks." He saw Sophie started to get excited then curbed it. No doubt she worried it would hurt his feelings.

"Sophie, you don't have to worry about hurting my feelings because you want to see your mother. The two of you need to have a good relationship." Sophie looked at him and smiled.

"It's fun to be with mom, but will I have to be alone on the plane again?" She asked.

"No, absolutely not. Your mother will pick you up here, and I will come to get you in Italy."

Sophie jumped off the bed and clapped her hands, "really, Daddy, you'll come get me?"

"Yes, and we will spend a few days in Italy together. Would you like that?"

Sophie hugged him, "yes, that would be so much fun." Her smile left. "Daddy, two weeks is a long time. I got so homesick; do I have to stay that long?"

"You only see your mother a couple of times a year. How long do you want to stay?" She thought about it.

"One week."

"Sophie, that's not enough. How about ten days?" She thought about it for a second and nodded.

"Ok, ten days. Deal. She put out her hand to shake on it." He laughed and shook her hand.

"Deal."

"Hello?" Clair answered.

"Clair, I talked to Sophie, she wants to see you, but she won't stay for two weeks."

"What did you say to her?"

"Clair, she only wanted to stay a week. I talked her into ten days. As she gets older and you show that you want to spend the time with her, she will want to stay longer." There was a pause on the other end.

"Alright. When can Sophie come?"

"When do you want her to come?"

"I can fly in next Friday morning, and we could get a flight back on the same day. That way, I wouldn't have to stay the night."

"That works for me. I'll make sure Sophie's ready for you."

They finished the conversation, and he went to let Sophie know when she would be leaving.

Northern Border of Syria

Malak walked with the small band of soldiers for hours. They only took one more break when she insisted she needed to check on the Major. The Lieutenant was concerned they might be spotted and expressed to her they needed to move quickly.

It was almost dusk when Malak smelled smoke. At the top of a steep hill, she saw a welcome sight. A camp perfectly situated in a valley. There was a small waterfall that likely supplied all their water needs. Further down the small river, there was a barrel lifted on stilts that she thought might be a makeshift shower. There were probably a hundred identical two-man Army issue, 'desert tan' tents on the valley floor. There was one large cook tent nearest the water. On a shelf, about 20 feet above those were three larger tents. They headed for one of those.

The smell of food cooking on the fire was making Malak's stomach growl. She had shared what Rima sent with her for the trip. They took Major Jabban into his tent. It was larger inside than

147

it looked, easily 18 by 12. It had that strong canvas odor that's hard to explain. Rolled wool blankets lay at the foot of an army cot with a sleeping pad laid out. A tent stove sat in the corner next to a table and chairs. There were stackable plastic storage bins against the furthest tent wall.

The Major was lifted off the stretcher and onto his cot. Then Lieutenant Arabi gave the men some instructions. They left, taking the stretcher with them. Malak didn't understand much of what he said, but it had to do with the supply tent.

"Lieutenant, we need to get the Major out of these clothes, and he needs to be washed down. Can you take care of that?"

"Yes. I have the men working on getting you a private area in the supply tent."

"Thank you. But what I need is medical supplies. What do you have?"

"I know there are some in boxes in the supply tent. You can go through them. I have not seen them myself."

Malak went over to check on the Major. She worried about infection. When she touched his skin, it was too hot. It confirmed her suspicion. She wondered if she had left some dirt particle or part of the bullet in the wound. She needed to reopen it and irrigate it again. It was the last thing she wanted to put him through.

"Lieutenant, he has a high fever. While you clean him up, I'm going to check on your medical supplies, see if you have anything that will help lower it." He nodded as he started to take off the Major's uniform.

The supply tent was even larger than the Major's tent. Men were putting up a divider. She asked if they would help her go through the boxes looking for medical supplies.

After going through all of them, she found they had a decent collection of wound care items. A lot of the boxes said, Syrian American Medical Society. She found fluids for intravenous rehydration and all sorts of instruments for surgeries. There were

148

a few doses of pain killer. What she needed was more pain medication and antibiotics, at the very least. One box had gloves, masks, and bandages of all sorts; another had medicated wraps for burns and infected cuts. She started setting up a triage station. The soldiers finished with the divider and left. The only soldier still there was standing at the door. She noticed him when she stepped outside.

"What is your name." She asked.

"Private Kilic," he responded.

"Private Kilic, can you get me a table, chairs, and a cot for the clinic?" He didn't understand, so she took a pencil and tablet from one of the boxes and drew out what she needed. He nodded and called out to a man working outside the tent on a latrine for her.

Private Kilic followed her back to the Major's tent and stayed by the entrance outside.

"Lieutenant, why is that man following me?"

"He is your guard."

"My guard? Am I a prisoner?!" She gasped.

"No, no. The Private is your protection." The Lieutenant said.

"Do I have to worry about your men?" Malak asked as she laid the items she brought from the supply tent on the table.

"No, but the Major insisted you have protection." He watched as she put a catheter in the Major's arm and set up an IV drip. He held up the bag of fluids while she looked for somewhere to hang it. She took it from him and hung it on a loose pin on the inside aluminum frame of the tent.

Malak removed a paper from her pocket and handed it to the Lieutenant. "You have medical supplies, but you need these items. Immediately."

He read it, "We have no access to antibiotics or pain medication."

"Every country has a black market. And I'm sure the nonprofit medical group that takes care of the refugees has what we need.

149

"I am sure they do, but they are not going to give it to us."

"You'll figure it out. I need those antibiotics for your Major. His body is not strong enough to fight off this infection on its own. And as soon as he's conscious, I will be using up what little pain medication you have in your supplies." She said.

The Lieutenant went to the guard at the door and gave him an order. He stepped over to the storage bins. He uncovered a container and discretely removed something in an envelope from it. Then replaced the cover; he moved to the table and wrote out the items needed on a pad.

In a few minutes, a Sergeant came in. The Lieutenant gave him what he took out of the box and the list. He then gave him some orders, and the Sergeant responded and left.

Incirlik Military Base

Clair knocked on Luke's door right on time. Sophie ran to open it. "Mommy," she hollered, hugging her. Luke was a few steps behind her pulling her suitcase and carrying her backpack.

"Hello, Clair," he said.

"Hello, Luke. Thank you for having her ready. Our return flight is in two hours, so we need to get right back to the airport. A driver stood behind Clair and asked if he could take Sophie's things. Luke handed them to him.

Sophie turned to her dad, and her eyes started to water. He got down in front of her. "Daddy, are you going to be lonely?"

"I will miss you, princess, but I want you to have a nice time with your mother."

"Will you call me every day?" Sophie asked.

"Yes. I love you so much," he said. Sophie hugged his neck for a long time. Before she let him go, she whispered. "I love you more, Daddy. I'll miss you. You'll come for me, won't you?"

He pulled away from her so she could see his face. "Of course, I will. I would never forget to pick you up." She smiled. Clair took her hand and headed to the town car. Sophie looked back and threw him a kiss and waved. He did the same. Luke stepped out in the yard and watched until the car was out of sight.

Luke kept busy while Sophie was with her mother. He bought a new canopy set for her bed, put up hooks for her medals, then rearranged and cleaned her room. He also hung more pictures on the memory wall.

Luke kept his promise to call Sophie every day. On the last call, she asked if there would be a party for her like last time. He had no answer for her since the last party was a spontaneous gesture from their friends. He didn't want to ask them to put that expense out unless it was their idea. He considered what to do, finally deciding to talk to Ruby about it.

Ruby was at her desk. When he was ready to leave on his short vacation, he stopped to talked to her. Ruby spoke first.

"Captain Star, I bet you're excited about picking up Sophie."

"I am, Ruby," he paused before going on. "Ruby, the welcome home party you all gave Sophie last time meant so much to her. If I paid all the expenses, would you make the arrangements for me?"

"Luke," she never called him that at work, but she was whispering. "Don't you dare insult us by offering to pay. Sophie is part of our family. Of course, we have a party planned."

Luke's eyes got a little misty. He thanked God for putting such good friends in their lives. He looked at her and said, "thank you, Ruby; you have no idea how glad I am to hear that. But I insist on contributing." All she did was shake her head.

He headed to the elevator and turned around. "Thank you, Ruby. I'll text you our arrival information."

"Goodbye, Captain. Have fun."

Milan, Italy

Sophie was watching out the window of her mom's Milan apartment for her dad. Clair tried to explain the parking was underground, and she wouldn't be able to see him. She waited at the window anyway. Sophie enjoyed her time with her mother but was ready to go home; her bags packed. Sophie thanked her mother for sending clothes for Lizzy last year.

"Mama would it be ok if I asked you to send something for Ricky too."

"Of course, sweetheart; I don't mind at all," Clair said. She hated to see Sophie go home and a little hurt she was so anxious to leave.

"Thank you, Mama. Daddy and I went to the PX and bought him some things last time, so we didn't hurt his feelings."

"I'm going to miss you, honey." Clair got down in front of Sophie and hugged her. Her eyes misting up.

"Oh, Mama, don't cry. I'll miss you too. Will you be coming down for Christmas?" Sophie asked.

"I hope so." She said and hugged her again.

A knock came at the door; Sophie ran to open it.

"Daddy!" Sophie wrapped her arms around him; Luke picked her up and twirled her around.

"Princess, I missed you so much." Clair looked on a little jealous over their relationship. But she knew it was her choice to leave, and this was the price she paid, but it still hurt.

Luke set her down and said hello to Clair. Wesley heard the commotion and came out from another room to say goodbye to them. Sophie gave him a small hug and said goodbye, then hugged and kissed her mother again.

Luke grabbed her suitcases, and Clair helped Sophie put on her backpack. She stayed at the door until they got on the elevator. Sophie threw her a kiss, and they were gone.

Luke took his time driving with Sophie to Venice, stopping to enjoy all the touristy spots. The Islands won't allow access by car past a specific point. Luke parked at Garage San Marco Venezia; his travel agent set it up along with a hotel room close by. They arrived at the AC Hotel Venezia twenty minutes later and got their room with a water view. After freshening up, they headed to walk and do the touristy things.

Luke heard that on hot days the smell of some of the canals could be unpleasant. If it was true, he didn't notice it that day. He carried a light backpack with a sweater and some snacks for Sophie if she got chilly or hungry later in the day. Their first stop was Saint Mark's Square. They went through the Basilica, the Tower, and the Doge's Palace. Luke stopped at several Bacardi's so Sophie could experience finger foods. Then they decided to get off the beaten track and see the real city. The city was enchanting in every way, and they walked for hours. Luke knew he had to find a restaurant to feed Sophie and get her off her feet for a while. They passed a cozy place not far back, so they headed there to eat and rest.

"Oh Daddy, isn't this place like a fairy tale?" Sophie said as they waited for their meal.

"It is princess; it's enchanting." The waiter brought their first course. Luke nodded to thank him, then asked Sophie, "did you have fun with your mother?"

"I did. Mama took me all over Milan. We did lots of shopping too." Sophie stopped to take a bite of her food. "She took the whole time off to spend with me. Wasn't that nice, Daddy."

"Yes, it was. Your mother wants to spend time with you. She loves you." Sophie nodded her head. Luke couldn't tell what she was thinking, but he knew Sophie had her own opinions about her mother leaving them.

After an excellent meal, they headed for a gondola ride. Luke wanted her to experience it at night so that she could see all the lights.

153

Sophie's reaction to the ride was as memorable as the ride itself. Luke ended up carrying her back to the hotel at the end of the night. Sophie was exhausted, and so was he.

The following day Luke and Sophie found a wonderful bakery. They ate breakfast, then headed further out to the other Islands. Sometimes walking the bridges, sometimes taking the gondolas.

Each island offered its own treasures making for memorable experiences. He captured it all on the expensive camera his secret Santa gave him.

The last stop of the night was at a Gelati shop. They agreed it was the best they ever tasted. Tomorrow was Sunday, and they would be heading home.

Before they headed to the car and then the airport, they stopped at their favorite bakery. Luke bought pastries hoping they would make it through the security point at the airport.

Sophie slept on a pillow on Luke's lap for five of the six-hour flight. He didn't wake her for the meal. The last few days had been a workout, and Luke wanted her to be awake to enjoy the party when she got home. He paid for first-class tickets; he rode coach on the way to Milan.

His SUV was in long term parking, and by the time they pulled into their driveway, it was after 6 pm. Luke had no idea they were going to have the party at his house. It was a great idea, and Sophie was bouncing in her seat at all the balloons and signs. Lizzy was waiting for them and started jumping up and down, hollering when they pulled in. When the others heard the commotion, they came out to greet them. Sophie barely let the car stop before she was out and hugging everyone.

Luke went to get their things out of the car and headed to the house. David came and took one of the suitcases from him and followed him in.

"How was the trip, Luke?" David asked.

"We had a wonderful time, but I'm glad to be home. I'm glad Sophie's home. I missed her."

David patted Luke on his back. "I understand; it would be hard for me to handle. How was it, seeing Clair again?"

"David, it is so different now that the Lord delivered me. I can see her, and even though there's still some lingering attraction, there is no anger or resentment."

"Praise the Lord."

Sophie ran into the bedroom with Lizzy. "Daddy, I need my presents." He opened the suitcase that held all the presents from Milan and the gifts from Venice. Sophie and Lizzy filled their arms up, and then David and Luke carried the rest.

Having everyone together again felt good; it felt like home.

CHAPTER FIFTEEN

Northern Syria close to the Turkish border

*M*alak rechecked the Major's temperature; it wasn't going down. She put up another bag of fluids.

"I'm going to have to reopen the wound to make sure there is nothing in there causing this infection. I was hoping his fever would go down so I wouldn't have to put him through that." Malak spoke her thoughts out loud.

"Can you wait to see if we get the antibiotics?" The Lieutenant asked.

"I don't think so. We need to get the Major's fever down." She walked away from his bed and checked on how much water was in the small water barrel. "I need this filled." Touching the barrel. "We'll need to stoke the stove so we can heat the water. I cut up a sheet in the supply tent; I need someone to grab those for me."

They put cold wet cloths on the Major's body for over an hour. His fever only went down one degree. He was unconscious.

"Lieutenant, do you still have that stretcher?"

"I believe so."

"You need to take him down to the river, take his clothes off, and submerge him. I'll send the thermometer with you. If you get it down three more degrees, I'll open his wound and see what I can find." She moved to take out his IV as the Lieutenant went to the door and called for some men and the stretcher.

Malak grabbed his arm as he was leaving with the stretcher.

157

"Do not let his injured leg get wet." He nodded and continued out the door.

"Malak disinfected the bed the Major had been lying on. She sterilized the instruments she would use. She went to the supply tent to get two more bags of fluid. Malak knew the cook was using the river as a refrigerator. He set a container in the river to keep their perishables safe to eat; it held the few bags of blood they had.

"Private Issawi, go to the cook and ask him to retrieve two bags of 'O-' blood for the Major." She had no way of typing the Major's blood, but 'O-' was the universal donor blood type. He had lost a lot of blood before he made it to Maleh's home and on the trip to the camp.

An hour later, the Lieutenant brought the Major back. "His temperature has gone down four degrees." The Lieutenant said as they lifted him off the stretcher. They had a sheet over him. They didn't put his clothes back on in case they had to submerge him again. Malak asked that the Lieutenant pull him up further on the cot, so the top of his head was over the edge.

After putting on gloves and a mask, Malak put up the blood bag and hooked it to the catheter. She moved the sheet above the wound and disinfected the area.

"I'm going to need a magnifying glass and a flashlight."

The Lieutenant went to retrieve those items. After he disinfected them, she handed him a mask and gloves.

"I want you to hold the magnifying glass over the wound when I ask you to. The flashlight needs to shine on the wound so I can see what's going on in there." He nodded.

After removing the stitches, she had to cut the skin where it started to mend. She started irrigating the wound. She used gauze to dry the wound after she was sure there was no more pus. Malak began to search for any foreign objects left in the wound.

"There it is. I need you to hold the magnifying glass over this spot." The Lieutenant did as she asked.

158

"There is a tiny fragment of the bullet that is pressing against a small vein. If I remove it and it is plugging a tear in the vein, the Major will lose more blood. I can't let that happen. We have precious little to replace it with." She stood straight up and considered the dilemma.

"Give me a long strip of cloth and that spoon on the table, please."

"What are you planning to do, Malak?"

"I'm going to tourniquet his leg above the wound. Then I'm going to remove the fragment and see if the vein is damaged."

"And if it is?"

"Then we will have to deal with it." She tightened the cloth around his leg and used the spoon to twist it tighter. "I'll need you to hold this spoon in place and still shine the flashlight into the wound. I'll hold the magnifying glass myself." The Lieutenant looked on as she took the tweezers, and delicately removed the fragment. She was trying not to damage the vein.

"Got it!" She smiled under her mask, showing the piece. "The vein looks like it's holding. I'm going to rinse it again, and then I want you to slowly loosen the tourniquet so a small amount of blood can flow."

The Lieutenant loosened the spoon. Blood started flowing into his leg. Malak watched through the magnifying glass to see if the vein would hold.

"It's holding. Loosen it a little more." She watched and kept having him slowly release the tourniquet a little at a time. She was afraid to put too much pressure on the vein at once if there was a weak area that might tear. When she saw there was no weakness, they released it to a full flow. She took a deep breath. "Ok, now I need to sew him up again. Can you take his temperature?" The Lieutenant did as she asked.

"It is back up to 104 degrees," he said.

"While I'm sewing him up, can you go back to cooling him down with water?" He rushed to get the water and some cloths.

Malak sewed up the wound and wrapped it. Then she covered him up with a sheet and checked the blood. She moved to watch

159

the Lieutenant pour cold water from a basin over his forehead. It flowed over the Major's head into a basin on the floor, then he traded them and repeated it.

After twenty minutes, she took the Major's temperature. It had gone down to 102°. She wrapped some cold cloths on his head, praying his body could start cooling itself.

Malak took a chair and sat next to her patient. The Lieutenant took a chair and sat in the center of the tent.

"You must be hungry," the Lieutenant said. "You haven't eaten except for the bread and cheese Mrs. Maleh gave you. And you shared that with the men on the way here." He went to the guard outside the tent and spoke with him.

After Malak ate her fish soup and flatbread, the Lieutenant said, "It's been a long day. If you wish to go to your tent, I will stay with the Major."

"I appreciate that, but I want to stay until the blood transfusion is complete. Malak sent the other bag of blood back to the cook. I'll put up a bag of fluids when the transfusion is complete. If his temperature has stabilized, I'll take you up on it. You'll stay in here with him tonight?"

"Yes, of course."

Sitting across from the Lieutenant, Malak saw he was much younger than she thought. His black hair had some gray at the sideburns, but his face was not aged. He had dark brown eyes, as did the Major. The Lieutenant was over six feet tall and built solid; now she guessed he was in his late thirties. The Major was at least a few inches shorter, and although he was solidly built, he was not as big as his Lieutenant. The Major would be considered handsome in his country. The Lieutenant would be regarded as ruggedly handsome in America.

"Malak, although I appreciate you are here and an excellent healer, I wonder what you are doing in my country?"

"I don't know, Lieutenant. I was in an accident. I have no memory of it or why I am here."

"Is that why they called you Mumarada?"

"Yes. I had no ID on me when the Maleh's found me. When they found out I was a nurse, they called me that.

She decided to change the subject. "Lieutenant, how was your Major shot?"

"Please call me Aden, my given name." He smiled at her. The first time she had seen him do that. "We were lured down to the city by a message, sent by the head of the President's guard. It said that the President would like to find a way to bring us in from the cold, as you Americans say.

When we were almost to the door, someone came up to us and whispered it was a trap. We turned to run, but the guards hidden inside came after us, two of our men were killed, and the Major was shot. We got far enough ahead of them to hide. When it was safe, we took backroads out of town. The Major wouldn't let us dress his wound until we were safe. He collapsed not far from the home of the Maleh's. You know the rest."

"What will you do now?"

"Before the message came, the Major was talking about discharging the men who wanted to try to find their families. There are a few parts of the country that have not been decimated. Suweida, Tartous, parts of Afrin Canton, and the extreme NE parts of Rojava are safe.

The problem is the people have no food. Some of the world's charitable organizations send in emergency aid. But the government takes most of it for themselves. The men could take their families to the refugee camps. I would not do that, if I had a family; so many countries refuse to take refugees. They could be there for a long time. But we do not have the supplies to keep this many men for much longer."

"If you were on the run, how did you get the supplies you have?"

"The Major saw the writing on the wall. When it looked inevitable that this President would be elected, he started requisitioning supplies and stipends for the men. He did that for many months in advance of the election and hid them up here. When the new administration labeled us terrorists, he moved the men here."

"I must say it is a perfect setting."

"It is, but there is still a lot of fighting going on up here between the Kurds and the Turks. ISIS is gone, at least for now, but the fighting goes on. Not to mention a civil war is still a possibility." He dropped his head for a moment, "you may not believe this, but Syria used to be a nice place to live."

"How is it you speak English so well?"

"My mother was English, my father Syrian. They both went to college in London, where they met. My father got a job in London right out of college."

"Was?"

"Yes, they have both passed away. I was born in London. When I was ten, my father's contract ended, so we moved here. My mother never liked it here, but she loved my father."

"Well, that explains it. Will you be leaving with the others?"

"No, I have no family left now," Aden said, dropping his head again for a moment.

"I'm sorry... How many will go, do you think?" Malak asked.

"A hundred, at least, which will leave us about forty men. The Major has set aside a small amount of money to send with each man."

"What will happen to the rest of you?"

"The Major is trying to get in contact with the Turk who trained us. We understand he is a General in the Turkish Army now. We are hoping he can let us attach ourselves to one of his units. At least until the political climate changes in Syria, so we can come home."

Malak got up to check on the Major. The blood pouch was empty. She took it off, and while she was switching to a fluid bag, she asked, "would you ever come back to Syria once you leave?"

The Lieutenant got up and moved to the Major's side. "I always believed I'd never leave this man's side." Aden touched the

162

Major's shoulder. "He is a great leader and cares for his men. But unless he becomes President, I don't think I'd ever come back."

The Major started to rally. Malak asked Aden to grab the pain medication on the table in the supply tent.

Together they lifted the Major up far enough to give him the medication and some water to swallow it. The Major opened his eyes and saw his Lieutenant. He tried to lift his hand but dropped it, it took too much energy. Instead, he smiled at him. Then he turned his head and saw Malak, but he was looking past her again. She thought she saw fear in his eyes. He kept repeating, "Malak haris, Malak haris." Then he closed his eyes again. They laid him back down.

"Why does he keep looking behind me?" She asked. "He looks like he's scared of something."

"I don't know." Aden moved away from him. She took his temperature. It was holding steady, at 102 degrees. She readjusted the sheet over him and moved over to the door.

"I think I'll get some rest now." She said.

"I'll walk you over." Aden opened the tent flap for her, and they went to her tent.

Malak thanked him then walked over to the separated portion of the tent they had made for her. There was a cot sitting next to the inside divider. On one wall of the tent was a small table with a battery-operated lantern. Her father had a Black Diamond Lantern, just like it. Next to it was a chair. On the south wall was a water barrel and a pitcher in a basin on a wooden box. She was thirsty, but she would have to wait to boil some water in the morning. She saw they put in a tent stove, there was wood in it, but it wasn't lit. The boiled water Rima gave her in a thermos was gone. She couldn't afford to get dysentery.

Malak stepped outside. She asked Private Issawi, "Is there a latrine close?" He couldn't understand her. She pointed to the one the Major and Lieutenant used on the valley floor.

He nodded and beckoned her to follow him. At the back of the tent, she saw it—her personal latrine. Malak went inside and turned on a battery-operated lantern.

163

On her cot, Malak found her carry-all. Rima had made it from bits and pieces of leftover upholstery material. It was beautiful. She pulled out her nightgown, and after praying, she laid down to sleep.

Incirlik Air Base

For the last few weeks, David had weighed up whether to tell Duke that Faiz found out his mother is still alive. If he told him and then she died before Faiz could get to her, Duke would have to go through the grief all over again.

It was so hard on Duke when the news came that Anna had disappeared. Many nights Duke laid in his bed crying. David went in to hold and comfort him, as Anna would have done if she had been there. But he was grieving too, and he was gone for weeks looking for her. Zoey was the one who picked up the slack when he and Jonathon were gone. Even now, there were nights he could hear Duke crying. David encouraged him to have faith that his mother would find her way home. It became more difficult as the months dragged on.

Duke was in a good place now. He was doing well in school; his friendship with CJ was as solid as ever. And now Sophie and Lizzy had joined the tight-knit circle of friends. Deciding to tell him now could jeopardize all his progress. So he decided against it.

Duke came into the study as David was pondering all this.

"Hey, Dad, Sophie called. She said Uncle Luke is dropping her and Lizzy off at the matinee on Base; she wanted to know if CJ and I wanted to go. Then we could spend a few hours at the Rec Center. Is it, ok?"

"Sure, I didn't have anything planned for you today. I was going to do some work in the yard. Next Saturday, we'll do something together."

"Thanks, Dad. I'll need some money."

"What happened to your allowance?"

"I spent it."

"I'll help you out today, but we are going to have to talk about budgeting," David said. He didn't mind Duke going over his budget. He knew he spent most of it on his friends, and he didn't want to discourage his generosity.

The matinee got out at 1:15 pm, and Duke and CJ were heading to the Rec Center with Sophie and Lizzy. They were taking a short cut at the back of the Base by the fence. Sophie noticed something moving in the bushes along the outside of the fence. She stopped to look. Duke and CJ didn't notice because they were reenacting one of the fight scenes in the movie. They were wrestling each other to the ground. Lizzy was busy trying to get them to stop.

Sophie started to walk over to the fence when Lizzy caught up with her, giving up on her efforts to stop the boys.

"Where are you going, Sophie?" Lizzy asked.

"A man just left something in those bushes. I'm going to go see what it is." By the time the girls were almost to the fence line Duke, and CJ realized they were no longer with them. They ran to catch up.

"What are you guys doing?" Duke asked.

"Sophie says there's something in the bushes," Lizzy informed them. The boys ran ahead to see what it was.

"Hey, wait for me; I'm the one who saw it." Sophie hollered at them as she ran to catch up.

When they got to the fence line, they had to maneuver around the bushes to see beyond the fence. "CJ, look Sophie's right. There is something; it's a duffle bag." They bent down to take a closer look.

"Move over; I want to see." Sophie tried to get around Duke; he made room for her. She didn't like that the boys were hijacking her discovery.

"Look, the fence is cut down here." CJ moved it to show them. Duke reached through the fence and dragged the duffle bag to this side of the fence. When he opened it, they all went silent.

"Duke look at that. That's a lot of money." CJ spoke first. Before anyone else could say anything, Lizzy heard a vehicle coming.

"Quick, put it back; someone's coming," Lizzy whispered.

"Move back into the bushes, so no one sees us. We don't want to get in trouble." Duke whispered. CJ moved the duffle back where it was, and they all moved about 15 feet away, behind the bushes on the fence line.

A few seconds later, a vehicle stopped, a man in an MP uniform got out and headed for the fence.

Lizzy gasped. "That's Private Phillips; he came to help when Buster's dad tried to hurt you and mom." She whispered. CJ put his finger to his lips so she wouldn't give them away. It was clearly him.

Private Phillips got out of the police SUV and looked around to see if anyone was nearby. Not seeing anyone, he grabbed a bag from the back of his vehicle and walked to the fence. He looked around once more, then bent down to exchange the duffle with the one he brought.

As soon as he traded bags, he looked inside, then headed back to the vehicle and drove off.

Duke told the others not to move until they were sure he was far enough away that he couldn't see them.

"We need to get out of here," Lizzy said.

"Not until I see what's in that bag," Duke said.

"Sophie, you and Lizzy be our lookouts, while Duke and I see what's in the bag."

"No way, I want to see too," Sophie argued.

"Alright, Lizzy, you be our lookout." CJ relented.

Hurrying to the spot in the fence, Duke pulled the bag back through. Inside were large bags of pills, and some white powder wrapped up like bricks. They zipped it up and pushed it back under the fence when they heard a noise from the street. They

166

moved back to their hiding spot but this time on the opposite side of the bushes. They didn't want to be seen by whoever was coming for the duffle.

They watched as a Turkish man walked right to the bag. He took a quick look inside and left. They all got a good look at his face as he got up to leave. Once they were sure he was gone, they ran to the Rec Center.

They stopped running at the picnic tables that were distributed outside the Rec Center. They all sat down, trying to catch their breath.

"What are we going to do?" Sophie asked, gasping for air from the sprint.

"We have to tell someone. That was a drug deal." Duke said.

"Maybe it's a sting," CJ added. "Private Phillips could be working undercover."

"Yeah," Duke responded.

"We need to tell my dad," Lizzy said.

"Will he believe us?" Duke asked.

Lizzy stared at him, "of course he will. He's my dad."

"Ok, Lizzy, go inside and call Uncle Manny. Tell him where we are." Duke said.

"Sophie, come with me." Lizzy got up and grabbed Sophie's arm to get her to come.

The One Who Stayed: Sophie's Story

CHAPTER SIXTEEN

S ergeant Diaz drove to the Rec Center at the request of his daughter. She seemed upset, and he wanted to find out why. He pulled in front of the Center and saw the kids sitting at one of the picnic tables.

As he headed over there, his daughter ran up to him and hugged him.

"What's going on, sweetheart?" He asked as she pulled on his arm to hurry him.

At the table, he asked the same question. They all began speaking at once.

"Hold on. One at a time. Duke, what's happened?" Manny asked. Duke looked at Sophie, who had crossed her arms and was pouting because she wanted to be the one to tell. Duke caved and let her.

"Sophie was the one who saw it first. Can she tell?" Sophie smiled at him and started talking.

"We were heading here after the movie, and I saw a man put something under the bushes outside the fence. We went over to see what it was, and it was a duffle bag. Duke drug it through the cut part of the fence. When we opened it, it was filled with money. Lizzy heard a car coming, so CJ pushed it back under the fence, and we hid in the bushes."

"It was Private Phillips, Daddy." Lizzy broke in. "I remembered him. He came to our apartment when Buster's dad broke down our door."

"Then what happened?" Manny looked at CJ.

"Private Phillips took another bag, a little bigger than the other one, and traded it; he looked inside and left." CJ recounted.

"Yeah, when we were sure he was gone, we took a look inside, and there were pills in big baggies, and white powder wrapped up like bricks." Duke finished the story. "Then we ran over here to call you."

It took a minute for Manny to soak in the ramifications of what he heard. He looked around to make sure no one else had listened to the conversation. "Ok, kids, I need you to come with me."

"Are we in trouble, Daddy?" Lizzy asked. He leaned over to her, "no, of course not. You did the right thing calling me."

Manny loaded the kids in his police SUV and headed off Base. He called Luke, "Luke, can you call Jonathan and David and ask them to meet me at your house. I'll be there in ten minutes." He slowed at the gate so the guard could recognize him and wave him through.

"What's going on, Manny?" Luke asked.

"I've got the kids. I'll explain when we are face to face."

Luke called David and Jonathan. And as Manny pulled up in the driveway, David and Jonathan walked up the sidewalk to Luke's house. The kids got out of the car and started talking.

Manny hushed them, "not out here. Go inside." They all moved inside.

David and Jonathan sat on the couch. Luke sat on the edge of the recliner, and Manny sat in the overstuffed chair. He motioned for the kids to sit on the floor.

"What's going on, Manny?" David asked.

"I'm going to let the kids tell you." Manny turned to them and nodded. They told the story again, just as they had to Manny.

When they finished, there was total silence. The implications were enormous.

Sophie got up and went to her dad, "don't you believe us, Daddy?"

He pulled her close. "I believe you, Sophie."

Manny spoke next. "Listen, kids, I wish you had called me instead of investigating yourself. Next time you see anything suspicious, call me first. OK? Now that I know, I'll open an investigation. You must tell no one what you saw. Do you understand me?" Manny looked at them one by one as they nodded. "That means not Liam, not Ricky, not your other friends. No one. If this gets out, it will hinder my investigation. If you talk to each other about it, you have to make sure no one can hear you and not over the phone. Have I made myself clear?" Manny finished.

"Are you mad at us, Uncle Manny?" CJ asked.

"No." He got up and moved to where the kids were sitting on the floor and knelt next to them. He put his hand on CJ's shoulder. "No. I'm not mad, CJ. It's just that this is serious. I want you to be careful, that's all."

Luke asked the kids to go out back and play so they could talk this over.

"We're hungry, Daddy."

"Ok, then why don't I put some frozen burritos in the microwave, and when it dings, you can bring them out here to eat. There are also some chips in the cupboard and some juice in the refrigerator. You can put a movie in and watch it until we finish talking in my office." He heard the kids arguing about what movie to watch as he headed to the kitchen.

The others waited for Luke in his office before discussing what they heard. When Luke came in and sat down, David asked.

"What do you know about this, Manny?"

"It's no secret that drugs have been running through military bases on a small scale for years. But a few months ago, I was part of a virtual conference called with General Masters at the Pentagon. MP Sergeants from all the overseas bases were linked in. General Masters said he had credible intel that some officers and enlisted men formed a drug-smuggling syndicate. The syndicate forms alliances with local drug lords near the bases.

The syndicate is running large amounts of drugs through transport containers or crates. These crates carry household items

171

with overseas destinations. Even cars are being used to traffic drugs. Somewhere down the transit line, someone opens the crates and places contraband in. They want us to go through everything that comes through Housing Transit. So far, we haven't been able to find anything. It's hidden too well; we would have to break up the furniture. We can't do that since the contents belong to soldiers who have no part in this. We need dogs, but they have a limited number. We've been told we are on the list."

"What kind of drugs, and how have they been distributing the contraband once it gets to the base?" Jonathan asked.

"The drugs are mostly what the kids found, cocaine and opioids. We didn't know how they've been distributing them. This is our first glimpse at how they are doing it." Manny answered.

"What are you going to do. We can't let the kids be involved with this." Luke said.

"No. You're right about that. I am not going to tell anyone about this until I have independent proof." Manny replied.

"I've got two questions. Why that particular spot? And why not do it off Base? It seems too risky." Jonathan asked.

"They chose that spot because it's a dead zone. The base surveillance system has about five of them. I'm going to place a surveillance camera facing that part of the fence line. If they used that spot once, they'll use it again. As for why not go off Base, I can answer that. They're American citizens, and if they get caught with drugs, they don't want to be tried by the Turkish government." He paused for a moment. "When I have the exchange on tape, I will approach Private Phillips and try to get him to turn on the others. Then I will get other agencies involved."

"That sounds like a good plan. And it will eliminate the kids from the equation. Man, I wish they hadn't gotten mixed up in this." Jonathan said, rubbing his hands over his face.

"I'd like to know how the US Military builds a surveillance system that has dead zones?" David asked a little unnerved that something like that could happen.

"I'd like to know the same thing. Whoever installed it didn't bother to have someone drive around the Base to see if he lost sight

172

of him anywhere. I noticed it after I went through some surveillance tapes I requested for a case I was working on." Manny replied. "I told them about it, but there is a lot of red tape involved with putting in a new updated surveillance system. I think the brass doesn't want to spend the money. There are still rumors this Base may close."

"I suggest we keep a close eye on the kids for the next few weeks. They assume no one saw them, but we don't know that for sure." David said.

"Agreed. And we have to reemphasize the importance of not telling anyone." Luke said.

"Manny, you may need help. And I'm sure you want to keep this under wraps. If you need help with surveillance or whatever, I'm willing." David offered.

"Count me in," Luke added.

"Me too." Jonathan chimed in.

Northern Border of Syria

Malak got up in the middle of the night and wrapped a blanket over her nightgown. She startled Private Issawi when she stepped out of the tent. He jumped up from the overturned bucket he was sitting on and kept repeating what sounded like an apology. As they walked to the Major's tent, she heard the waterfall in the distance. She stopped, closed her eyes, and listened to the symphony of God's creation. The waterfall was the percussion, the crickets the string section, and the frogs the horns. It made a beautiful melody just for her. She took a deep breath inhaling the sweet fragrance of the cedars of Lebanon. Her guard broke into her revelry. She understood enough Arabic to know he was asking if she was alright. She turned and smiled at him, nodded her head, and moved on to the Major's tent. The music was gone.

Malak crept into the tent, moving to the Major's bedside; she wanted to check his temperature. The Lieutenant was sleeping in his clothes on a cot next to him. He woke at the first sound of movement.

"I'm sorry to wake you, Aden. I wanted to check his temperature and clean his wound." She whispered.

"No need to apologize. I will help." He got up and moved to the Major's side. Blood had seeped through the gauze. She checked to see if there was any pus mingled with the blood, but it looked clean. She changed the wrapping on his wound, and Aden checked his temperature. It was almost down to 99.6°. He showed it to her.

She covered the Major back up and moved away from his bed, not to wake him. "Aden, tomorrow we are going to have to get him up and moving. I don't want him to get a blood clot." She said.

As she was going out the tent door, she heard him moan. She moved back to his bedside. "Aden, help me get him up enough so he can swallow some more pain medication." She grabbed the bottle and a glass of water.

"Hold on, Major, we are getting you some pain medication," Aden whispered to him in Arabic.

After laying him back down, the Lieutenant walked her to her tent. "If there is anything I can do for you, let me know."

"I do have one request."

"Anything."

"Are you a Muslim?" He looked at her, unsure of why she was asking.

"I was born into a family of mixed faith. My mother considered herself Christian, although she did not practice her faith. My father was born into a Muslim family, but he too did not observe the traditions. So I would say I am neither Christian nor Muslim." He watched her face to see if that answered her question. He couldn't tell. "Why do you ask."

"I didn't want to offend you by asking you this favor."

"Which is?" He furrowed his eyebrows, still unclear.

"Rima gave me her Bible, but it's written in Arabic, and I can't read it." She hesitated, "would you be willing to read it to me?"

He smiled, "yes, bring it with you to the Major's tent in the morning."

She touched his hand, "thank you." Then she turned and went into her tent. She knelt by her bed and prayed for the men in the camp. She prayed that God would open their eyes to the truth of who He is. She fell asleep on her knees.

In the morning, after using the basin to clean up, she got dressed and went to check on her patient. She grabbed her Bible and put it on the table as she walked into the Major's tent. "Lieutenant, can you have the cook bring the Major some type of thick broth? And some mashed fava beans?"

The Lieutenant went to the guard to order some food. Malak was checking and rewrapping his injured leg. She checked his temperature and then used the stethoscope to check his lungs. 'It looks like he is improving. I don't understand why his body won't rally. The infection he had must have gotten in his bloodstream before I could stop it. If he goes septic without antibiotics, we will lose him. When do you think your Sergeant will be back with the supplies I asked for?"

"It depends on how far he has to go for them and if he gets captured."

"If I didn't need the antibiotics for your Major, I would never put your sergeant in such danger, Aden."

"I know that, Malak."

The food came, and the lieutenant propped the Major up so Malak could feed him. He was weak but able to eat a fair amount of food. She saw that as a good sign.

"Aden, after you clean him up and change him, I need you to help him to walk as much as he is able."

She went back to her tent, and the Lieutenant ordered some food sent up for her.

Malak watched as the lieutenant took the Major for a walk outside. He managed to walk for five minutes before he was too weak. Malak checked on him again once he was back in bed. The Major was groaning, so she gave him some more medication.

Once the Major was asleep again, she took a seat close by. The Lieutenant took the Bible off the table and sat down. "Where is it you would like me to read?"

"There is a marker in there. If you would start there." She said. The Lieutenant spoke softly and began reading, translating it into English. He read of the virgin birth, the Wise Men's visit, the escape to Egypt to hide from Herod. He read about Jesus' baptism by John and going into the wilderness and Satan trying to tempt Him to sin. Then came the stories of the ministry of Jesus and all the miracle healings.

The Major was half-awake hearing words spoken softly in a language he didn't understand. He opened his eyes and look over to his Lieutenant. He saw him reading to the woman who was taking care of him. His eyes moved to the Angel, who was behind her. He was bowed from the waist with his wings covering his head. Somehow he understood. Whatever was being read was so holy that the Angel was humbling himself before it. He needed to understand the words he was hearing. He spoke in a weak voice.

"Please read in Arabic so I can understand." He said. The Lieutenant quit translating for Malak and began reading in Arabic. Loud enough for the Major to hear.

The Major listened as the Lieutenant read of healings and deliverance at the hand of Jesus.

Malak had no idea what prompted the Major to want to listen, but she knew it was the hand of God. She raised her hand to pray quietly as the Lieutenant read the Bible.

The minute she raised her hands, she felt the presence of God. As the Lieutenant continued to read, she felt the Spirit of God move like a breeze, electrifying the air in the tent. She slipped to her knees and bowed her head to the ground, continuing to pray. The Spirit of God kept sweeping over her as He moved.

The Major continued to listen to the spoken Word; his body started to regain strength.

"...So when Jesus came, He found that he had already been in the tomb four days. Now Bethany was near Jerusalem, about two miles away. And many of the Jews had joined the women around Martha and Mary to comfort them concerning their brother.

Then Martha, as soon as she heard that Jesus was coming, went and met Him, but Mary was sitting in the house. Now Martha said to Jesus, 'Lord, if You had been here, my brother would not have died. But even now I know that whatever You ask of God, God will give You.'

Jesus said to her, 'your brother will rise again.'

Martha said to Him, 'I know that he will rise again in the resurrection at the last day.'

Jesus said to her, 'I am the resurrection and the life. He who believes in Me, though he may die, he shall live. And whoever lives and believes in Me shall never die. Do you believe this?'

She said to Him, 'yes, Lord, I believe that You are the Christ, the Son of God, who is to come into the world.'

And when she had said these things, she went her way and secretly called Mary her sister, saying, 'The Teacher has come and is calling for you.' As soon as she heard *that*, she arose quickly and came to Him. Now Jesus had not yet come into the town but was in the place where Martha met Him. Then the Jews who were with her in the house, and comforting her, when they saw that Mary rose up quickly and went out, followed her, saying, 'She is going to the tomb to weep there.'

Then, when Mary came where Jesus was, and saw Him, she fell down at His feet, saying to Him, 'Lord, if You had been here, my brother would not have died.'

Therefore, when Jesus saw her weeping, and the Jews who came with her weeping, He groaned in the spirit and was troubled. And He said, 'Where have you laid him?'

They said to Him, 'Lord, come and see.'

Jesus wept. "

The Major sat up on his own, gaining more strength as he continued to listen. He looked over and saw the woman on her knees. The Angel also was on his knees, covered by his wings. He felt a black cloud lift from his mind. He understood the truth of what he was hearing.

"...Then the Jews said, 'See how He loved him!'

And some of them said, 'could not this Man, who opened the eyes of the blind, also have kept this man from dying?'

Then Jesus, again groaning in Himself, came to the tomb. It was a cave, and a stone lay against it. Jesus said, 'Take away the stone.'

Martha, the sister of him who was dead, said to Him, 'Lord, by this time there is a stench, for he has been *dead* four days.'

Jesus said to her, 'did I not say to you that if you would believe, you would see the glory of God?' Then they took away the stone from the place where the dead man was lying. And Jesus lifted up His eyes and said, 'Father, I thank You that You have heard Me. And I know that You always hear Me, but because of the people who are standing by I said this, that they may believe that You sent Me.' Now when He had said these things, He cried with a loud voice, 'Lazarus, come forth!' And he who had died came out bound hand and foot with graveclothes, and his face was wrapped with a cloth. Jesus said to them, 'loose him, and let him go.' (John 11:17-44)

The Lieutenant stopped reading and closed the Bible. He could see something was happening and looked at the Major sitting up on his own and Malak on her knees.

The Major looked at him and said, "keep reading."

The Lieutenant reopened the Bible randomly and read.

"...that if you confess with your mouth the Lord Jesus and believe in your heart that God has raised Him from the dead, you will be saved. For with the heart, one believes unto righteousness, and with the mouth, confession is made unto salvation. For the Scripture says, 'Whoever believes on Him will not be put to shame.' For there is no distinction between Jew and Greek, for the same Lord over all is rich to all who call upon Him. For 'whoever calls on the name of the Lord shall be saved.'" (Romans 10:9-13)

The Major slipped to his knees. When he did, the Spirit of God moved on him, and he wept and prayed for the first time in his life.

The One Who Stayed: Sophie's Story

CHAPTER SEVENTEEN

*T*he Lieutenant could no longer read. He slipped to his knees and bowed his head to the ground. He knew about salvation from hearing it on TV when he was young and living in London. He remembered watching the televangelist speak of salvation. He was moved by the words spoken, but he never accepted the Lord into his heart. But now feeling the power in this tent and seeing a man he considered the strongest man he ever knew on his knees, receiving Christ into his life. He knew he wanted to do the same.

How long the Major was on his knees, he couldn't determine. But he knew instantly when the Spirit of God lifted. He raised his head and saw the Lieutenant and the nurse getting off their knees. The Major looked for the Angel, he could no longer see him, but he knew he was still there.

The Major got up and went to his friend and wrapped his arms around him, kissing his cheeks, as was the custom. He stepped back and smiled, saying, "I believe, Aden. What you read; I believe." He then patted him on the back and moved over to the nurse. He took her hand and said, in his limited English, "thank you." He turned his head to the Lieutenant and spoke in Arabic while still holding her hand.

"The Major wants to thank you for taking the risk of coming and taking care of him." The Lieutenant translated to her.

"Tell him. The Lord directed me to do so." She smiled back at the Major as Aden translated her words.

The Major nodded at her then went back to speak with Aden again in Arabic. "I need to talk with the men. We need to move forward with our plan to discharge those that wish to go back. Then we have to find a way to communicate with General Tabib Ozer. We need to move from here before we are detected."

"Yes, sir." The Lieutenant moved to the covered box and opened it, reaching in for his and the Major's sidearms. After closing the box again, he handed one to the Major. They left the tent nodding to Malak as they went.

"My name is Anna, Major. The Lord restored my memory." Both men looked at her and nodded with a smile.

Anna stood there, amazed at what she witnessed. Not just for the others but for her. As she was on her knees before the Lord, her memory came back. She remembered everything, but it was a two-edged sword. Before, she had no one to long for, no one to get home to. Now she knew her family was mourning her disappearance. She needed to find a way home. She bowed her head and prayed, "Lord, get me back to my family."

As she walked out of the tent, the Sergeant walked into camp and handed her the medications. She thanked him repeatedly, knowing he risked his life to get these for his Commanding Officer. He had no idea that God had healed the Major; he no longer needed them. She knew his risk was not without purpose; these medications would eventually save others in the camp. She took them to the clinic and stored them away.

Incirlik Military Base

Manny and Jonathan had agreed to fill their wives in on the situation. The next morning Manny got up before daybreak and headed to the office. He went to the locked cage that held their surveillance equipment. The Army had just updated their equipment. He found what he was looking for; cameras that could be monitored by his cell phone or his personal computer.

Manny drove to the Transportation Department and signed out a maintenance vehicle. They never asked him why he needed it, and he didn't offer. Manny spotted a tree directly across from the cut fence; he climbed the tree using the truck's extension ladder. The dim lights from the streetlamps gave him enough illumination to install it. Connecting his cell phone to the camera, Manny made sure it was positioned where he wanted it. He put the ladder back on the truck and got out of there. He didn't want any of his patrol vehicles spotting him.

Manny returned the maintenance truck and headed to the station. He needed to link up his computer to the camera to start recording.

After a week of surveillance, there was no activity at the fence line. Manny started wondering if that drop site was a one-off. After thinking about it, he realized there is probably more than one person on Base doing drops. They each may have a different spot. Since there were five dead zones, he decided to check them all.

The next morning, Manny got up before dawn and walked the other dead zones' fence line. Sure enough, three of them had cuts in the fence like the one Private Phillips used.

Manny picked up three more cameras and signed out the maintenance truck again. After putting up the cameras, he connected them to his phone and computer on a split screen.

Later in the day, he called the others and told them what he found. He asked if they could help him monitor the cameras when he was on patrol. They all agreed, and Manny gave them the link.

Two days later, Sergeant Diaz was doing paperwork in his office, with the surveillance running on his computer. He noticed some movement on the computer in his peripheral vision.

Manny watched a man get out of his vehicle, look around, and walk over to the fence. He squatted down between some bushes and pulled something through the fence. After checking what was inside, he then pushed his duffle through to the other side.

Manny needed to catch the man red-handed. So far, he hadn't seen the man's face, but based on his build, he could tell it wasn't Private Phillips. When the man got up and headed back to the car, he recognized him. It was the day sergeant of the Housing Transit Unit, Viktor Roschin.

Sergeant Diaz called the Base Surveillance Station. He asked that they track a vehicle for him until he could catch up to it. He gave them the make and model and told them it was just leaving Sector 17. They immediately made visual contact and started reading out the location to the sergeant.

Sergeant Diaz ran to his vehicle and sped off, listening to the directions on his cell. When he got behind Roschin's car, he turned on his lights and sirens, thanking the man on his cell, and hit the off button. The vehicle pulled over and stopped; Sergeant Diaz approached the car.

Sergeant Roschin didn't appear nervous; in fact, he was friendly and at ease. When Sergeant Diaz asked him to get out of the car, his demeanor changed. Manny asked Sergeant Roschin to turn around. He handcuffed him and led him to the back of his Police SUV; Sergeant Roschin repeatedly asking what he had done wrong. Sergeant Diaz didn't respond; he searched the vehicle, found the bag filled with money, and took custody.

"I'm going to have your car towed to the impound, Viktor."

"What are you doing, Manny? Why are you arresting me?"

"Are you serious? You have a duffle bag full of drug money, and you're asking me why you're in custody?" Manny read him his rights.

"Look, Manny, I'll split it with you; please, man, don't do this."

"Shut up, Viktor. Don't make it worse."

"You didn't have probable cause."

"So now you're not just a crook, you're an attorney?"

Sergeant Diaz called Major Scott to ask if he could bring Sergeant Roschin to his office. He didn't want anyone to know he'd been arrested; in case he could still catch one of the other perpetrators.

"Sure, Sergeant, bring him into the conference room. I'll have Ruby direct you to it when you get here." Major Scott answered.

Twenty minutes later, Sergeant Diaz was in the conference room. Major Scott, Major Young, and Captain Star sat in on the interrogation.

"What am I doing here?" Roschin asked.

"I have you on tape trading drugs for cash at the fence line in Sector 17," Manny said.

"I want a lawyer," was the next thing out of Roschin's mouth.

"And you will get one. But first I'm going to allow you to help yourself. I'm willing to work with you if you will help me take down the syndicate running drugs through this Base." Major Scott offered.

"I want a lawyer," Roschin repeated.

The other men left the room and went to Major Scott's office.

"None of us can handle this one. If it ever got out that our children were the informants and this went to trial, we would have to recuse ourselves." Major Young said.

"That only leaves Captain Maya Patel. Where is she?" Major Scott asked.

"I'll go check with Ruby." Captain Star left the room. A few minutes later, he came back with the answer.

"She's talking to a client in holding at the Police Station. She's supposed to be back in an hour."

"Manny, we can keep him here until she gets back. After he speaks to his attorney, are you thinking of taking him to your holding tank?"

"No, if word gets out he's arrested, we may not catch the others in the act. I found two more dead drops along the fence line, both in areas the surveillance doesn't cover. I'm hoping we can grab the next one with the drugs and the cash. But I don't know how long I can keep this quiet."

"Yes. Catching the courier with the drugs and the money would be hard to explain away." Major Young said.

"I'd like to catch Private Phillips. I can't believe I misjudged him." Manny said.

After Captain Patel spoke with her client, she went to talk to Major Scott.

"Sir, Sergeant Roschin is not inclined, at this time, to make any deals. He feels his arrest was without probable clause."

"That's ridiculous. Sergeant Diaz has him on surveillance video. But if that's his choice, he will be held at the Stockade in solitary confinement. We don't want him warning the other couriers. Do you have any concerns about that?"

"As long as his constitutional rights aren't trampled on."

"That's your job, Captain."

"Yes, sir."

"Sergeant Diaz will be coming for him in an hour. He is not to make any calls, and you are not to contact anyone for him. Is that understood?"

"What about his wife?"

"I thought she didn't accompany him to Base. Did I hear wrong?"

"No, sir. "

"Then, do not contact her. Sergeant Diaz asked for 48 hours, and I intend to give it to him. He is entitled to a lawyer, but he is not entitled to any other contact. Are you onboard?"

"Yes, sir." Captain Patel left the Major's office and went back to speak with her client again.

CHAPTER EIGHTEEN

Syria

*I*t took months for Faiz to get a legitimate reason to leave headquarters for an extended time. A call came in that a notorious anti-administration dissident was spotted. The President wanted him in jail because his flyers and speeches encouraged insurrection. Faiz got permission to hunt him down.

Faiz left at 4 am. He took his camping gear and some of his personal items he didn't want to leave behind. If he found Anna, he had no intention of coming back. He had a plan to get them both across the border. He drove as far as he could, then parked and headed on foot, with his gear, into the mountains. He had a vague idea where a Company of FSA were last seen and followed their trail. He knew there was more than one Company of FSA hiding in the mountains. He had no idea if he was following the ones with Anna. By 3 pm, he was close enough to hear fighting in the distance. It was probably the Kurds and the Turks.

He finally came upon the Company he had been tracking. What he found when he got to the camp was an Army that had been decimated. It appeared they had been caught in a firefight between the Turks and the Kurds.

He found the Commanding Officer and asked if they had a nurse traveling with them. He said if he had a nurse, his men would have a chance to survive. Their medic was one of the first ones hit. Faiz gave him all the food he had and what few first aid items he carried with him.

"What will you do now, sir?" Faiz asked.

"I will try to keep as many of my men alive as I can."

"Have you considered letting them go home to their families?"

"My men are not deserters, sir."

"But you are no longer considered a legitimate part of the Army by the Administration. What would they be deserting?"

"We will be reinstated; the President has been lied too about us. He will come around."

Faiz knew there was no way to reason with the man so he

went back to the fork in the trail and traveled the other direction.

Incirlik Military Base

Captain Patel went back to the conference room to tell her client where he was to be held.

"Sergeant Roschin since you do not wish to cooperate. Sergeant Diaz will take you to the Stockade and put you in solitary confinement. They want to be sure you don't warn the other couriers."

"Solitary?"

"Yes. You will have no contact with anyone except me. No phone calls, no visitors."

"Can I call my wife?"

"Not until the investigation is complete." She watched as he lowered his head into his hands.

"I only did this to supplement our income. I don't make enough to keep us out of bankruptcy. At least not until my wife finishes her degree program and gets a job." He lifted his head. "Captain, I'm not part of a syndicate. I don't have any information. All I do is get a one-word text on a burner phone that directs me to a crate or a car with the product. On the crate or the windshield of the car is another code. That code tells me where to look. Then I take the product to specific gym lockers, put the merchandise in it, and lock it up."

"How is it then you were caught switching drugs for cash?"

"One of the curriers transferred to another Base, so that left an opening. I could get extra money if I took the risk of switching duffels."

"How many men do the tradeoffs?"

"There are three, including me." He said.

"How much do you make?"

"Before, I made $5,000 a month. Now for doing both, I make $10,000 a month. But I don't know the others, and I have no information on the people who actually run the syndicate. Everyone is in the dark, so no one can snitch if they get caught." He watched his hands as he wrung them, then forced himself to stop. "That's why I didn't answer the Major's questions. I don't know anything. Do you think he would make a deal with me if I tell him what I told you?"

"I don't know. You don't have much to offer. Do you want me to approach Major Scott?"

"Yes." He looked her in the eyes, "do what you can for me. Please."

Major Scott was in his office with Major Young and Captain Star. "It looks like Sergeant Roschin is refusing to make a deal. That is going to prolong this investigation."

"Maybe he is more afraid of them than going to the Stockade." Major Young said.

"That's possible. I will have to ask one of the Air Force Jags to prosecute for us." David started to reply when Captain Patel knocked on the door.

"Enter." Major Scott ordered. The Captain walked to his desk and saluted the Major, who reciprocated and said to stand at ease.

"What is it, Captain?"

"My client would like to try to negotiate with you for what information he has. Unfortunately, he doesn't have much. The syndicate plays it tight to the vest, sir." Captain Patel said.

"Have a seat, Captain, and bring me up to speed." The Captain relayed everything her client told her.

When she finished, Major Scott looked over at the others in the room. "What do you think?"

"Sir, the Captain is right, he doesn't have much to offer, but I have an idea that could work. We would have to run it by Sergeant Diaz first." Captain Star replied.

"Ok. Captain Patel, we need to get your client to the Stockade while we work this out. But I have a couple of questions I'd like answered before he's gone."

"What would you like to know, sir?"

"I want to know how they recruited him and why him?"

"I'll ask, sir," Patel said.

"I'll call the Sergeant over, and after he gets Sergeant Roschin settled, we'll go over Captain Star's idea. Is that acceptable to you?"

"Yes, sir." She stood up and saluted him again. After he reciprocated, she headed for the door. She stopped before she opened it and turned to him. "Sir, why aren't one of you handling this?" The question had been bugging her all day. "This case is high profile usually handled by one of you".

"You're excused, Captain." She saw she wasn't going to get her questioned answered.

Once Sergeant Diaz took Roschin to the Stockade. He instructed that the prisoner is not allowed communication with anyone. He went to Major Scott's office, where the others were waiting for him.

"Let's move to the conference room." Major Scott suggested.

"Please, Captain Star, tell us your plan." Major Scott said as they were seated.

"Sir, if we can get Sergeant Roschin to cooperate with us, I think we might be able to arrest the other drug couriers."

"Go on, Captain." Major Scott encouraged.

Captain Star turned to Sergeant Diaz. "Do you think you could trust Sergeant Roschin to go back to his post and help us with a sting?"

"From what he has said and what I know of him, he is not a bad man. He found a way to make some extra money and didn't consider the consequences. I think he would do anything if it helped him get a shorter sentence." The Major turned to Captain Patel for her read on the man. She agreed that Sergeant Roschin would do anything to shorten his sentence.

"Major Scott, what I'm thinking is we let Roschin go back to work until the next shipment comes in. We have him handle it, as usual, putting it in the lockers." He turns to Sergeant Diaz, "that's where you would come in, Sergeant. From there, you could have men following them to the drop site. One of them may know more about the syndicate, or at least have some insight about it." Captain Star finished.

"And, if we can time it right, we may get the drugs and the money on this side of the fence when we arrest them." Sergeant Diaz added.

Major Scott thought the idea through. He turned to look out the window and felt the warmth of the sun filtering through. "We are taking a big chance that Roschin won't warn the others. Can't we watch the cameras you set up and catch them in the act?" Major Scott directed his question to Sergeant Diaz.

"Sir, that would have to assume they haven't already made the drops from the last shipment. And the fact Sergeant Roschin has disappeared doesn't spook them."

"I see your point." Major Scott sat up, putting his forearms on the table. "What do you think, Major Young?"

"It's a sound plan," he turned to Captain Patel, "it relies on the cooperation of your client. We will have to trust your judgment on Roschin's earnestness if he agrees."

I'll make sure he understands that if he warns anyone, it could add more time to his sentence." Captain Patel said.

"And let him know we will have a camera on him at all times." Sergeant Diaz added.

"What incentive does he have to do this?" Captain Patel asked.

Major Scott turned in his chair to face her directly. "He won't get off without jail time, Captain." He said a little too harshly, then adjusted his tone. "There is no getting around a dishonorable discharge. But as far as jail time and where he does it, I might be open to an agreement on that."

"If you approve eighteen months in a stockade close to his home in the States. I think he would agree."

Major Scott looked at the other Jag officers. "Do you think we could sell that to the Judge?"

"Are you requesting the Air Force Judge to sign off?" Major Young asked.

"Yes, I think we should have an outside judge look at it in case down the line there are any inquiries."

"I agree." Major Young replied.

Captain Patel looked directly at Major Scott with her eyebrows furrowed. "Is there something here I need to know? Why aren't you signing off on this, sir? You have the authority."

Major Scott took a moment and scrolled over everyone's faces. "Captain Patel..."

The Captain broke in. "Sir, if there are mitigating circumstances that can affect my client's disposition. I need to know."

"Like I was about to say, Captain. The fact that you were called in to handle his defense. And the plea agreement will be overseen by an outside Judge, ensures your client is getting a fair treatment."

Captain Patel looked down at her hands that she folded on her lap. After a moment, she said, "Sir, do I have your assurances that there is nothing you are privy to that could clear my client?"

"Indeed, Captain. If there were information you were not privy to, it would only seal your client's fate, not clear him."

"But my problem, sir, with all due respect, is I can only take your word for that." Major Scott bristled at the accusation; he had never had his integrity questioned. He calmed himself and answered.

"Mine, Captain and every other person in this room." He finally said. She looked around.

"You can all attest to this?" She asked, watching as each man agreed. "Ok, I have no choice. I will take this to him and get back to you."

"So, are we all agreed that it's worth the risk?" He turned to each one in the room for a yea or nay.

As Captain Patel got up to leave, she turned back to Major Scott. "Sir, about the questions you wanted answered. He said one day, a burner phone was left in his car outside a bar in Adana. When he got in the car, the phone rang, a man on the line offered him a way to make money."

"But why him?"

"They needed someone who had access to the incoming transit crates and vehicles. They must have done their research on him and found out the Sergeant needed money."

Northern Border of Syria

In the months that followed the Major's healing and conversion, Anna spent her time in camp working in the Clinic. She stitched up cuts and among other things she tended infected ingrown toenails, a common ailment due to the hard structure of the combat boots. She even dealt with a severe allergic reaction. A perimeter guard stepped on a beehive that had fallen from a tree and got stung a hundred times. Luckily EpiPens were on the list of items the sergeant brought back with him.

The Major and Lieutenant spent their time talking to each man. They gave them the option to be discharged so that they could go back to their families. The Major also shared his testimony on how he came to believe that Jesus was the Son of God. The ones who chose to leave were given two months' pay, discharge papers and permission to take their tent and gear. He knew many of these men would have to move their families if the bombings had not already displaced them.

By the time he spoke to everyone, only forty men were left in the camp. They either had nowhere to go or just chose to stay. Several of his men gave their hearts to Jesus. Including both of Anna's guards.

The Major told the men of his plan to contact the Turkish General who trained them. He gave the men another chance to leave. He offered to take Anna with them across the border. The Major was less than optimistic about their chances. She assured him she wished to go; choosing to trust God would make a way. They planned to leave in a few days.

When things were quiet, the believers often spent time together. They would pray, and she would teach them out of the only Bible they had while Aden translated their questions.

Anna was in the Clinic when she heard a commotion outside. She stepped out of the tent and saw some men bringing up the cook. He was holding his arm. She could see men running to the cook's tent in the distance, putting out a fire.

Anna rushed the men into the tent and sat the cook on the cot. The burn on his arm was severe. The men who brought him in were trying to explain to her what happened in Arabic. She picked up enough of what they said to understand he stumbled into the cook's fire. His arm landed on the hot cauldron he cooks in.

"I need lots of cool water and a raw potato." She ordered as the Lieutenant came in to see what happened. He made sure the men understood what she wanted.

"Lieutenant, can you get that pitcher and basin," she pointed to what she wanted. "and I'll start running water over the burned area." He grabbed it and held the basin as she poured the pitcher of water over it. The man moaned. When she had cooled the burn a while, she inspected it.

"It looks like a second-degree burn. Can you get me the gauze in that box under the table, and the Hydrocolloid Dressing? And I need some pain medication." The Lieutenant found what she asked for. The men came back with the water and the potato. She asked his friends to cut the potato into thin slices. She placed the thinly sliced potatoes on the burn for pain relief until the pain relievers could kick in.

Fifteen minutes later, she ran more water over it, dabbed it dry, and applied the dressing, wrapping it with gauze. She placed the cook's arm on several rolled-up blankets and a pillow to get it elevated above his heart. Private Kilic came in and whispered something to the Lieutenant. The Lieutenant spoke to her as he left with the Private.

"The Major needs me. I'll be back as soon as I can."

"Thank you, Aden.

The Lieutenant walked into the Major's tent. Standing there was a perimeter guard with his gun aimed at a man who looked familiar to him.

"Lieutenant Arabi, you remember Sergeant Major Faiz Nayef." He pointed to Faiz.

"Yes, of course, your department has been hunting the FSA for months. How did you find us?" The Lieutenant responded while walking into Faiz's personal space.

"I'm not here for you. I'm looking for a woman you took from the home of Nabil Maleh." Faiz took a step back so he would not appear to be challenging the Lieutenant.

"What makes you think she is here?" The Major asked.

"Nabil told me you were gravely wounded, and she agreed to take care of you. But to look at you, it appears he may not have told me the truth." Faiz answered.

"What does the Directorate want with her?" The Lieutenant asked, giving him some distance.

"Not the Directorate, me. She is my friend, and she disappeared."

"I don't believe you." The Lieutenant retorted.

"I understand your reluctance to take my word for it. But if Anna is here, I guarantee you she will want to see me." Faiz said.

"The woman you are looking for. Her name is Anna?" Faiz nodded.

The Major motioned the Lieutenant to move outside with him. "Do you believe him, Aden?"

"I believe he is looking for her, but I don't think we can trust him. Just in case he is telling the truth, I will ask Anna if she knows him." The Lieutenant said as he walked to the Clinic. The Major nodded agreement.

The Lieutenant walked in as Anna was using a wet rag to stroke her patient's face and head. Her compassion was the reason the men had such respect for her. It was something they were not accustomed to.

"Anna." He got her attention and waved her over.

"What is it, Aden?"

"Do you know a man named Faiz Nayef?"

"Faiz? Yes. How would you know that?"

"Is he out to harm you?"

"No, he is a dear friend. Why do you ask?"

"Did you know he works for the Directorate? The Unit the President uses to hunt and imprison his enemies. Of which Christians and anyone who opposes his administration are included."

"No, Aden. Faiz is a Christian. He uses his position as a cover to get information." She touched his arm, trying to convince him he wasn't who he seemed. "Why are you asking me these questions?"

"One of our perimeter guards found him and brought him to the Major..."

"Are you telling me Faiz is here?" She started out the door. When she stepped out, she saw her tent surrounded by the men in the camp. She turned to the Lieutenant; her brows furrowed. "What's going on?"

"They heard someone from the Directorate was here looking for you. They didn't know if he was by himself, so they came to protect you." She looked up at him. Her eyes filled with tears.

"Please tell them how much I appreciate them."

When Anna walked into the Major's tent, she immediately saw Faiz. A Type-56 assault rifle pointed at him. She rushed over to him and wrapped her arms around him, saying, "Faiz, I had no idea what happened to you." The guard lowered his weapon. When Anna let go of Faiz, she turned to the Major and introduced him as her dear friend.

"You have brought no other men with you?" The Major asked. They were speaking in Arabic. The Lieutenant translated for her.

"No, I am not here for the Directorate, as I said. I am here to take Anna home." Faiz responded.

The Lieutenant dismissed the guards waiting outside and the one in the tent.

"Faiz, you can talk freely, they are believers, and as you know, they are out of favor with the President." She turned to the Major. "Major, Faiz is a member of the same organization I belong to. We help Christians who are in danger of being imprisoned or killed for their faith. We find a way to get them out of the country. This Organization, Mission of Peace, works all over the world. I was on a mission with Faiz to get a family out of your country when we had the accident." She turned back to Faiz, "were you able to get them to safety?"

"Yes, after the accident I looked for you, but I could not find you. I knew I had to get the family out, so I left. I hurried back and hunted for hours, through the sandstorm." He put his hand on her shoulder. "David, Jonathan, and Jared came with forged papers to help me look for you. We looked for weeks. It became dangerous for them to stay. I promised them I would not leave until I found you." He lowered his head. "I'm so sorry, Anna. Maybe if I hadn't left with the family..."

"You did the right thing, Faiz. We all agreed to the policies when we signed up." She smiled at him.

"Please be seated." The Major pointed to the chairs, and they all sat down. "So, how is it you work for the Directorate, but you are not a threat to us?" The Lieutenant asked.

"I only worked for them as a cover. Now that I have found Anna, I plan on taking her home, and I'm not coming back." Faiz said.

"How do you plan on getting her across the border?" The Major asked. Faiz looked at him, not sure if he should answer. The Major understood his hesitancy and continued. "I am trying to get my men to General Ozer in Turkey. I am hoping he will allow us to join him until it is safe to come home."

"Are all of your men in agreement with this? Can you trust them?" Faiz asked.

"There are a few I am not sure of."

"I can get you across the border. But I will only do that if you are certain there are no Administration sympathizers or spies with you." Faiz said.

The Major looked at his Lieutenant, who nodded. "If I can assure you of that, will you take us with you?" Faiz translated for Anna. She agreed.

"Yes. I can get you safely across the border. From there, I can contact someone for you who will connect you with the General."

The Major stood. "Thank you, Sergeant Major. You are an answer to prayer." He stood, triggering the others to do the same. He put his hand on Faiz's shoulder. "Now, please go to the cook's tent; one of my men will find you something to eat." Anna walked out with Faiz.

When Anna walked out of the tent, she asked Private Cemal Issawi to have someone take Faiz for some food. Then she turned to Faiz.

"I have a patient to take care of. When you're done, come to the Clinic. We can talk there." She pointed to her tent and started to move, then she turned and hugged him. "I'm so glad you're alright."

When Anna and Faiz left, the Lieutenant stood by the door and watched them for a while. He turned when the Major spoke to him.

"Can we trust him?"

"I do not know. But I trust Anna." Aden responded.

"Major, do you have a plan to separate the wheat from the chaff?"

"Yes. I need you to pray with me about it."

CHAPTER NINETEEN

Incirlik Air Base

*L*uke pulled into his driveway; glad he was home. He had spent little time with Sophie this week. The group was focused on a solution to keep the drug syndicate from finding out the children were the informants.

As soon as he walked in, Sophie jumped off his recliner and ran to hug him. Deniz came out of the kitchen, drying her hands on a dishtowel.

"Good evening, Mr. Luke. There is leftover spaghetti in the refrigerator. Would you like me to heat some for you?"

"No, Deniz. You have done too much already this week." She grabbed her coat, hugged Sophie, and headed to the door.

Luke handed her a white envelope with her paycheck and watched her get into her car, saying, "have a nice weekend Deniz."

"You too, sir." She hollered back as she shut her door.

Luke went to his room to change out of his uniform and into jeans and a T-shirt. Sophie went back to the book she was reading in her dad's recliner with a throw over her. When he headed for the kitchen, he asked, "do you want some ice cream, Sophie?"

"No, daddy. I already had some." Luke took the spaghetti bowl out of the fridge, scooped some onto a plate, and put it in the microwave. He saw some garlic bread wrapped up and grabbed a few slices, then poured himself some milk.

"How was your day? Anything interesting?" He said loudly enough so she could hear him.

"No." Then she sat up, "except Duke and CJ got in trouble."

"They did? What did they do?" Luke came to the kitchen door to hear better while the spaghetti was warming up.

"CJ asked Aunt Zoey if he and Duke could go to the Park. When she said no, they pouted about it." Sophie giggled. "I thought only girls pouted. Anyway, when Aunt Zoey saw how they were acting, she said, 'if you boys can't figure out a way to occupy your time. I will do it for you'. She made them go to the garage and reorganize Uncle Jonathan's tools and sweep up. It took them over an hour." Sophie giggled again.

"Well, I guess that will teach them, huh?" Luke smiled.

"It did. They found something to do after that."

Luke brought his meal out to the living room and sat on the couch. He pulled the coffee table closer so he could set his plate on it.

"What are you reading, princess?"

"Nancy Drew, remember Aunt Zoey bought me them for my 9th birthday. I love them, but what will I do when I've read them all?"

"Honey, there are 54 books in the original series. I will buy you more when you are done with these."

"Really, daddy?"

"Of course. And you can always read the Hardy Boys when you finish with Nancy Drew." Sophie scrunched up her face, letting him know that there was no way a boy detective could be as good as Nancy Drew. He laughed at her.

"Daddy, I want to be a spy when I grow up."

"A spy, not a detective like Nancy Drew?" She thought for a moment.

"No, a spy. They go to far away countries. Then they steal secrets and bring them back to the President, and he gives them a medal."

"Really, it's as easy as that?"

"Well, maybe not that easy, but close."

"But I would miss you so much, Sophie."

"Well, you could be my partner; you know every spy needs a partner."

"That's true enough, but what about my job?"

"Oh, daddy, you would be retired by then."

"I suppose so." Luke laughed to himself. He loved her imagination. Although knowing Sophie, she could do it.

"Shall we look at the stars tonight through the telescope? The sky is clear." Sophie got excited; it was her favorite thing to do with him.

"Yes, daddy. Hurry and eat."

Sergeant Roschin was back at his post with an ankle monitor the following Monday. The next drug shipment showed up the same day. He retrieved the drugs from the crate, divvied them up, and put them in the lockers. Then he contacted Sergeant Diaz.

Sergeant Diaz didn't know who to trust. Private Phillips blindsided him. Who else had he misjudged? There were two of his MP's he was willing to take a chance on, PV1 Zac Coulter and PV2 Noah Adams. He called them into his office while Private Phillips was on patrol and told them everything he knew so far, leaving out the kid's involvement.

"I expect both couriers to do a dead drop sometime today. I will take care of monitoring Private Philipps. I have no idea who the other courier is, but I know his dead drop location. I want you two to surveil it. You need to time his arrest, so we get the drugs and the money. You will have a window of about thirty seconds while he does a quick check that the money's all there. Then he will push the merchandise through the fence. We need them both on this side."

"Understood, sir," Coulter responded.

"Are you sure about Private Phillips, sir? Could it be a mistake?" Adams asked. Manny leaned back in his office chair and let out a deep breath, looking at the group picture of them on the wall.

"I wish I were wrong. But there is no doubt." He sat back up in his chair and continued. "The drugs are already in the lockers, so I need you out there right away. Sign out an unmarked car, get a dashcam out of tech, and make sure you wear body cams."

"Yes, sir," they both answered and got up to leave.

Private's Adams and Coulter headed to the dead drop. As they arrived, they saw that there was nowhere to hide their vehicle close to the fence. They decided to park in the gas station parking lot further down the street and watch with binoculars.

"If this guy comes while it's light outside, it's going to be impossible to sneak up on him."

"Yeah, I see that" Coulter said while trying to come up with a plan. "When he gets out of the car, we can move behind his car. When he bends down to trade bags, we will have to hustle to catch him before he moves the drugs through the fence."

"Can you believe Phillips is involved with this?" Adams asked.

"I wouldn't have six months ago. But Phillips confided in me his fiancé put Earnest Money down on a house. She pushes him to live above their means. She wants this house. She told him he needed the down payment for the bank by August or the Earnest Money agreement would run out. He's afraid if he can't show he can support her, she'll leave him. She came from a poor family and said she wouldn't marry anyone who can't support her in a comfortable lifestyle." Coulter replied.

"She knew he was in the Army when she accepted his proposal; how much did she think he makes?"

"He's only in for a short stint so he can get his college paid for when he's out. He plans on being an architect. They make good money." Adams nodded.

"It's getting late in the day. Maybe we will have the cover of darkness to catch him," Coulter said.

Sergeant Diaz parked his unmarked car in the Rec Center and walked to the fence. He knew he could hide in the hedges because the kids had told him that's where they hid. The last time Phillips made a drop, it was in the middle of the day. If he stayed true to that, he could be here anytime. Manny settled behind a full Boxwood hedge, squeezing through a damaged spot in the bushes. No doubt the same place the kids hid. He moved closer to the dead drop by moving forward in the two-foot space between the fence and the back of the hedge.

It was less than an hour when Manny heard a vehicle pull up to the curb. He looked between the branches and saw it was Private Phillips. Phillips got out of his car and looked around. When he didn't see anyone, he went to his trunk, pulled out a duffel bag, and headed to the fence.

Manny didn't move, didn't even breathe. He was waiting for Phillips to pull the duffel, filled with money inside the fence. When he did, the Sergeant stood; gun drawn. He was five feet away from Phillips.

"Put your hands up, Private." Diaz aimed his gun at Phillips's chest while he squeezed through a break in the hedge by the cut fence.

Private Phillips was stunned to see Sergeant Diaz standing there. He looked around to see if he had backup. Manny could tell he was going to make a run for it.

"Don't do it, Phillips. You have nowhere to go. Get down on your knees. If you try to run, I will shoot you." Manny could see Phillips's mind racing, deciding what to do.

"I said, turn around and get down on your knees." Manny moved closer to him.

"Sergeant, listen to me; I will share the money with you; please don't arrest me. No one will know."

"On your knees now!" This time Phillips turned around. Manny moved closer and kicked his foot into the back of Phillips's knee to get him to drop.

"Sergeant, please, you can have it all."

"Shut up, Phillips." Manny put his gun in its holster and grabbed his handcuffs. He helped Phillips up and used the handcuffs to control him, causing Phillips to bend over slightly. Diaz moved him back to pick up the two duffle bags, which were heavier than he expected. Diaz carried them both with his free hand and started walking Phillips to his unmarked car, reading him his rights on the way.

Sergeant Diaz dropped the bags and placed Phillips in the back of the unmarked car; he then put the evidence in the trunk. He called Private Coulter on the phone, not wanting to use the police radio.

"I've got Phillips. What do you see?"

"Nothing yet, sir. We are exposed until it gets dark. We're hoping he waits until then." Coulter responded.

"Ok, he'll show up." Coulter was quiet for a moment.

"So it's really Phillips, sir?"

"Yes, I'm sorry to say it is." Manny hung up and headed to the station to lock up his friend.

Sergeant Diaz drove to the Police Stations bay area. He brought Phillips in without fanfare through the back door. They had one holding cell separated from the rest. They used if for quarantine or confinement. He didn't want anyone talking to Phillips. Once locked up, he had him put his hands through the slot to take off the cuffs. Phillip's turned and grabbed the bars. He looked Sergeant Diaz in the eyes.

"Please don't do this, Manny. I'm not a drug dealer; all I do is drop off a bag. I'm not a criminal."

"Are you kidding me, Gavin? You know the law. You gave up everything for a few extra bucks." Manny took a step and looked at the handcuffs he took off him. "I thought you were a friend," Manny said and walked away. Phillips kept talking until Manny was out of sight. Manny gave the MP on guard orders that Phillips was to have no visitors and no phone privileges. The MP had a hard time believing it was Phillips in the cell.

It was dusk when Coulter saw a car approach that looked suspicious. It was traveling too slow. It went past the dead drop and drove another fifty feet before making a U-turn. The car pulled over to the curb close to the drop site.

"This has to be him," Coulter said. They had scooted down in their seats and turned the dash and body cams on. They watched as the target sat in the car for five minutes before he stepped out.

"He's an Air Force mechanic. I've run into him a few times at a bar in Adana when they called to get a drunken soldier out of their establishment." Adams said.

The target took a slow, deliberate look around. The men scrunched down even further in their seats. Convinced there was no one watching. The Airman moved to his trunk, took another look around, and opened it. He grabbed the duffle and moved toward the fence.

Coulter and Adams slipped out of the vehicle, quietly closing the car doors. They ran squatted down to the target's car. When the Airman got to the fence, he looked around one more time. The MP's had to get to the Airman as soon as he pulled the bag through the fence. When the Airman squatted down to pull the money through, Privates Coulter and Adams rushed up behind him.

"Stop right there and put your hands up!" Coulter said. The target jumped up and rushed the MP, knocking him to the ground. He started running to his car. Adams ran after him and tackled him to the ground before he got to his car.

"Put your hands behind your back," Adams yelled; he had his knee in the Airman's back. Coulter ran up and helped to cuff him. Adams took him to their vehicle as he read him his rights, and Coulter grabbed the evidence. They called transportation to tow his car.

Private Adams called Sergeant Diaz on his cell and informed him they had their target.

"Bring him in the bay area and take him to interrogation. I don't want anyone talking to him." He paused and took a breath, "is he one of ours?"

"No, he's an Air Force mechanic."

The fingerprints came back to Airman First Class Kalinin. Diaz and his two officers were watching the Airman through the one-way mirror in the next room.

"I want you both to recount the evidence in both duffle bags, to make sure it matches up with what Roschin gave us. Then I want you to take it to the Lab to see if there are any fingerprints they can lift." Sergeant Diaz turned from the window and looked at his men. "I don't want any mistakes that can get this thrown out."

Manny sent a text to Captain Star before he entered the interrogation room.

Luke was going through files of closed cases. He double-checked to make sure nothing was missing. Of the twenty files he was putting in storage, he had two that were missing notes he took during an interview with a witness. One was short the court transcript; another was missing the picture and fingerprints. He separated those files and boxed the others to go to storage.

Luke was walking back to his desk when he got the text from Manny. He took a deep breath. With the men in custody, the danger to the children decreased.

Luke considered going to watch the interrogation but decided it was best to stay out of it.

Sergeant Diaz walked into the interrogation room with a yellow pad, a pen, and his computer. All the interrogation rooms had cameras that recorded the interviews; he turned it on before he entered. Sergeant Diaz kept his eye on the Airman, pulled out the chair across from him, and sat down. He didn't speak. He wanted Kalinin to initiate the conversation so that he could get a feel for his temperament. Nervous people always want to fill up the silence.

"Why am I here, Sergeant? Your MP's accosted me while I was out for a jog."

"In uniform?" Manny asked.

"Yes. I do that on occasion." Manny put a smirk on his face.

"Unfortunately, my men tell me a different story."

Kalinin leaned back in his chair, arrogant, believing he could talk his way out of this. "Their word against mine." He smiled.

"We have duffle bags full of evidence, Airman," Manny said.

"I noticed the bags when I was jogging. All I did was go to see what was in them. I planned on turning them in to the police station when your men accosted me."

"Let's see if that will hold up in court. Shall we." Manny opened his computer; it was queued up and turned it so they both could see. He started the video and gave a running dialogue of what was happening.

"So, there you are parking your car. You get out and walk to the back of your car. Let's see what you do next. Oh, well, there you are, taking a duffle bag, one that looks exactly like the one in evidence out of the trunk. Let's see what you do next. You look around to see if anyone is watching. Hmmm, I don't see you jogging. All I see is you heading to the fence and pulling a similar duffle from the other side. And there you go; my men catch you red-handed." He slammed the computer closed. It startled the Airman, and he jumped. Manny sat back in his chair, waiting for a comment from the Airman.

The winds were out of Kalinin's sails, his arrogant demeanor disappearing. Kalinin slumped forward with his elbows on the table, his head in his hands.

"You can make things a little easier by telling me what you know about the drug trafficking on base. I will recommend you get a lighter sentence to the prosecuting Jag."

Kalinin dropped his hands away from his face to look at the Sergeant, "I don't know anything."

"How were you recruited?" Manny asked.

"One day after I left the bar my buddies and I go to after work, there was a burner phone in my driver's seat."

"You don't lock your car?"

"Yes, of course, I don't know how they got in, but they did."

"Then what happened?"

"When I got in the car and shut the door, it rang. I answered, and a man on the other end asked if I wanted to earn some easy money."

"Why you? Why choose you? He would be taking a big risk if he weren't confident you would agree." Manny leaned forward, interested in his answer.

"My buddies and I complain all the time when we're at the bar about how poorly the Military pays its men. You know yourself; the pay scale is ridiculous."

"You knew that going in. Why join."

"So I can get the big bucks as a Commercial Airline mechanic, you have to have experience. Airlines usually give preference to military applicants. But I still have three years to go, and my paycheck never makes it to the end of the month. I'm here in Europe; I could be going to Paris or Italy on my days off. But I can't afford anything other than a drink at lousy dives."

"More than a drink, Airman. I have a file here that shows you have been picked up for drunk and disorderly from the bars in town several times. So someone overheard you?"

"That's what I figure. When the voice asked if I wanted to earn money, I said I would consider it."

"What happened then?"

"He told me what I had to do and that I would get $5000 a month for one or two deliveries a week. I was pumped."

"You didn't ask what you would be delivering?"

"Sure. He said drugs. He wasn't more specific." He sat up straight and looked Manny in the eye. "A lot of States back home are legalizing drugs, so I figure it's not that bad."

"Not cocaine and opioids, Kalinin!"

"Well, maybe not, but me saying no is not going to stop the drug trade, and I needed the money." Manny sat back, disgusted by his attitude.

"I told you everything I know. Will you talk to Jag?"

Manny stared at him for a long time before he spoke. "I'll do what I said. Now I suggest you ask for a lawyer."

"Yeah, I want a lawyer."

Sergeant Diaz called the Air Force Military Police and handed him over. He told them the situation and that the evidence was in the Lab if they wanted to inspect it.

"He asked for a lawyer," Manny told the Air Force MP, that came to collect Kalinin.

CHAPTER TWENTY

Sergeant Diaz considered the interview with Kalinin. More than likely, Phillips's would be more of the same. He was getting nowhere. *I need to get the attention of someone a step higher up.* He considered that a few minutes and got an idea. He called Major Scott.

"Major, these guys know nothing. But I have an idea."

"I'm getting ready to go home. You want to come over for dinner?" Major Scott asked.

"Yes, thank you. Will you see if the other guys can come?"

"Yes." Major Scott asked, "will seven work for you?"

"I'll be there."

By seven, the steaks were on the grill, and Duke went to visit CJ.

Jonathan was the first one there, helping put the meal together.

When the others arrived, they prayed over the meal and enjoyed the food and the company. After clearing off the table, Major Scott turned to Manny.

"Ok, Manny. What's your plan?"

Manny took a sip of his coffee and started. "After I called you." He nodded to David, "I watched Phillips's interview again. His story is identical to the others. I realized I'm going to have to do something to get one of the higher-ups in the syndicate to come out from behind their cloak." He looked around, "we have confiscated their funds, but I'm sure they have no idea yet. What if

I keep Roschin in play and continued confiscating the drugs that come in. They will start to wonder where their money is. And when the drugs stop showing up at the dead drops, someone is going to want answers."

"Which means one of the syndicate men is going to have to come to base to get some answers," Jonathan added.

The men considered what Manny was saying. "Did you find out how Roschin got the cash to the syndicate?" Luke asked.

"Yes. Roschin puts it in a crate or car headed back to the states. If one doesn't go that week, he holds it until the next week. Then he sends a text on the burner phone of the transit number on the crate. And the corresponding code to where it is hidden."

So they might not be aware they have a problem right away unless the local Mafia has contacted someone about their missing drugs."

"You confiscated both money and drugs on the last two busts, right." David asked.

"True. If we keep Roschin in play, we could confiscate a lot more. Somebody is going to have to show up," Manny said.

After a few moments of silence, David spoke, "wow, Manny, that's a risky plan. What if they kill Roschin, thinking he's stealing from them?"

"I doubt anyone higher up would know what Roschin looks like. I could put one of my men undercover."

"Do you think we should contact CID? Maybe the intelligence unit should take it from here." Luke said.

David nodded, "he's right, Manny. Why take the chance one of your men gets killed? Send it up the chain. It will take the pressure off us worrying about the kids getting found out." Manny didn't respond.

"Manny, I know how hard it is to give up a case you were so essential in developing. But David is right. Your office doesn't have the same resources the CID does." Jonathan sympathized.

Manny nodded his head, "you're right. My office did its part. I'll pass it on."

"Make sure you tell them about your plan. It's a solid plan." Luke added.

They spent another hour or so having a Bible study. It had been a while since they were all together for anything other than work.

Northern border of Syria and Turkey

Major Jabban asked his Sergeant to call the men together so he could speak with them. Fifteen minutes later, he stepped in front of his men.

"Men, as you know, Major Nayef from the Directorate has located our position. Although he is not here on Directorate business, it follows that if he found us, others will too."

Faiz was standing with Anna on the shelf above where the Major was speaking. He was translating for her.

"Faiz, how is he going to know who to trust to come with us?"

"I don't know. But when I spoke to the Major earlier, he said he had prayed about it." She nodded, and he went back to translating the Majors speech.

"...it has been my great honor to serve with you. But it is time for you to leave here and try to find a safe place until we are no longer on the terrorist list.

I will give you discharge papers and two month's pay, so you have some resources. The documents will protect you from being tried as a deserter if they capture you, and FSA is once again recognized.

You may take your tent and anything else that you feel will help you. The cook will split up the balance of our food supply. I suggest you do not travel in your uniform and do not travel in more than groups of twos.

Get your things together tonight and then leave in the morning.

Again, I want to tell you what an honor it has been to serve with you. The Sergeant will send you in one at a time to get your discharge documents and pay."

When he finished, the men came to attention and saluted; the Major reciprocated.

Incirlik Military Base

Sergeant Diaz was in his office; it had been ten days since he had heard anything from CID. They had thanked him for doing a good job and summarily dismissed him. He'd always wanted to be in the intelligence unit, but he didn't have the College degree required. Manny decided to look into the possibility of taking the classes online. He would ask next time he spoke with one of the men in CID. His thoughts were interrupted by the Police receptionist, Private Sorensen. She poked her head in his office door.

"Sir, there is someone here to see you from CID."

The kids wanted to go to the Mall that had the Arcade for days. It took a lot of begging to get the ok from all the parents.

There was no indication that anyone knew the children were the informants that led to the drug bust on Base. So their parents relented.

Zoey drove the kids to the Mall and showed them where the bus would pick them up to take them home.

"I don't want you to stay past 3 pm and take bus 2236. It will say Incirlik." Zoey said as the kids jumped out of the SUV.

As they were walking into the Mall, Duke said, "I can't believe they finally let us out of the housing complex. It was like we were under house arrest. I think it had something to do with the drug deal we saw about a month ago."

216

"I think you've been around Sophie too long; that's a little dramatic." CJ laughed.

"What is that supposed to mean?" Sophie asked with her hands on her hips.

"Ignore them, Sophie, let's go to Claire's and get some new barrettes."

Lizzy pulled Sophie along.

"Wait, we're supposed to stay together. You know the rules. And Duke and I do not want to go to Claire's."

"Let's go to the Arcade," Duke suggested. The girls scowled at him.

"Claire's is next store. As long as you promise to come straight to the Arcade when you're done. I think that would be ok." CJ said.

"Ok. But we don't want to stay in the Arcade for hours. There are other stores we want to go to." Lizzy said.

"Once you get to the Arcade, we will only stay one more hour. Fair?" Duke asked.

The girls nodded.

Two stops at the food court, visits to seven of their favorite stores, another hour at the Arcade, and the kids were ready to go home. They had been at the Mall for four hours.

There was a shelter with benches at the bus stop located at the main entrance. They were twenty minutes early, so the bench was empty. They were a few feet from the shelter when a van squealed to a stop next to them.

Before they realized what was happening, a man in a mask opened the sliding door and grabbed Lizzy. Duke and CJ started punching the man. Sophie bit the man's hand, and he let Lizzy go. Then the driver came around and grabbed Sophie's arm. CJ turned from the first man and ran a hard football type tackle on him. Pushing his shoulders into the man's ribs and forcing him up against the side of the van.

"RUN!" he yelled. Lizzy started to run, Sophie turned to go too, but the first man had shoved Duke to the ground and caught her. The driver pulled out a gun and hit CJ over the head with it. He went down hard on the concrete sidewalk.

The first man had his arm around the front of Sophie with his hand under her arm. He was using the other to fend off Duke. Sophie bit him again, but he didn't let go this time.

Lizzy turned when she realized the others weren't behind her. She headed for CJ, who was on the ground, not moving. She started yelling for help. The commotion was getting people's attention.

The driver said something to the first man and tried to shove Sophie into the an. Duke refused to let go of her. So they shoved him in with her. The men slammed the door as Sophie hollered something to Lizzy. The driver got in the van and drove off at high speed.

"I promise, Sophie," Lizzy yelled at the moving van, holding CJ's head.

"Let him in," Sergeant Diaz told her. He stood when Agent Lance Marquez came in, and Manny moved around his desk to shake his hand. Lance was at least four inches taller than Manny and built like a linebacker. He had met him a few times and became friends. His grandfather was one of the first black men to make General after WWII.

"Sit down, Lance. Do you have news about the case?" Lance took a seat while Manny leaned against his desk in front of him.

"It's not good, Manny." He looked to make sure the door was closed. "Roschin has been compromised."

"What are you saying? Compromised how?"

"They got to him."

"Who?"

"The syndicate." Lance paused and looked Manny in the eyes, "they worked him over pretty bad. He's in the hospital unconscious."

Manny stood up, "you were supposed to protect him, Lance."

"We had men protecting him. They're dead." Lance lowered his head to swallow a lump in his throat.

Manny started pacing. "What did they get out of him?"

The ambulance driver said before he went out, he was mumbling."

"What."

"He kept saying they wanted it back. I have to assume he meant the drugs and money. The paramedic said he kept saying to tell Sergeant Diaz he was sorry." Lance finished.

"Sorry for what?"

"My guess is he told them you had the evidence."

"But I turned that over to you when the Lab got done with it."

"Roschin didn't know that," Lance said. "I think they plan on going after you," Lance hesitated.

Manny stared at him, "and."

He looked up, "or your kids." Manny froze in place.

"My kids? What makes you say that."

"I've done some research on the different Turkish Mafia families. Our intel says that it's one of them that's involved with the syndicate. They have been working together trafficking drugs through this Base for quite a few years. We captured communication from the Mafia to the syndicate. Lance pulled the message up on his phone and read it:

We will get our money back and the merchandise too.
But we will keep the money for the inconvenience
you have caused us. You need to take care of whoever
is plugging up the flow of the business. Or we will
find another supplier.

They have no compunction about taking kids to get what they want. They have done it to the local Polis."

Manny called Luke to let him know there was a threat and asked him to tell the others.

"Listen, Manny; we will do whatever we have to, to make sure your family is safe." Lance stood.

Northern border of Syria and Turkey

By 7 am the next morning, the camp looked almost deserted. The Major had spoken with the men, giving them their documents and pay. He told them he would pray for their safety.

Faiz was sitting on a cot in the Clinic when Anna stepped around the divider. He had insisted on sleeping in the Clinic, not wanting to take any chances he would lose sight of her again. Faiz got up and handed her one of two cups of tea he had in his hands. She thanked him, and they stepped outside.

"It is strange. Seeing how quickly the men can tear down a camp." Faiz said.

"Yes, I had no idea it could happen so fast. It's as if no one was ever here."

"That's the point. The Major wants to make sure no one knows they camped here. There are a dozen men still here. A few more will be leaving after they tear down the rest of the camp. The cook's tent is down, but his assistant is still serving breakfast. Would you like me to get you some?"

"Yes, thank you. And bring some for my patient too." She heard the cook moan inside the Clinic. She went back in to give him more pain medication.

Anna had filled up her field pack with the rest of the medical supplies and anything else she thought might be useful. Whether she would be able to carry it was another story. The rest of the supplies in the tent were divvied up among the men last night. She took several blankets and a mess kit for herself. She filled the thermos Rima gave her with boiled water to drink. Then she filled one of the canteens with water for washing. Anna also took the few personal items she had. She separated a small bag of supplies to tend to the cook's burn without having to tear her field pack apart.

Anna and her patient stepped out of the tent. Men were outside, waiting to tear down the Clinic. She smiled and moved out of the way as Faiz came up with breakfast. Faiz grabbed chairs from inside for her and the cook to sit on before the men tore everything down.

Anything that was too big or clumsy to take, they would usually burn. It was protocol, so an enemy could not have the use of it. But a big fire would give away their location. So they planned on breaking up any crates, boxes, furniture, and the large tents and bury them. They would fill the hole and cover it with foliage.

Major Jabban and Lieutenant Arabi came up to the shelf from the cook's station with hot tea.

"Good morning, Anna." The Major said in his limited English. He nodded to Faiz, who he had spoken with earlier. He waved them into his tent.

"Good morning, Major," she turned to look at Aden, "Lieutenant." They acknowledged her greeting — the Major pointing to the chairs for them to sit.

They reverted to Arabic. "We should be leaving in a few hours. You can see all but my tent has been dismantled."

"How many will be traveling with us?" Faiz asked.

"Ten, including the Lieutenant and I."

"Are you sure we can trust them?"

"I have no doubt. The ones staying are the men I prayed about. I encouraged them to leave, but they said they had nowhere to go."

"I trust your judgment," Faiz said.

"Can you tell us a little about the direction we will be going?" Faiz moved to the door to make sure no one could hear.

"My grandfather worked with the black market his whole life. He was a courier. He would pick up merchandise at the border and take it through a one-mile tunnel between Syria and Turkey. Then he would haul it down the mountain. He had a holding shack hidden in the woods down below somewhere. He would take me with him on occasion.

It will take at least one day, maybe two from here. But once we get to the tunnel, we will be safe."

"How close to the fighting is it?" Lieutenant Arabi asked. Faiz stood again and walked back to the door.

"I'm afraid it will be close. That's why I said it might take two days. If we get too close to the fighting, we may have to travel at night." The Major turned to Anna.

"It is rough terrain, Anna. Will you be able to handle it?" Faiz translated for her but didn't give her a chance to answer.

"I will take care of her. If there is any delay, I will give you directions, and you can leave us behind." Faiz said. The Major laughed.

"You misunderstood, Major. There is no way I would leave Anna behind. I only asked to see if there is some way to make it easier for her."

"Thank you for asking, Major, but I will be fine," Anna said. The Major stood.

"I must make ready to dismantle the tent. It will take us another hour to discard what we can't take. Then a few more men will leave. I suggest we wait for another hour to make sure they are truly gone. Then we can go."

"Do you have a map?" The Lieutenant asked.

"My father taught me how to use a military projector to find MGRS coordinates. So I mapped out my grandpa's route for him. I still have a copy." Faiz answered. "But from here, I'm not sure. You will have to navigate us to a coordinate on the map. Then I can take it from there."

Faiz and Anna left the Major to his packing.

Incirlik Military Base
Manny called Ruby to find out where the kids were.

"Zoey took them to the Mall. We talked about it last night, remember? You said you were off the case." Ruby could hear the panic in Manny's voice. "What's going on, Manny?"

Ruby turned to see the men come out of their offices and into the conference room. "What's happened."

"CID thinks they might be in danger," Manny said.

"What kind of danger? No one knows the kids saw anything. Right?" Manny heard Ruby's voice tremble.

"The syndicate finally sent someone to locate the problem in the assembly line. They came after Roschin and killed two CID agents. Lance thinks they might take one of the kids as a way of forcing me to give back the drugs and money."

"But the CID has them."

"They think they are still in evidence at the Police Station." Manny rubbed his hands down his face. "I've got to pick up the kids. Which Mall are they at?"

"The one with the Arcade."

"Don't worry, sweetheart, I'm going after them now."

Lance insisted on driving Manny to the Mall. Luke was heading that way with David and Jonathan, as well. They were still a few miles away when a bulletin came over Lance's radio about a kidnapping at the Mall. The dispatcher said an ambulance was taking two of the victims to the hospital.

Manny got on his cell and asked for the dispatcher who called out the bulletin. "What do you know about the victims?"

"Young, white male, blond hair, unconscious. A little girl with him, also blond. They are taking them to the Base hospital. The little girl said her dad was an MP on Base."

"That has to be Lizzy and CJ," Manny said, turning to Lance.

"What about the other kids," Manny asked dispatch.

"That's all we have, sir." Manny hung up and called Jonathan.

"Jonathan, you need to get to the hospital. CJ and Lizzy are on the way there." Manny heard him suck in a big breath.

"What do you know?"

"Only that CJ is unconscious, and Lizzy is with him." Jonathan hesitated to ask.

"What about Duke and Sophie?"

"I have nothing on them. Go to the hospital; I'll send Ruby. I'm going to the Mall."

"David and Luke will meet you there once Luke drops me off at the hospital," Jonathan said.

"I'm putting you on speaker. Tell us everything you know." Manny filled them in.

CHAPTER TWENTY-ONE

*L*ance and Manny made it to the Mall in record time. Turkish Polis vehicles spotted the area, red and blue lights flashing, causing a light show on the bus shelter. Manny saw his friend Sergeant Metin Demir talking with a man, hopefully, a witness. Manny jumped out of the car before Lance had it in park.

Running over to Sergeant Demir, he asked, "Sergeant Demir, what do you know?"

Demir turned to him, "give me one minute." Then he finished writing down what the man was saying. Manny didn't know enough Turkish to understand what was said, so he stepped a few feet away. He also didn't know if any of the other officers spoke English, so he waited.

Lance stepped up behind him and put a hand on Manny's shoulder. Manny nodded, understanding the gesture. He calmed down, knowing being professional in this situation would get him further.

Sergeant Demir stepped over to him, "Sergeant Diaz, how can I help you?"

"My daughter is one of the victims. She was with her friends."

Demir looked surprised. "I'm sorry, Sergeant. I can tell you what I know so far."

"Thank you." He turned to Lance, "this is Agent Lance Marquez of the CID." Lance stretched his hand to Demir, who shook it.

"The man I was speaking with is a witness. He was getting in his car about 75 yards, that direction," he pointed over Manny's shoulder. "He heard a scream and turned to see what was happening. When he saw a man trying to grab a little girl, he

225

started running toward the commotion. He said the first thing he saw was a man in a hood grabbing a blond girl. Then two boys, a dark-haired one and a blond, started punching the man, a dark-haired girl bit the kidnapper and he let her go. Someone yelled 'RUN' and the little girl took off. The other little girl tried to follow, but the driver had come around and grabbed her. Then the blond boy tackled him against the van, and he let go. She tried to run again, but the first man had pushed the dark-haired boy down and grabbed her. The driver pulled out a gun and hit the blond-haired boy on the head with it. He dropped to the ground. The driver grabbed the dark-haired girl shoving her in the van, but the dark-haired boy wouldn't let go of her. So the man pushed them both in and took off."

"Did he get a description of the men or the van?"

"The men wore masks. By the time he made it to the scene, the van was too far away to get a plate. But we have the description. It was a locally manufactured older dark blue Ford E150 Econoline Van."

"Are there other witnesses?"

"Yes, but my witness was the first one to make it to the scene. The others didn't see much."

Manny walked over to the witness; he was speaking to others who had stayed to talk to the Polis.

"Yardım etmeye çalıştığınız için teşekkür ederiz." Manny thanked the man for trying to help. It was one of the few phrases he had learned since he moved here. The man nodded and shook his hand. Manny moved back to where Sergeant Demir stood.

"What has been done so far?" Manny asked.

"We have a call out to pull over any similar vans in a thirty-mile radius." Sergeant Demir looked Manny in the eyes, "we will find them. That I promise you." He put his hand on Manny's shoulder.

Before Manny could respond, David and Luke ran over. "Manny, what do you know?" After he introduced them to Sergeant Demir, he asked the Sergeant to repeat what he knew. Sergeant Demir repeated everything he told Manny and Lance.

"Sergeant Demir, our CID will want to coordinate with your effort to find these children. They are United States Citizens kidnapped in your country. We will put all our efforts into locating them and bringing them home." Agent Marquez said.

"I understand, but remember you are in our country. And we will want to take the lead on this. If we can work together, I am happy to do so, but I can't promise how my superiors will feel." Sergeant Demir said.

"I appreciate that, Sergeant Demir. But you must realize the United States will not stand by and do nothing." Sergeant Demir acknowledged the Agents response. Another officer called Sergeant Demir over, and he excused himself.

"Agent Marquez, how are we going to get our kids back?" Luke asked.

"The fact they want the children in trade for drugs is good." The men looked at Lance, questioning his statement. "They won't hurt them if they want to trade them. It won't be long before they contact you."

"We can't just wait," David said.

"You guys go to the Hospital. I'm going to CID and see if the Command Center has any satellite images over this area about the time of the kidnapping." Lance said.

David looked hopeful. "Do you think there's a chance there is footage?

"We monitor this part of the country continually, but I can't promise anything. And even if we do, this happened in such a short window of time. The Satellite may not have caught it." David and Luke nodded.

Manny and Lance went to look at the scene. David and Luke went back to their car and headed to the Hospital.

Lizzy wouldn't let go of CJ's hand on the ride in the ambulance. The nurse asked Lizzy to let go of CJ when they took him into an emergency room. But every time they tried to force her

227

hand out of his, she started screaming. They decided she had been through enough trauma. They didn't want to add to it, so they let her go back with him.

It took twelve stitches to close the wound the butt of the gun caused. Lizzy closed her eyes for that part. When it was time to get CJ a CT scan, a nurse knelt in front of her. "Sweetheart, you have to let us get a look at his brain so we can make sure he's ok. I promise you we will bring him right back, and you can stay here and wait for him."

Lizzy's eyes looked panicked. "You promise?"

She crossed her heart and put up the Girl Scout three finger salute. Lizzy let go of his hand but grabbed his backpack and held it to her chest.

Ruby and Jonathan showed up at the Hospital about the same time. The lady at the desk pressed the door release and told them what room to go to. When they opened the door, CJ wasn't there, but Lizzy was in a chair waiting. Her eyes stared straight ahead, her body shaking. It looked like she might be going into shock. Jonathan ran out and got a nurse.

The nurse tried to take Lizzy to another room to have a doctor look at her. "Noooo, I can't leave CJ. Sophie told me to take care of him. I promised her." She looked up at her mother.

Ruby picked her up off the seat and sat down, putting her on her lap, holding her close. The nurse grabbed a blanket from the cabinet and placed it around Lizzy's shoulder. "Thank you. It's alright, nurse. I'll call you if I need you."

Jonathan stepped out of the room with the nurse. "Where is my son?"

"They took him for a CT scan. He was unconscious when he came in. They stitched up the wound on his head." She gently laid a hand on Jonathan's arm. "He should be fine, Major. I'll let the Doctor know you would like to talk to him."

"Thank you," Jonathan replied. He called David before he headed back to the room. "David, what do you know?"

"It appears two masked men in an older van have taken Sophie and Duke." David's voice trembled as he recounted what he knew.

"Where are you now?"

"We are heading to the Hospital. How are CJ and Lizzy?"

"I think Lizzy's in shock. She screams anytime they try to move her away from CJ. Sophie made her promise to take care of him."

"What about CJ?"

"I haven't seen him yet. He's having a CT scan. The nurse says he had an injury on his head they sewed up."

"Man, I don't know what I would do if I got my hands on these guys," David said.

"Me either, David."

Jonathan called Zoey to see if Deniz came over to watch Liam and Ricky yet. She didn't answer her cell.

"Why did you get me involved with this? These are not local kids. They are from the American Base. The whole of the United States will be after us." The driver screamed at the man sitting behind him.

"I'm sorry, Kader. I told you they said if I did this, they would wipe out my debt." He looked at the driver, "they threatened Paša if I didn't pay up."

"Well, now, you have a bigger problem. Who is going to take care of your wife when we are both in prison...or dead, kardesim?"

Kader slowed the Van down; he had been driving way too fast trying to get out of Adana. He didn't need the Turkish Polis stopping him for speeding. They were still twenty minutes from the abandoned ranch they planned on holding up at.

"I'm telling you right now. If Sandalli wants us to kill these children. I will not do it. Do you hear me?"

"I hear you. You know I would never kill a child, Kader."
"I don't know what you would do, Mesut."

Half an hour after being shoved in the Van's third row, Duke still had both arms around Sophie. He held her close as she cried and shook. The men talked too fast; Duke couldn't understand what the driver said. But it was obvious the driver was angry. He did recognize one word, 'kardesim': brother.

Duke tried to memorize the street signs, so he could find his way back when they escaped. It was more challenging now that they were in a rural area. Sophie had stopped crying, but he didn't let go of her.

Sophie looked up at him and whispered, "what's going to happen to us, Duke?"

Duke looked down at her, "don't you worry, I'll take care of you." She nodded and wiggled out of his arms to try to see where they were.

A short time later, the van turned onto a dirt road. Duke could see an old, dilapidated farmhouse down the road to the left. Fifty feet to the right, there was a large barn. The once bright red roof, now ugly brown, had fallen in on the side of the barn that had caved. There was one more building that looked like it could be a bunkhouse. That was the building the van stopped in front of.

The man sitting behind the driver opened the sliding door and got out. He waved his hand, directing them to come. Duke took Sophie's hand and led her out. The driver was opening the bunkhouse door.

The room they walked into was old, but it looked like it was still maintained and used. The old planks on the floor were sturdy, and there was a newer table and chairs. A couch and a small TV with an antenna sat on the east side of the room, opposite a kitchen sink and a hot plate. On the wall that faced them were two doors. The man took them to one of the doors and tried to take Sophie away from Duke.

230

"No, No. She stays with me." The driver must have understood him because he said something to the other man, and he let them both go in together.

They stepped into a long room about half the width of the other. There were two sets of bunk beds without mattresses on the left side of the room. A window separated them against the wall. There was a door open at the end of the room. A sink was visible through the door. On the right side were two cots with thin, stuffed pads; a window separated the cots. Duke led Sophie to a cot, and they sat down. The man shut the door when he left. Duke didn't hear it lock.

Duke ran to the windows to see if they would open, but they were both nailed shut.

"What are we going to do?" Sophie's voice trembled.

"We're going to find a way to escape," Duke said.

"My daddy will find us."

"Yes, our dad's will find us." Even though he had no idea how anyone would find them, he smiled at her. It was up to him to get them home.

"Look, Sophie, I still have my backpack. I don't know how it stayed on through all that, but it did. It has your purse and your packages from the Mall." Duke said, trying to get her mind off their situation.

"Will you keep them safe for me?"

"Don't worry; they'll be safe in here." Duke patted his backpack.

"Duke, what about CJ. He was on the ground, not moving when we left."

"I think the driver hit him in the head with something. The doctors at the Hospital will fix him. He has a hard head." Sophie seemed to be alright with that explanation.

"I'm scared, Duke. What do they want with us?" Duke got up and checked out the room with the sink.

"My guess is it has to do with the drug deal we saw."

"You think so?" He walked back to the cot and put his arm around her again.

"I don't know for sure. We need to pray and ask Jesus to send his Angels to protect us." Duke said. A big smile came over Sophie's face.

"Yes, Jesus will send his Angels to protect us." They closed their eyes and prayed together.

Shouting outside the door interrupted them. Duke went to the door to listen, trying to hear something he could understand.

Northern Syrian and Turkish Border

Faiz explained to Anna that the Major would be leading them to the closest coordinate on his map.

"He knows this area better than I do. The first fifteen miles are steep. I will walk with you and carry your field pack."

"Thank you, Faiz. But I don't want to be a burden."

"I don't have medical supplies...or much of anything else, for that matter. You can carry mine." He took the field pack next to her. It was at least three times the weight of his.

The Sergeant, who was one of the men who stayed, called for everyone to come together. Anna was glad both of her guards decided to travel with them.

When everyone assembled, they headed on the first leg of their journey. It was already late morning, not ideal, but the men had to make sure they left no trace behind.

Four hours later, the Major stopped to give the men a break. Anna sat on a felled tree and took her canteen from the field pack Faiz had carried for her. She also grabbed the small sack of medical supplies and headed to where the cook was sitting.

Anna motioned for him to roll up his sleeve. She undid the bandage and saw that the blisters had not yet burst; there was no sign of infection. Anna ran some water from her canteen over it and patted the surface dry. She laid a clean medicated gauze on the burn and wrapped it. If the environment wasn't so rugged, Anna might have left it unwrapped. But she didn't want to take the chance he would scrape it on a branch and get it infected. Anna reached into the bag and pulled out the pain medication, handing him two. He thanked her, and she went back to her seat. She grabbed her thermos and took a short drink.

Faiz came back from talking to the Major. "The Major says we can probably make it to the intersect point by the end of the day tomorrow. But he warned we might get caught up in some fighting when we get closer." He took the thermos Anna offered and took a drink. "We will have to be careful not to be seen."

"Once we get there, how long will it take to get to the tunnel and across the border?"

"It will take a day's walk to get to the tunnel. The tunnel is only a mile long; we come out the other side in Turkey."

Anna prayed with Faiz that the Lord would keep them hidden and that they would all make it safely.

Incirlik Military Base

The Doctor sent CJ to a room on the second floor by the time Luke and David got to the Hospital. Lance had gone back to CID to start the search effort for the Van, using the Satellite.

Manny finally made it to the Hospital, nodding to the two guards at the door as he walked by. CJ had a room to himself because of the security concerns. David walked up to Jonathan and hugged him. Zoey was sitting next to CJ's bed opposite Lizzy, who still wouldn't let go of CJ's hand.

"How's CJ, Jon?" David asked. The other men listened in.

"He has a serious concussion. The CT scan didn't show any cranial bleeding, but there is swelling, and he still hasn't woken up." David patted Zoey on the back. She looked up and smiled at him.

"What does the Doctor think?"

"He was a little concerned CJ hasn't woken up yet, but he is confident CJ will make a full recovery," Jonathan said.

Manny knelt in front of Lizzy. Putting his hands on her arms. "How are you, sweetheart?" Her mind hadn't registered anyone had come into the room.

"Oh, daddy! They took Sophie and Duke." She threw herself at him and wrapped her free hand around his neck. He held her close, stroking her hair and whispering to her, "everything is going to be fine."

Luke stepped next to them; he saw tears running down Manny's face. Luke reached out to stroke Lizzy's hair.

"We'll find them, Lizzy," Luke said.

She turned to him, "Uncle Luke, we couldn't stop them." He knelt next to her.

"Of course, you couldn't. The men were much bigger. But I know how hard you all tried. We'll find them." Luke stood and went to talk to David and Jonathan. Manny picked Lizzy up and sat in the chair she vacated and put her on his lap. He needed to hold her.

Manny asked Zoey where Ruby had gone. "She stayed with me until Luke and David showed up a few minutes ago. Deniz picked up Ricky and then came to the house to watch Ricky and Liam while I came to the Hospital. Ruby went to relieve her. She said Liam could stay with you guys as long as needed." She looked at him, "Is that alright."

"Yes, of course, you don't even have to ask that question, Zoey." She just nodded.

Manny got up and put Lizzy back in the chair. She grabbed his hand. "Daddy, where are you going?"

He patted her head, "I'm going to talk to Uncle David." She let go of his hand.

The men moved out into the hall. Manny asked the nurse if there was an empty room they could use. She directed them to a room two doors down.

"Thank you." He said as they headed in that direction.

CHAPTER TWENTY-TWO

*O*nce they all found a spot to sit, David spoke, "no offense Manny, but there is no way I am going to sit back and wait for someone else to find Duke and Sophie."

"Of course, David. We will let CID and the Turkish Polis do their investigation, but we will do our own."

"Where do we start?" Jonathan asked. Manny rubbed a hand over the stubble on his face.

"Someone will be contacting me for the trade. It's the drugs we confiscated they want, not the kids." He lowered his head. "I'm so sorry, guys. It was Lizzy they were after. Sophie and Duke got in the way."

Luke moved to his side. "How would it have been any better if they had Lizzy instead? We love them all like they're our own."

"He's right, Manny. I would never wish it had been Lizzy instead of Duke."

Manny's phone rang. He put it on speaker when Lance's name popped up. "Manny, it's Lance; we found the van. They drove East out of Adana. Our satellite moved out of position when the van reached a rural area. We were able to get a license plate number."

"Who does it belong to?"

"A man named Mesut Sari. We checked his background; he isn't involved with the Mafia, as far as we can tell. He works with his brother in construction." Manny stood.

"When do we go to his house?"

"Look, Manny, my bosses say we have to turn this information over to the local Polis. Since he's a Turkish citizen, we can't arrest him without a lot of red tape. I'm going to give it to Sergeant Demir and see if he will let me tag along to the house."

235

"I will come with you." Manny insisted.

"It would be better for you to wait for the call from the kidnappers. Can I have the CID tap your cell phone?"

"Yes. Do what you have to."

After Lance hung up, the phone immediately rang again. No number came up. He put it on speaker.

"Hello?"

"Sergeant Diaz. You have caused me a great deal of trouble." The man spoke English well but had a heavy accent.

"Who is this?"

"That's not important." There was something familiar about his voice. "What *is* important, is I have your little girl and her friend. And you have my money and drugs." Manny didn't tell him he had the wrong girl. It made no difference anyway.

"That's the cost of doing business. This can't be the first time you lost drugs." Manny said.

"That is true, Sergeant Diaz. But you have stopped the flow of my access to more, and that is not acceptable. Besides, the value of those drugs on the street is over a million dollars. Do you see my dilemma?"

"I do but using a Military Base as your funnel to get the drugs was not your smartest move. You had to know the Military would eventually find out and stop it."

"No, not at all. It has been working well for years. Everyone gets a small piece of the pie; everyone does their part, and we all walk away happy."

"What is it you expect me to do?"

"I want my money back! And the drugs too. Who says you can't have your cake and eat it too?" The voice said with a laugh.

"I can't get it back. The drugs are destroyed." That part wasn't true. They wouldn't destroy them until after the investigation was over, but he didn't think the man would know that.

"Well, you have a problem then. I have your child, and you have nothing to trade for her."

"You have kidnapped American Children. Do you really want the entirety of the United States of America coming after you?"

"They will never find me. But if you want your girl back, you better figure a way to get me the money and the drugs. You have twenty-four hours."

"How can I get in touch with you?" Manny asked.

"I will call you back." The voice hung up. No one said a word for a full minute.

"We need to call Agent Marquez." David finally spoke.

Manny sat on the edge of the hospital bed and dialed Lance, putting his cell on speaker.

"Hi Manny, I can't talk; we are on the doorstep of Mesut Sari."

"He called."

"There is no way CID recorded it. They are just now putting a tap on your line."

"I figured."

"I'm sorry, Manny. What did he say?"

"He wants his drugs and the money back," Manny said.

"What did you tell him?"

"That we already destroyed them." There was dead air on the other end.

"How'd he take that." Lance finally asked:

"He said I had twenty-four hours."

"That gives us time to locate the children." The men heard another voice in the background. Lance responded, "ok", then redirected his attention back to Manny. "Hold tight, and I'll get back to you." Lance hung up.

Somewhere East of Adana

"Paša, just text me. She said the Polis are on our porch."

"What! How on earth could they find us so fast?"

"I don't know."

"You got us into this. I need you to call Mr. Sandalli and tell him we did our part. Now he needs to come and pick up these children."

"Kader, that's not how this works. I have to hold them until the trade. Besides, I've never talked to Oguz, only to Mert his underboss."

"How did you get involved with the Sandalli brothers?"

"I didn't know it was the Mafia. I have seen how Oguz operates; he is crazy. I would never have taken a loan from him. I had no idea the man who gave me the money was a front man for the 'Brothers'. My brother-in-law told me about this guy who makes private loans when I asked him for money so Paša could finish the treatment she needed. The Sosyal Güvenlik Kurumu wouldn't pay for anything experimental...I had to, Kader. Or she was going to die!" Mesut hung his head. "I didn't mean to get you involved in this."

Kader moved over to his brother. "How did you expect to pay him back?"

"I thought I would find a bank who would loan me the money, given some time, and I could pay him back. Except no bank would approve a loan for me."

"I'm sorry I didn't have the money to give you," Kader said.

"When I couldn't pay it back on time. I got a call from Mert. He said if I did this job for Oguz, he would forgive my debt. Up until then, I had no idea the 'Brothers' were involved."

"And no one can trace the kidnapping back to them. We are the ones the Polis are after, and we are the ones going to jail if we get caught. Call and ask him when the exchange is happening?" Mesut pulled out the burner cell that Mert gave him to communicate and hit the programmed number.

"Hello, Mesut. Has something happened?"

"No. No, I just wanted to know how long before we trade."

"Sergeant Diaz said the drugs are destroyed." Mesut gasped.

"What about asking for money to cover the loss."

"The money they confiscated isn't a tenth of what the drugs are worth on the street. There is no way that man could come up with the difference."

"What will Oguz do?"

"Oguz does not believe they would have destroyed it yet. He thinks they still have it in the evidence lockup. The Sergeant lied, thinking Oguz would be willing to cut his losses and take the money in trade. He'll give up both if he wants to see his daughter again."

"I don't know how long we can stay here, undetected."

"Stay put. I'll get back to you." Mert hung up.

Incirlik Air Base Hospital

After the call from the kidnapper, the men moved back to CJ's room. Jonathan checked on his wife and son, and Manny lifted Lizzy to his lap and sat down.

"David, there is no need for you guys to stick around here. Go home and get some rest." Jonathan said. David walked over to him.

"Jonathan, I don't want to leave you guys," David put his hand on Jonathan's shoulder.

"Really, David. Zoey and I are fine. Go get some sleep." David nodded and stepped away.

"Come on, Lizzy; we'll come back tomorrow. I'll take you home."

"No, daddy, I can't go." Manny looked over to where Jonathan and Zoey were, on the other side of the bed.

"Let her stay, Manny. We'll make sure she gets some sleep," Zoey said. Manny eyed a recliner on the far side of the room and pushed it over. He switched it out for the hard chair Lizzy had been sitting in. Jonathan grabbed a couple of blankets from the closet and laid one out on the chair. Lizzy climbed up. Manny pushed it back so it would recline, then covered her with the other blanket and kissed the top of her head.

"Good night, sweetheart."

"Daddy, did you find Sophie and Duke yet?"

"Not yet. But we will, don't you worry." Lizzy still had CJ's hand in hers.

239

The men said their goodbyes to Jonathan and Zoey and headed out.

Luke walked into his home, the reality that Sophie wasn't there hit him hard as he walked in. Tears spilled out of his eyes onto his cheeks and landed on his shoes. He walked to the living room couch; he sat with his elbows on his thighs, his hand over his face. He slipped to his knees.

"Lord, I have never needed you more than I do at this moment. I trust you, Lord, with everything in me, I trust you. Please take care of my girl and Duke." He prayed, staying on his knees until his home phone rang. He reached for the extension on the end table next to the couch.

"Hello?"

"How are you doing, Luke?" David's voice.

"Not too good. How about you?"

"The same. It hit me when I walked into my house."

"Me too." Luke took a deep breath.

"I'm scared. But I trust God will take care of them, and we have taught the kids how to pray," David added.

"I know, David" He sat on the couch. "My biggest fear is that this trauma will change who she is," he paused and took a deep breath. "I don't want that. She has always been so fearless and sensitive." Luke laughed to himself as he remembered an incident and decided to share it with David.

"I remember when she was four. We lived in a duplex on base in Fort Bliss, Texas. It had a concrete walkway to the house that had a waffle pattern. Clair would tell Sophie when it was time for me to come home, and she waited for me on the steps every day. That day she was on the steps crying. I sat down next to her.

'What's wrong, sweet pea?' I asked.

'I killed him, Daddy.' She lifted up a leaf with a little roly-poly bug on it. 'I was playing with him. Rolling him in the cracks, and he stopped moving.' Tears were running down her face. 'His family is going to hate me.' I wrapped my arm around her. Thinking it would make her feel better, I said, 'Oh, I know this one, honey, he doesn't have any family.' She started crying harder.

'Daddy, he was all alone. That's so sad.'" Luke could hear a chuckle coming from the other end of the line. He couldn't help but smile at the memory too.

"So I said, 'Yes, but now he will be in roly-poly heaven, and he will have soooo many friends.' She sucked in a hiccup.

'Really?'

'Yes,' I said.

'Then we have to have a funeral for him.' She told me. We moved to the small flower bed in front of the house with honeysuckle vines growing. She dug a hole in the soft dirt, put the leaf in the ground for a cushion, and laid him on top. Then we covered it up.

'He needs a cross, Daddy.' I cut off a small piece of vine and pulled the honeysuckle off it. Using the vine, I formed a crooked cross. She laid it on the grave.

'Now Daddy, you have to pray, like they did for grandpa,' she said. So I said a little prayer. She visited that grave for a week."

David chuckled, "She really is special." Luke realized he was being insensitive.

"I'm sorry, David. I know you're just as worried about how this will affect Duke. I hope you won't hate me for saying this." He paused, wondering if he should say it out loud. "I don't think I'd survive the night if she were all alone...if Duke wasn't with her." David didn't answer right away.

"I'm not offended, Luke. I'm just as glad Duke isn't alone. Though I wish neither of them was in this mess. But I know one thing about my son and CJ, for that matter. They are born protectors. If Duke hadn't hung on to her, he would be emotionally devastated. More so than being taken with her. He would have never forgiven himself. I know when CJ wakes up and finds they are gone; he will be broken up that he's not with them," David said.

"I have never seen a group of kids take care of each other the way our kids do. I remember when Duke and CJ carried Sophie on their backs when she was so sick. Their bond is special." Luke said.

"I agree. Jonathan and I have had a strong bond since we were infants. The gifts God gave us complement each other. We accomplish more together than we would individually. But you're right, the kids have been through a lot together, they have formed a special bond." They were both quiet for a while.

"David. Thank you for calling."

"Get some rest. We have to come up with a plan to get our kids back. I'm not waiting on the Turkish Polis or the CID to do it for us."

"I agree. Goodnight, David."

Near the Turkish border

The group had walked until it was so dark they couldn't see a foot in front of them. The temperature had dropped significantly when the sun went down. Anna's body couldn't adjust. She laid a blanket on the ground using Faiz's backpack as a pillow. She kept on the winter coat she found in the supply tent and put another blanket on top of her.

Faiz could hear her teeth chattering. He placed his blanket over her. The Major and the Lieutenant did the same. Finally, she stopped shaking and fell asleep.

Anna woke up as the first sliver of light started to creep up the horizon. She rolled up the blankets to return them when the others woke. She grabbed some personal items out of her field pack next to Faiz.

Whispering, he said, "stay as close as you can and be quiet. We are not alone in this area." She nodded.

Anna found a private spot about twenty-five feet from the others. She grabbed her cloth and canteen and was able to wash up and felt better. She brushed her teeth and ran a brush through her hair. She gathered her hair back with a ribbon at the nape of

242

her neck, then wrapped the scarf over her head. Anna's blond hair would be a dead giveaway she wasn't a local. She stood and headed back to the camp. Anna froze when she heard a man behind her, whisper something in Kurmanji. Even never hearing the language before, she understood. She put her hands up.

The man moved behind her pushing her forward with the tip of his AK 47, a weapon the US still denies providing for the Kurds. He moved her closer to the camp, her eyes searching to see if anyone was looking her way. Her eyes stopped on the guard on duty. He nodded his head and moved undetected behind some trees. He hurried, planning to position himself behind the Kurd. The armed man spoke to the group who were standing with their guns aimed at him. The men moved back, lowering their weapons, and made room for the man with the AK 47 aimed at Anna.

Anna knew Private Issawi had a Kurdish mother and would know the language. He stepped forward to say something when there was a commotion behind her. When she turned, she saw the gunman crumpling to the ground. Faiz grabbed her out of the way. A couple of the men took the Kurdish soldier to the camp's center and tied him up. They didn't know how close the rest of his unit was.

The men were discussing what to do with him. Anna moved closer to the prisoner to check his injury. The guard watched closely. She motioned him to move the prisoner to a rock so he could sit and she could tend the cut on his head. She cleaned up the cut and used medical glue to close the open wound. Then she covered it with gauze.

"We are out of uniform, so we have to come up with a plausible explanation for who we are and what we are doing here." Major Jabban said.

"I have an idea. Private Issawi, will you translate for me?" Faiz asked. The men moved toward the prisoner.

"Undo his restraints," Faiz told the guard. He turned to Issawi and said, "ask his name." The man responded after Issawi translated.

"The man says his name is Simco Chelki," Issawi said. Faiz nodded and said, "translate this. We are not your enemy. We are government workers assigned by the President to track and map black market routes. He wishes to confiscate their merchandise for the State." Issawi translated it, and the man nodded.

"Tell him the President himself sent us on this mission, and he is to tell no one." Issawi translated. Although the Kurds did not answer to the Syrians, they had a truce of sorts. As long as the Kurds didn't interfere in government business, the government would leave them alone.

The prisoner stood, nodding his head. "I do not wish any trouble." The Kurdish soldier said.

The Lieutenant spoke up. "Do we dare trust him, Major? His unit could be close. If he goes back to them and tells where we are, there are not enough of us to win that battle." The Major thought about it.

"Our only other alternative would be to kill him." The Major said. Faiz turned back to Issawi. Translate this.

"They are discussing whether to kill you to protect the mission. You have one chance to persuade them you will not betray us." Issawi translated. The prisoner started repeating the same words.

"Do not kill me. I will not tell." Faiz believed him. "How far away is your unit?"

"Five miles. I was sent out to relieve the sentry watching the border. We are making sure the Turkish Army doesn't cross the border into the 'safe zone' again. We have been moderately successful in keeping them back, but every day is a new battle. We do not need trouble from both sides." Chelki said.

Anna saw that the man's uniform was threadbare and he had no jacket. She was sure he had no food either. Anna took off her coat and gave it to him. Then she went to her field pack and took out her food and brought it back to him. She didn't speak; there was no way to explain an American in their midst.

The others agreed to let him go. As soon as he was out of sight, they got as far away as possible.

CHAPTER TWENTY-THREE

Rural area outside Adana, Turkey

*I*t was quiet outside the room where Duke and Sophie were. Duke listened to the men argue, hoping he could understand a few words, but they spoke too fast.

"Duke, I need to go to the bathroom." Sophie half whined, afraid to move from her spot on the cot. Duke took her hand, walking her to the bathroom. He turned on the light and checked it out.

"It's safe, Sophie, go ahead." She walked in, not closing the door all the way. Duke went to check out the windows again, trying to figure out if there was a way to get the nails out. If he had anything flat and metal, he could do it. He started checking the bunk bed frames, looking for any piece that might be useful. Sophie came out of the bathroom.

"I'm hungry," she said. He moved back to the cot where his backpack was sitting on the floor.

"I have a juice box and three granola bars. Which one do you want?" She took a carob chip granola bar. She started to take the juice box but hesitated. He saw she didn't want to take the only one.

"We can share the juice box," he said. She smiled. They sat down and ate.

"How long will it take daddy to find us?" Sophie asked, chewing her last bite.

"Not long, Sophie, but we'll be fine. I promise." Duke put his arm around her.

As the sun went down, Duke heard the men talking again. He moved back to the door to listen.

"Mesut, we have to think this through." Kader started pacing after putting a kettle of water on the single electric burner. "The Americans are never going to give Oguz the drugs or the money. And he will never give back these kids if they don't."

"You think he will want us to kill them?" Mesut asked.

"I don't know, but I'm not killing any children! After he asks us to do his dirty work, he will kill us to tie up loose ends." Kader sat at the table across from his brother. "When cousin Nijaz married the woman from Dubai, he told me her father has hotels there. He said if we ever want to come, he will help us get visas and a job."

"And leave our home?"

"What home, Mesut! You sold your home to get Paša's treatment and still had to borrow money. You're living with your in-laws. All I have is my fire restoration business, and I can do that anywhere." He rubbed his hands over his face and through his thick black hair. "If we stay here, we are dead men, and Paša too. I'm sure the Polis and Mafia are both watching your house. We just need some money."

"Where, Kader, where are we going to get the money?"

Duke hadn't realized it had gotten so dark outside. He was concentrating so hard, trying to understand what he heard. He was going to flip the light switch when he noticed Sophie was fast asleep on her side, in a fetal position. She was using his backpack as a pillow. It was chilly in the room, so he took off his light jacket and laid it over her. He sat on the floor, using the cot to rest his back. He wrapped his arms around his legs and put his head on his knees. For the first time since this started, he let the tears he'd been controlling all day fall from his eyes.

"O Lord, I know you hear me, and You know where we are. I promised Sophie I would protect her and get her home. But You know I can't do that unless You help me. Please let my dad know where we are. I love you, Jesus. Thank you."

"We can make our own deal with the girl's father. He's an American; he can get his hands on some money." He took the water kettle that was whistling off the burner and poured some into two cups for tea. "You need to call Paša, have her shove as many of your things as she can in a duffle bag and a backpack. Make sure she gets your passports and papers. Then have her sneak out of the house."

"Where will she go?"

"Tell her to take the first bus to Iskenderun, ask her to go by my house to get my passport. It's on the way to the bus station. Give her the address of our job in Iskenderun. The owners said they weren't coming back until the restoration is complete. So the place is deserted. We will be safe there. Ask her what the Polis said." Mesut stepped outside to make the call.

Kader finished his tea and grabbed a pen and paper. He needed information from the girl. He walked into the adjacent room, flipped on the light switch, and walked to the cot. Duke watched his every move. Kader reached over him and grabbed Sophie's arm. It startled Sophie awake, and she started screaming. Duke shoved the man's arm away.

"Don't touch her!" Duke growled. Kader stepped back, putting his arms up in a surrender motion. Duke moved to the edge of the cot and wrapped his arms around Sophie so she would stop screaming.

"Need your papa name and..." his broken English was so accented Duke couldn't understand what he was saying. Then he gestured with his hand the universally understood motion for the phone.

"Sophie, I think he wants Uncle Luke's name and phone number." He whispered to her.

"Should I tell him?"

"Maybe he is going to tell him where we are." She put her hand out for the paper and wrote it down. The man took it and left the room, flipping the light off as he went.

Mesut came back into the bunkhouse. "She is leaving now."

"Good, we need to get out of here too. We cannot be here if Mert sends men to get the kids. What did the Polis say?"

"They wanted to know if I still owned the van and where I was. She told them I did own the van but sometimes lent it out, and that I was at work."

"Did they believe her?"

"I don't know. The Polis didn't take her to the station, but they have men watching the house. And she said there was an American with them."

"Can she get out undetected?"

"She thinks so."

"Pull the van out front, and I will get the children and meet you outside," Kader said. Kader opened the door to the bedroom and motioned for the children to come as he said, "come, come." Duke put on his backpack and grabbed Sophie's hand.

"Come on, Soph."

"Are they taking us home?" Sophie asked.

"I don't know." Duke doubted it.

Mesut took every back and access road he could to avoid roadblocks or Polis cars.

Duke and Sophie were in the third-row seat like last time. Sophie looked up at Duke and whispered, "I don't think this is the way back home, Duke." He took her hand.

"I don't know where they're taking us, but don't worry. If these men want money, my dad will give it to them."

It took over two hours to get to their destination at Iskenderun, taking the back roads. Mesut pulled into the building's bay area, and Kader told him to take the plate off the van. Kader slid the side door open and motioned for Sophie and Duke to come out.

Kader walked them upstairs and directed them to the master bedroom. "We're hungry; you need to feed us," Duke spoke up now that he knew the man understood English. The man nodded and left the room.

When Mesut came upstairs, Kader went to the little store down the street. He came back with bread, peanut butter and jelly, and some boxes of juice. Kader made a stack of sandwiches and took two of them, and two boxes of juice to the children. He told them to eat then go to sleep.

"Do we know when Paša's bus will come in?" Kader asked Mesut while taking a bite of his sandwich.

"She looked up the schedules when we were on the phone. The bus will stop at the Lukoil gas station at 11 pm. I'll meet her." Mesut put on a kettle of water for tea.

"In the morning, we will call the girl's father. I'll tell him we had no choice; we had to do this. That we want to give the children back but we need money to leave the country. Or Oguz Sandalli will kill us for double-crossing him."

"How much will you ask for?"

"One hundred thousand American dollars."

"One hundred thousand? How will her father come up with that kind of money? It's too much."

"He's an American. He will figure it out."

A few hours later, Mesut picked up Paša at the Lukoil gas station. Kader could hear Paša's angry voice as she stepped into the apartment. "You are taking these children home right now; do you hear me?!" Paša yelled at Kader.

"How could you do this thing? Kidnapping children. Why would you borrow money from the Mafia?" She turned to Mesut.

"I did it for you...I couldn't lose you." Mesut plopped down on a chair in the kitchen. "I didn't know the money came from the Mafia. I was desperate to get you the last treatment." His hands covered his face making his words muffled.

Paša moved over to his chair and knelt in front of him. "Look at me, Mesut." She took his hand when he lowered it from his face. "Can you imagine a world that I would want to live in while you were in jail, for life or worse, dead?" She asked.

Kader never loved a woman the way Mesut loved Paša. He watched as Mesut wrapped his arms around her. He laid his head on her shoulder, tears falling as they hugged. She kissed his cheek.

"Paša. When Sandalli demanded the money back, he threatened to kill you. He gave Mesut a choice; pay up or do this job and he would forgive the debt." Kader explained.

"Then let's take back the children and leave." She said, releasing Mesut from her arms and standing.

"Paša, we won't get very far without money," Kader said. She moved to the bedroom door to check on the children.

Paša saw Sophie and Duke lying on a mattress with only a sheet covering it. Not even a blanket to keep them warm. She searched the apartment and found a few blankets in a closet and covered them up. She went back to the kitchen.

"What have you fed them?"

"We gave them peanut butter sandwiches earlier," Mesut said.

"In the morning, you will go to the store and pick up some groceries, so I can feed them breakfast. Pick up Sucuk, Gozleme, and some Feta cheese; after they eat, we will take them home."

Near the Syrian, Turkish border

There was only an hour of daylight left when they reached the intersection on Faiz's map, hearing gunfire on and off all day. They moved fast and only took two short breaks to rest. When they finally stopped, they slept in a tight circle. The Sergeant put two men on guard duty, rotating men every three hours.

Anna whispered to Faiz, "how far are we from the border?"

"It will take another six hours to the tunnel. The border is at the halfway point in the tunnel; we will walk right under the wall. Once we come out of the tunnel, we will be passed the border guards. But we will need to wait until dark before we step out; we can't take the chance of being seen."

Incirlik Military Base 3 am

Jonathan and Zoey finally laid down on the other bed in the room about midnight. Around 3 am, CJ opened his eyes. His head hurt, and in the dark room, he had no idea where he was. He turned his head and saw Lizzy in a recliner asleep holding his hand. That's when he remembered what had happened. He pulled on Lizzy's hand.

"Lizzy, wake up." She slowly opened her eyes.

"CJ," she said too loudly. He hushed her.

"Are you ok?"

"You're the one in the hospital, silly." She smiled.

"What happened?"

"That man hit you, and you were unconscious."

"Where are Duke and Sophie?" He was almost afraid to ask.

Tears came to Lizzy's eyes, "they took them. Those men took them."

CJ was distraught, "noooo." He cried, the tears dripping onto his pillow, creating a wet spot.

That woke up Jonathan and Zoey; they ran over to his bedside.

"CJ, what's the matter? Are you in pain?" Zoey asked as she stroked his forehead. He turned his face to her.

"They took Duke and Sophie," he cried. Jonathan moved in closer. "Dad, the men, they took Duke and Sophie; I couldn't stop them."

"Son, you did everything you could. Don't worry, we will find them."

Zoey ran out of the room to get a nurse. The nurse came in to check on CJ and paged a doctor.

"How are you feeling, CJ?" The nurse asked. The doctor came in as he answered.

"My head hurts." The doctor used his light to check his eyes and then checked his reflexes.

The doctor turned to Zoey and Jonathan. "He will have a severe headache for a few days. I will prescribe something for that. But he is going to be fine." The doctor turned to the nurse and instructed her to give him a sedative so he could rest. He saw that CJ was agitated. The doctor answered Zoey's questions then left the room.

CJ kept hold of Lizzy's hand; soon, the sedative put him back to sleep.

David had texted the others to meet at Luke's around 7 am. They had to figure out how to do their own investigation.

Jonathan was the last one to make it.

"How's CJ, Jonathan?" David asked.

"He woke up around 3 am. The doctor on duty said he would have a bad headache for a few days but that otherwise, he will be fine."

"Thank the Lord." They all said.

"The first thing CJ asked when he saw Lizzy was where Duke and Sophie were." Jonathan had to gulp back a lump in his throat. "He was distraught when he found out the men took them," Jonathan said.

"I know Duke would have felt the same way, Jon," David said. He barely spoke the last word when Luke's cell rang. He didn't recognize the number.

"Hello?"

"Luke Star?" The heavily accented voice said. Luke put it on speaker.

"Yes, who is this?"

"That not matter. I have daughter." Luke stood to his feet.

"I want to talk to her."

"NO! You listen. We forced to do this thing. Not want to. If you not give drugs to Sandalli, he will tell us to kill them. We do not want to do. Need money to hide in different country. So he not kill us." Luke looked at the others; he was having a hard time understanding the man. "If give us one hundred thousand American dollars, we give you son and daughter."

"How do I know you have them? I need to talk to them." The men heard what sounded like the man walking, a door opened, and more walking.

"Daddy?" Luke collapsed into the chair.

"Sophie, are you alright?"

"Yes, but I need you to come to get us, right now, Daddy!" She started crying. "is CJ…" The man grabbed the phone and gave it to Duke.

"Uncle Luke?"

"I'm here too, Duke."

"Dad, we couldn't stop them. How's CJ?"

"Duke, you did everything you could. CJ is going to be fine."

"And Lizzy?"

"She's fine too. They are worried about you."

"Dad, you need to find us…" At that point, Kader grabbed the phone away.

"Enough. You give money; we give children."

"There is no way I can come up with that kind of money fast," Luke said.

"How much?" David wrote on a scrap of paper, fifty thousand.

"Fifty thousand," Luke said. There was silence on the other end for a long time.

"Ok, fifty thousand. I call back at 3, tell you where." Luke clicked off the line and racked his hands over his face.

"I'll have to go to the bank and get a loan. Can they do it that fast?" Luke's leg was bouncing.

"Don't worry about it. I'll get the funds." David insisted.

"We need to tell Agent Marquez and CID," Manny said.

"No, Manny. I'm not taking any chance they get in the middle of this and mess it up. Let them deal with Sandalli until we get our kids back. Then we will tell them everything we know," David said. Luke agreed. Manny sat, looking at them, weighing it up.

"I'm good with that, and now we know it's the Sandalli Mafia family. We had no idea who we were dealing with. But are you good with letting these men get away with this?"

"Getting our kids back is the only thing I care about. The Turkish Polis can chase them down once we give them the information." Luke said.

"Can you live with that, Manny?" David asked.

"Yes. I'll keep working with the CID. Can I tell them who we're dealing with?" He looked around for agreement.

"I don't think that will affect our plans. But won't they want to know how you got that information?" David asked.

"I'll tell them it was a confidential informant," Manny responded.

Do what you need to," David said. Manny headed to the door when his cell rang. The caller was anonymous. He put it on speaker.

"Hello?"

"Sergeant Diaz. Do you have my drugs and money yet?"

"I do."

"Do you know where the rooftop café is in Adana?"

"Yes."

"Meet my man there at 2 pm."

"No."

"If you want to see your little girl again, you will do as I say."

254

"No. If I'm going to risk everything by stealing from the evidence locker. Then you are going to have to risk something too. And I want to look in the face of a man who would kidnap children. You want your drugs and money; then you meet me yourself." Diaz said. He had discussed this move with the Turkish Polis and CID. They wanted to get whoever was running this operation, not some minor player. They had no idea who they were dealing with at the time.

There was no sound on the other end. Manny looked at his phone to make sure he was still connected. Then he heard a laugh.

"Sure, why not. Just you and me?"

"Yes."

"Be there on time; I will leave at 2:01."

"I'll be there. You better have the children with you. No garbage about giving me their location later. Got it!" Manny said. He heard a laugh again.

"Sure. No problem." That was the last thing said before the man hung up.

The others let out a collective breath. "Manny, are you sure you're not walking into a trap?"

"I'm sure it is, but the Turkish Polis and CID will have snipers in place. We planned for every contingency; the best-case scenario was a public place. CID doesn't know it's the Sandalli Mafia family yet. Oguz is the only brother left. Cenk is dead, and Kaan is in jail, captured a year ago. If we get Oguz, it might be the end of this Mafia family for good. The other families will fight for control of their territory, I'm sure. But that's a problem for the Turkish Polis."

CHAPTER TWENTY-FOUR

Iskenderun 9 am

*P*aša took breakfast into the bedroom for Duke and Sophie. She saw Sophie's hair was a mess and brought back a brush to fix it. Sophie was hesitant at first but then let the lady fix her hair. Paša put it in a ponytail, humming a tune while she did.

Mesut's phone rang. "Hello?"

"Mesut, where are you? I sent a man for the children, and he said you were not at the bunkhouse." Mert spits out.

"We had to move. The Polis went to my in-laws looking for us. We knew they must have the van's plates, so we moved and hid the van." Mesut explained.

"Where are you? I need them here by noon. We are making the exchange at 2." Mesut didn't answer right away. "Did you hear me?!"

"Yes… Yes, I heard you. We'll have the children there at noon. I shouldn't tell you where we are, over the phone. In case someone is listening."

"You better be here at noon." Mert hung up before Mesut could say anything else. Kader saw the color drain from Mesut's face.

"What do we do, Kader?"

"We need to make the exchange now. Then get out of the country."

Kader called Luke's cell.

"Hello?"

"Luke Star, you must come with money now," Kader said. Luke put the phone on speaker. Manny had gone to CID headquarters, and Jonathan had gone back to the hospital, so David was the only one still there.

"The bank isn't open. I don't keep that kind of cash at my house. What's going on? We made a deal," Luke said.

"Sandalli called. Want children by noon. Mad we moved. He will come looking. Must go by 11."

"How far away are you?"

"One hour and half," Kader answered.

"The bank won't be open until ten. Then it will take at least an hour to have that much cash available. There is no way we can do it." More silence on the other end.

"How much here by 11?" Kader asked, desperate. Luke put his phone on mute and discussed it with David.

"I have three thousand in my savings, but I can only get one thousand out of the ATM a day," Luke said.

"I have money in savings too, but with the same ATM restrictions. Jonathan will take that much out for us. I don't know if Manny has that much in savings, but I can promise to give it back to him." David said. Luke took the phone off mute.

"All we can get out of the ATM is four thousand dollars. If you want it by 11, you'll have to accept that." Kader let out a long breath.

"Ok. Be at Lukoil station Iskenderun at 11. I will take you to children." Kader hung up. Mesut had heard everything.

"Can we make it to Dubai on that?"

"I have eight hundred in the business account. With that, and the four thousand, it should be enough. We'll take the company truck. It has all our tools; we can get work when we get to Dubai. And the Polis aren't looking for it." Kader ran his hands through his hair. "I don't trust Mert to wait. He will send someone to find us."

Sandalli family residence outskirts of Adana

Oguz's demeanor changed when he heard Mert's conversation with Mesut. He turned to his underboss, "I need you to find out where Mesut is. He works with his brother Kader. Find out where their last job site is and check for other vehicles." He turned back to his coffee. "I don't trust them. There was no reason for them to leave the bunkhouse or not tell you where they were."

"You do not believe the Polis tracked the plates from the van?" Mert asked.

"I know they did because I had a man at Mesut's house. They said the Polis showed up. But the bunkhouse was the safest place for them. It had no ties to them at all. Something else is going on."

"You want me to pick up his wife for security?" Oguz thought about it for a moment.

"Yes."

Incirlik Military Base 9:30 am

Before David and Luke met Manny and Jonathan at the ATM on Base. Luke drove David to his house to grab his gun. Luke already put his in the glove box.

"I'll pay you both back," Luke said to Manny and Jonathan. Jonathan laid his hand on Luke's shoulder.

"If you even try to. I will be offended. We are in this together." Jonathan and Manny agreed.

Luke grabbed an envelope from above the overnight deposit bin and slipped all the money in it.

"I want to come with you," Jonathan said.

"No, you stay here, backup Manny at his meeting with Sandalli. Luke and I can handle this," David said.

Then he and Luke got in the car and headed to Iskenderun.

Near the tunnel at the Turkish border

The gunfire was getting closer. The small troop tried to stay behind cover wherever possible. They were moving at a good clip since the first ray of light, trying to get to the safety of the tunnel.

The Major had two men moving parallel on both sides as lookouts. His orders were to keep within visual range.

"How far are we from the tunnel, Faiz," Anna whispered.

"Another 12 miles." He responded, grabbing her arm, keeping her upright when she tripped over a vine.

"Thank you." She said, being more vigilant with her steps.

One of the guards ran over to the Sergeant. The Sergeant motioned to the others to follow him. There was a large rock and a few thick bushes about 20 feet east. He directed everyone to stay quiet behind the cover.

Anna could hear men speaking Turkish, not Kurmanji. The Turks cross the border into the Safe Zone through the broken wall. They kill any Kurd who they find in what is supposed to be the unoccupied Safe Zone. It wouldn't matter that they were not Kurds. The fact they were in the Safe Zone was enough reason to kill them. It also didn't matter that the Turks weren't supposed to be there either.

The Turks crossed their path about 20 yards away in front of them. They were oblivious to the small troop hiding close by. They waited for an extra ten minutes before they moved and got back on the trail.

Iskenderun 9:45 am

"Sophie," Duke whispered after the women left. "This window isn't locked. I'm going to tie these blankets together, and we can use them to scale down the wall to the ground." Sophie's eyes got big.

"You want us to use blankets to get down there?" Sophie looked out the window. "It's too far down, Duke. I'll fall."

"No, you won't. Don't worry; I'll be at the bottom to catch you if you slip." Sophie kept arguing. Duke used the grapevine knot he learned in Boy Scouts to tie the blankets together. He pulled on the knot to make sure it wouldn't come apart. He pushed the bed closer to the window and tied one end to the bed frame.

"Go to the bathroom; it could be a while before we find another one." Sophie did as he said. Duke opened the window a slow as he could to not make noise.

When Sophie got back, he crawled over the bed to crawl out the window. He stopped, positioned himself, so his feet were on the outside wall, preparing to propel down.

"Watch me, Sophie. Do it exactly as I do." Sophie got on the bed and watched him drop into the alley next to the building.

"Ok, Sophie, now grab the blanket and climb out." Sophie kept shaking her head. Duke kept coaching her using a stage whisper. "You have to, Sophie. We need to find a way to get home." Finally, she grabbed the blanket and crawled out the window. She didn't position her feet against the wall and slid down as far as the knot, letting out a small gasp.

"Sophie, put your feet on the wall like you're walking down it." She made it to the bottom, and the two of them ran to the back of the building.

The town was small, and there weren't any businesses open yet. Duke was afraid the kidnappers heard Sophie when she gasped. He started looking for somewhere to hide. Most of the buildings were no more than two stories high with flat roofs. He looked for one with ladder access to the roof. Two blocks down, he saw what he was looking for, and they climbed up to the roof. Duke wasn't sure what to do next, but at least now they were away from the kidnappers.

10 am

"Boss, I sent Sevket to pick up Mesut's wife." The Underboss said, moving to the table Oguz was sitting at on the patio. The smell of the ground lamb, onion, and garlic coming from the Lahmacun Oguz was eating, caused his mouth to water.

"Good, where did he take her?"

"She wasn't there," Mert said. Oguz put down his tea.

"They have double-crossed me. I knew it." Oguz slammed his fist on the table, causing his cup of tea to rattle on the saucer.

"Did you locate them?"

"I think so. Kader has a permit to work on a job in Iskenderun."

"You need to get there now! Kill them and bring me the children." Oguz shouted, standing up and moving back indoors. "And I want you to do it yourself. Take Sevket with you."

"Yes, sir."

10:45 am

"I'm going to the Lukoil in case they get here early. If the traffic is light, they could be here soon. Load up the business truck and be ready. As soon as we get the money, we need to leave." Kader instructed.

Kader walked to the gas station. He leaned on the side of the building, peering out on occasion to see if anyone pulled in. He was nervous, afraid that Sandalli may have figured out where they were. He took in a deep breath, trying to calm himself. He could smell the spicy sausage on the grill the gas station made to sell to its customers.

At 11 am, Kader heard a car pull in. He looked around the corner and saw a man step out. When the man bent down and spoke English to the car's driver, he knew it was the Americans. Kader stepped out from the side of the building and next to the man. He motioned down the street and got in the back seat.

Luke drove in the direction the man had pointed. Kader put his hand in the front seat and pointed right.

"Stop," Kader said. Luke pulled over in front of a closed business and put the car in park. Kader got out of the car and motioned them to follow him. Luke grabbed his gun out of the glove compartment and put it behind his back in his belt. Kader took them up the stairs to the apartment. When they stepped in,

Mesut and Paša stood up. Kader moved over to stand with them. Luke and David closed the door behind them.

"Money," Kader said. Luke pulled it from his jacket.

"Kids," Luke said. Kader pointed to the bedroom door. Luke handed him the envelope and headed to the door. When he opened it, no one was there.

"Where are the kids?" He came back out and got in Kader's face, grabbing his shirt. Mesut ran to Luke and tried to pull him off Kader.

"In room," Mesut said in English. They all moved to the room. David saw the window open.

"Luke, over here. They escaped through the window." Luke and David scrambled for the door to find them.

Kader stopped, "Mesut, take the construction truck and hide until I can help them find the children. Then I'll take the van and meet you. I'm worried Oguz will send someone. We need to get out of here." He handed Mesut the envelope of money.

"Where will you meet us?"

"Just past the park is an old, abandoned logging road. Drive on it until no one can see you from the road. I'll call you once we find the children." Kader left to catch up with the Americans.

David and Luke were behind the building, calling out for Duke and Sophie. Kader caught up to them; he suggested they split up. David went South down the alley. Luke went North, and Kader went to the front of the properties. Shops were opening up, and customers were moving in and out on the sidewalks. Kader asked the shop owners and customers if they had seen a little boy and girl. No one so far had seen them. He was nearly back at the gas station when he saw a black SUV whiz past him and stop at the building they had just vacated. He hurried back to the alley to warn the others.

He found David. "Men! Oguz men, they come. We must go."

"There is no way we are leaving without our kids." David text Luke to come back and meet up with them.

Duke had been walking the perimeter of the roof, trying to figure out what to do. He knew most of the shops had opened. He figured he could ask to use one of their phones. He told Sophie to wait while he went down to ask.

"You can't leave me here alone, Duke! I'm coming with you." He tried to calm her down.

"You are safer here. I'm only going next store. I see people going in and out of there. I can call my dad. Sophie watched as he climbed down the stairs to the alley. Duke's foot touched the ground as a man came around the corner and grabbed him from behind, under his arms.

Sophie started yelling, "let him go; let him go." She screamed louder and louder. She started down the ladder. Duke was squirming and flailing his arms, trying to reach around, and hit the guy. Duke had the guy twisted around, his back to the ladder. Sophie got almost to the bottom; she turned around on the ladder and grabbed the railing backward. She started kicking at the man's head.

Sophie's first scream alerted everyone. Luke, David, and Kader headed in the direction of the screams from both ends of the alley. Sevket heard Mert yell for him to come.

Luke was the closest. When he had a visual of what was happening, he rushed to reach the man holding Duke. He kept punching the man in the kidneys. Mert let go of Duke and arched his back, letting out a gasp of pain. He turned to defend himself. Sevket came around the corner and pushed Luke off of Mert. Sevket grabbed Luke's arms from behind and held him up while Mert started punching him in the gut. Luke doubled over in pain. David got there and put Mert in a chokehold. Kader grabbed one of Sevket's arms and twirled him around. Luke got free, and they wrestled Sevket until they had him contained on the ground. David still had Mert in a chokehold. Mert was grabbing unsuccessfully at David's arms, trying to pull them off. Luke came up and punched Mert hard in the gut and again in the face. Mert

264

crumpled to the ground with David's arm still around his neck. David let go and pulled out his gun, telling Kader to translate.

"Stay on the ground, or I will shoot you dead." Kader translated. Luke searched the men and grabbed their guns.

"Daddy, Daddy." Sophie started screaming for him. She was still on the ladder. He ran to her and swung her off the ladder and held her close. Duke wrapped his arms around his father. David wrapped his free arm around Duke while holding the gun on Oguz's men.

"Are you alright, son?" David asked.

"I am now," Duke replied.

Luke put Sophie on the ground to check her over, making sure she wasn't injured. "Daddy, I knew you would find us." Throwing her arms around his neck again. Luke tried to stand, but she wouldn't let him go, so he lifted her with him and went to check on Duke.

"You ok, Duke."

"Yeah, Uncle Luke. How did you guys find us?"

"We'll explain later." Luke turned to David. "We need to get out of this alley. Let's take them back to the apartment and figure out how to handle this."

Kader interpreted David's instructions to the men on the ground. They all headed for the apartment. "Kader, do you have rope or duct tape?" Kader nodded and went to the van in the bay area and grabbed the duct tape.

Kader duct-taped the men to the kitchen chairs. Once they were secured, the men took a deep breath — while Sandalli's men kept shouting something over and over again.

"What's he saying, Kader," David asked.

"He is saying we are dead men." David walked over and picked up the duct tape from the table, taping the men's mouths.

David, Luke, and Kader moved to the other end of the room and spoke in whispers. Duke and Sophie sat on the couch, furthest from the men taped to the chairs. "It's 11:30. If we have the Turkish Polis arrest these men before Manny has his meeting with Oguz, he won't show up. They will lose their chance to arrest him," David said.

"And how do we know if any of the Polis are on the Mafia's payroll?" Luke added, looking over to the men squirming in the chairs.

"He will know when children not come back with men," Kader added in his broken English.

"He's right." David leaned against the wall by the door of the apartment.

"What if we send a text to Oguz from one of the men's phones? We could say they have the children, but their car broke down. Maybe that would satisfy Oguz."

"We could add that they already sent for another ride, so Oguz doesn't send help," Luke added.

"What do you think, Kader?"

"Yes. Could work." Kader took Mert's phone from his pocket and sent the text. In less than a minute, a response came.

Are Kader and Mesut dead?'

Kader sucked in a breath. He knew Oguz would kill them but seeing it confirmed shook him.

Yes. Kader texted back.

Will you make it here by 2?

"Kader, tell him he may be a little late," Luke said. Kader was already sending the message. A response came back.

Don't worry. If the children are not here on time,
I will kill the father and take the money and drugs.
I was thinking of doing that anyway. I can sell
the children. Make extra money.

"We need to call Manny and let him know," Luke said. Luke and David opened the door to step outside to call when Sophie came running.

"Daddy, where are you going. You can't leave us." He bent down in front of her.

"I would never leave you, princess. I just need to talk to Uncle Manny. I'll be right here on the stairs." He hugged her tight and stepped outside.

Manny answered on the first ring. "Do you have them?"

"Yes." Luke could hear Manny tell Jonathan the kids were safe.

"Manny, we have two of Oguz's men here. If we have the Turkish Polis come for them, Oguz will know, and you will lose your chance to arrest Sandalli."

"You're right. I can send two of the CID team members after them. We can hold them here until the sting is complete. Then they can turn them over to the locals," Manny said.

"We thought the same thing. We don't know who on the Polis force is on Oguz's payroll…" Luke hesitated. "Manny, Oguz plans on killing you and taking the money and drugs."

"We already have a plan in place for that possibility. You just get back home safe with the kids. I'll see you when this is over. Give me the address, and I'll send CID now."

"Thanks, Manny, but David and I plan on being at that meeting with you. You're not doing this alone."

"We'll talk when you get here." Manny signed off. They stepped back into the apartment.

"I go," Kader told the men. They nodded. "I sorry, no want to do."

"Where are you going."

"Far away."

"You will have to come back for the trial," David said. Kader s eyes got big.

"No, no." He shook his head. "I go to jail."

"No, Kader, we will get you an immunity deal?" David added.

"What?"

"You won't go to jail. We'll make a deal for you." Kader nodded.

"I need your phone number to get ahold of you when it goes to trial." Luke pulled out his cell and asked for Kader's number. Kader gave it to him, and Luke entered it in his contact list.

"I go." Kader left, David and Luke nodding at him in way of goodbye. They had mixed feelings about letting him go. They had not yet gotten past the anger to accept Kader's claim that they were forced to do it. But there was no question that Kader and his brother would be dead if Oguz found them. So they let him go.

CHAPTER TWENTY-FIVE

Near the tunnel at the Turkish border, NOON

*T*he small troop sped up as the gunfire got closer. The perimeter guards stopping them more often to hide as they encountered both Kurds and Turks, roaming the Safe Zone.

Faiz turned to the Major, who was walking behind him. "The tunnel is up here." They stopped at a small copse of trees and bushes. Faiz pulled a large bush out of the ground, it hid a wooden plank covering the tunnel entrance. The bush was planted in a plastic container.

Faiz pulled off the lid and used his flashlight to show the men the ladder that went down ten feet into the tunnel. The Sergeant went down; first. Faiz was last; he replaced the lid over the entrance, then pull the rope coming through a hole in the lid. The container holding the bush was attached to the other end of the rope. When he pulled the rope, it yanked the bush back into place.

Faiz moved back to the front of the line. Everyone had their flashlights out and pointed to the ground except Faiz, who had his leading the way.

It took ten minutes to reach the middle of the tunnel that passed under the border wall. When they got there, dirt and rock blocked the passage. Everyone stared in silence for a moment. "Faiz, what could have caused this?" Anna asked.

"They made some repairs to the wall a few years ago. It must have caused the tunnel to collapse."

"What do we do now?" The Lieutenant asked.

"If it was from work on the wall, then the tunnel may only be caved in a few feet. We could dig through it," Faiz said.

"But the dirt will keep coming down and maybe even part of the wall if we don't support the ceiling," The Major said. The Sergeant spoke up.

"We can take the ladder apart, use the wood to make a false ceiling, a barrier halfway down. If there is enough to support the cave-in, to within a few feet of the other side, we can dig a small tunnel underneath, and we could get through." The Sergeant's father was an engineer. He spent many hours at his side, inspecting earthquake-damaged buildings. His father's job was to make them stable enough so first responders could hunt for survivors. They all agreed it was worth a try.

It took 45 minutes for them to feel the makeshift ceiling was stable enough. They started digging a test hole underneath it. Private Kilic and Private Issawi grabbed their field shovels from their packs. Private Kilic laid on the ground and started digging a hole. Private Issawi took the dirt he shoveled and moved it out of the way. If this didn't work, they would have to abandon the plan and get across the border some other way.

Private Kilic had dug four feet; there was no sign of breaking through. He was almost at the point of no return.

He dug one more foot...two feet...three feet.

With the next shovel of dirt, he yelled. "We are through!" The Sergeant inspected the ceiling, and it hadn't shifted at all.

"Ok, on your way back, make it wide enough for us to crawl through and pack the sides with your shovel for extra support."

"Yes, sir," Kilic responded.

Twenty minutes later, they and all their field packs were through the tunnel and in Turkey.

They reached the end of the tunnel an hour and a half after they first stepped foot in the tunnel.

"We need to wait until dark before we leave. It's all desert between here and the closest town." Faiz said.

"Faiz, you said you knew someone who could get ahold of General Tabib Ozer?" The Major asked as everyone found a way to make themselves comfortable.

"I have a friend that can help you," Faiz said.

Adana near the Rooftop Café, 1:45 pm

Ruby had agreed to meet David and Luke in the parking lot of a big-box grocery store. She was standing outside her car when Luke pulled up. A smile as broad as her face came up as soon as she saw Sophie and Duke in the back seat. David got out of the passenger door and opened the back door for the kids. Ruby ran up to them as they got out and swallowed them up in a big hug, kissing them over and over on their faces.

"Aunt Ruby!" They both yelled as they wrapped themselves around her.

"I missed you so much." Her voice cracking as tears fell.

"Can we go see CJ and Lizzy?" Duke asked. Ruby nodded, telling them to get in the car. Sophie went up to her dad.

"Daddy, aren't you coming?" She asked, hugging his waist. Luke knelt in front of her.

"I have to help Uncle Manny for a little while; then, I will meet you at the hospital. OK." He kissed her forehead and stood. Sophie hesitated, not sure she wanted to be away from her father.

"Come on, Sophie, let's go." Duke hollered as he got in Ruby's car. She nodded and went with Ruby, looking back as she got in the car.

Luke locked the car, and they walked to the building across the street from the Rooftop Café. Manny was in the lobby to meet them. They moved to an office that the Polis and CID had commandeered. When they stepped in, they saw the commotion. Everyone was busy with a job, getting ready to take down one of Turkey's most notorious Mafia heads.

Agent Marquez went to greet them. "Sirs, Sergeant Diaz just informed me you were able to locate your children. I wish you had not done that on your own, but since you were successful, the point is moot." He moved them away from the entrance. "Agent Pamela Hill is working undercover on this." He caught her eye and motioned her over. He looked at David, "she will act as your date.

You will ask to sit outside, preferably on the westside; it's our blind side. CID and the Polis stationed men on the roof, above us with a sniper and a spotter, Jonathan is with them. Luke, you'll stay inside at the bar. We have two men undercover inside — one behind the bar and one a waiter. Manny will walk in at exactly 2 pm." He looked at his watch, "you better head over there now, Manny. Do you have your earpiece?"

"Yes," he grabbed the two duffle bags, looked at his friends, and left.

"Let me get you set up with comms so you can hear and speak if this goes awry." He walked over to the tech who was handling the computers and communication systems. When he came back, he handed them each an earpiece. "Ok, let's do this."

David and Agent Hill left first, heading across the street. Luke waited a minute and did the same.

Manny sat at a table on the rooftop. He saw David and Agent Hill come in and sit on the other side. He looked at his watch. It was 2:05. Manny couldn't see Luke seated at the end of the bar inside. "Oguz is late." He said it so those monitoring could hear. *Maybe he found out we rescued the children,* he thought. Luke broke in.

"I see him; he's walking in now."

Manny saw a man in an Alexander Amosu suit, flanked by two bodyguards wearing Hugo Boss. They walked out to the rooftop seating. The man looked around and spotted Sergeant Diaz; a smirk came on his face. He turned and said something to his men. They stayed at the doors as he walked to the table.

"Well, well. I wasn't sure you would be able to meet my demand, Sergeant Diaz." Oguz said as he seated himself. A waiter came up and tried to hand them menus. Oguz waved him off but asked for coffee for him and his guest. It was apparent the man was a regular when the waiter acknowledged him by name.

"Where are my children, Mr. Sandalli?"

"They will be here. There has been a slight delay." He looked at the duffels at Manny's feet. "Is that for me?" Oguz asked, nodding to the duffels.

"Yes, but they don't move from this spot until I see the kids."

"Yes, yes. I just want to inspect them. Please, open them up so I can see you are not trying to trick me." Manny unzipped them both and opened the bag far enough so Oguz could see from where he was sitting. A big smile came on his face.

"Good. Now I need you to re-establish my distribution line." The waiter came with the coffee. Manny zipped up the duffels and waited to respond until the waiter left earshot.

"No way, that was not the deal. I got you what I promised," he nodded to the bags. "You give me back my kids. That was the deal." Oguz laughed.

"You have cost me money, Sergeant. You will do what I say, when I say, until I say. And the children will stay with me until I decide." The smirk came back on his face again. "Or maybe I will decide to sell them and recoup some of my money." Oguz laughed. Manny had never heard such an evil laugh. This man was as evil as they came. Manny pushed the bags over to Oguz.

"I'm not sure I can do what you want." Manny knew they had what they needed to prosecute Oguz on tape now. The Polis just needed to wait until Oguz picked up the bags before they arrested him. Oguz pulled a gun. "I can kill you right now. But I need my distribution line re-established."

"I'll do what I can. But how can I trust you to give me back my kids?"

David saw the gun come out. "Do something," he said through the comm.

"We can't; we need him to pick up the duffels." A voice he didn't recognize responded.

"I'm not going to wait until he shoots Sergeant Diaz," David said.

"Oguz is in our crosshairs. We have Diaz covered. Don't do anything."

Oguz lowered the gun, "I planned to kill you, but I believe you can do what I asked. So for now, you are more valuable to me alive." He stood, "you will have to trust me that I will return your children." Oguz picked up the bags and turned to the door.

That was when everything broke loose. The undercover waiter and bartender pulled their guns on the bodyguards. And men in Polis uniforms came running out onto the rooftop toward Oguz. When he realized what was happening, he grabbed Manny around the neck, pointing his gun at his head. He spoke to the Polis in Turkish. But it was obvious what he was saying.

"Put your guns down, or I will shoot the American," Oguz ordered. The Polis kept their guns pointed at Oguz. David and Agent Hill were the only ones that were out of Oguz's peripheral vision.

"Jonathan, do they have a shot at Oguz?" David whispered.

"No, it's too risky. Can you get behind Oguz, without him seeing?"

"Major Scott, stand down," came a voice interrupting them. "Agent Hill will take the lead."

"David and Agent Hill moved slowly behind Oguz. Their weapons drawn. Agent hill stepped behind Oguz. She placed the barrel of her gun against the back of Oguz's skull, and speaking in Turkish, said.

"Put it down before I blow your head off." Oguz hesitated, trying to assess his chances of getting out of this alive. "I said, put it down. NOW!" Oguz dropped his gun and raised his hands.

He turned to her after one of the Polis officers cuffed him. "You will pay for this."

"Yeah, Yeah. I heard it all before from scumbags like you." She responded in English as the officers hauled him off.

David couldn't help but laugh at her bravado. "Well played, Agent Hill." She holstered her gun and smiled at him. David went to Manny and put his arm around his shoulder. "You gave me a scare there for a minute, buddy." Manny nodded; he was shaken up.

Luke came out of the cafe and walked over to his friends. He hugged Manny. You ok, man?" Manny nodded again. Agent Hill picked up the duffels and caught up to the Polis.

"What do you say we go see our kids?" Manny smiled, his hand still shaking from the adrenaline. The three of them walked together off the rooftop.

It took the men two hours before they could leave. They each had to give an account of what happened here and in Iskenderun. The Turkish Polis Chief was not happy with them. They had acted without authorization in his country. However, they did have Oguz Sandalli and four of his men in custody, thanks largely to them, so he forgave the oversite.

They drove into the hospital parking lot at 5:30 pm. When they walked into CJ's room, everyone was glad to see them. Sophie hopped off the bed that all four of the kids had managed to fit on and ran to her dad and hugged him.

"Look, Daddy, CJ is all better. They are letting him go home in the morning." She pulled him over to the side of the bed, then hopped back up. "And Lizzy held his hand the whole time and took care of him. Didn't you Lizzy?" Lizzy smiled and nodded.

Luke looked at her, "yes she did. She took real good care of CJ." Luke looked at CJ. "Do you still have a headache?"

"Yes, Uncle Luke, but it's not as bad. I feel better now that David and Sophie are back."

"Why don't we head down to the cafeteria and get this group some food." David said, happy to see the kids back together.

"Guys, what do you want to eat? Uncle David and I are heading to the cafeteria." Jonathan wrote their orders down on a notepad that sat on the bedstand and left with David.

In the tunnel -Turkish side of the border. 6:30 pm

Faiz looked at his watch. He knew it would be dark by seven. He also knew that a group this size would look suspicious in a little town like Reyhanh. He was afraid someone would call the Border

Patrol to check them out. His best chance was to get ahold of David and have transportation there when they arrived.

It would take two hours or more for them to walk through the desert in the dark. It would take about the same time for David to get there from Adana.

Faiz took the Major aside. "Sir, I'm going up to try to get reception on my phone. We need to have someone waiting for us when we arrive in Reyhanh." The Major agreed.

"Can you find a way for me to contact the General?"

"Yes, I have a contact that can get his number." Faiz climbed the ladder and slowly pushed up the lid and plastic planter until he could see from a small opening. He couldn't see 360°, but there was no one in his line of sight. He removed the lid and the bush and crawled out. He immediately replaced the bush so no one who came upon him would see the tunnel.

Faiz had documents for him and Anna. He had no idea at the time that they would have company when they snuck across the border. He spoke English well enough he could pass as an American.

Faiz moved away from the opening to some bushes that were about twenty-five feet away. He managed to get three bars on his cell and dialed David.

The hospital on Incirlik Military base.

Jonathan put their orders in with the lady behind the counter. David headed to the cashier to pay for the food. His phone vibrated; he saw that it was Faiz. He handed Jonathan the cash and moved away from the noise to answer the phone.

"Hello."

"David, I need your help."

"Of course, Faiz. What can I do for you?"

"I have Anna, and we have crossed into Turkey." David collapsed down into a chair, stunned, not believing what he heard. "David, are you there?"

"You have...Anna?" He covered his face with his hand. Jonathan looked over at him to get help to carry the food. He left the food when he saw David's face had gone pale.

"What is it, David?"

"Faiz has Anna." Jonathan took the seat next to him, speechless.

"Is she alright, Faiz?"

"Yes, David, she is fine. I don't have much time. We are waiting in a tunnel until it gets dark, then we will walk to Reyhanh. It will take us about two hours. But there are 12 of us, and we will attract too much attention. I only have papers for Anna and me."

"Twelve people. Who is with you?"

"We have ten Free Syrian Army soldiers who traveled with us. The President wants them in prison or dead."

"Just tell me what to do, Faiz."

"Can you meet us in Reyhanh? I also need the private number for General Tabib Ozer."

"Ozer? The head of the Turkish Army?"

"Yes, he trained these men. They believe he will let them attach to his command until there is an Administration change in Syria."

"That may never happen."

"I know David, but they believe the General will help them."

"We will leave immediately. Is there a hotel in Reyhanh? I can call ahead and get some rooms. That way, you would be off the streets."

"I have only been there once before when I smuggled a family across the border. I think there is a motel on the main street."

"I'll check it out. Call me when you get close to the town. I'll let you know about the General and if I was able to get you rooms."

"Is Anna close? Can I talk to her?"

"I'm sorry, David. She is in the tunnel."

"Ok. I'll get there as soon as I can. Be careful."

"Pray God makes us invisible."

"I will do that." David hung up, stunned by the news. Jonathan's voice brought him back to the moment.

"David, I'm going to call Manny to come get the food we bought. We can let him know what's happening." David stood.

"I'll get the car." David started to the door.

"No, you're too shaken up. I'll get the car. You tell Manny what's going on."

David and Jonathan spent the first half-hour of the drive praying. They asked the Lord to make the group invisible to the Border Patrol. Then he got online and looked for a motel in Reyhanh.

David called the hotel and reserved and paid for four rooms. He told the desk clerk that his brother might get there before him and asked him to give his brother the keys. Then he asked if there was a restaurant close to the motel and asked for the number.

Getting the private number for General Ozer was going to be more difficult.

"Jonathan, who do we know who could get the General's number?"

"Manny has a friend in the Turkish Polis. But I don't know if he would have the kind of clout it takes to get a General's private number." Jonathan kept his eyes on the road.

"What about Agent Marquez? He might be able to get it from someone in intelligence?"

"I'll call Manny and see if he can do that." David called Manny. Manny didn't ask any questions. He just said he would do it and hung up.

Dusk came at 6:45 pm, and Faiz removed the bush from the exit of the tunnel again. Once everyone was out, he put it back and took out his compass. He checked his coordinates projector to make sure he could navigate once there was no light left.

The moon was full and allowed them to move through the desert at a good clip. The Lieutenant heard a sound in the distance. He motioned for everyone to stop and lay flat on the desert floor.

"What is it, Lieutenant?" Faiz whispered.

"It could be a patrol vehicle." The sound of an engine became more recognizable. As it kept getting closer, they laid on the desert floor, praying. A dark cloud covered the moon and made the desert pitch black. The sound of the vehicle started to move away. They waited a few more minutes lying on the desert floor before they moved.

The One Who Stayed: Sophie's Story

CHAPTER TWENTY-SIX

*T*he group made it to Reyhanh in less than two hours. Faiz dialed David.

"Hello."

"David, we are behind the hotel trying to stay out of sight."

"I have reserved four rooms. I told them my brother would come in and pick up the keys. It might be good to take Anna in with you."

"Thank you, David."

"There is a restaurant next door. If you go in and have them call me, I can pay for food for everyone."

"I will do that. No one has eaten much in two days. Thank you."

"We are only a half-hour away." They ended the call, and Faiz and Anna went to the office and picked up the keys.

Anna took a shower; she wanted to look her best when she saw her husband for the first time in over two years. She used the hairdryer on the wall, but it only caused her hair to frizz up. Anna didn't have a curling iron to control it, so she put it in a ponytail. She looked at herself. Her face was so thin. *Will he even recognize me? What if he's moved on? He must have thought I was dead. Will he still love me?* The thoughts brought tears to her eyes. She didn't know what to expect; she would know soon enough.

Faiz ordered food at the restaurant next door. When he stepped in, the aromas coming from the kitchen made his stomach growl. Aden helped him take the carry-out containers back and hand them out. Anna sat there, moving her food around.

"Anna, you must eat," Faiz said. Anna looked up at him, tears welling up in her eyes.

"What if he doesn't love me anymore?" Faiz moved next to her and put his arm around her.

"Anna, he has never stopped looking for you. He loves you more than his own life." Faiz pushes the food in front of her. "Eat, please." Anna ate so Faiz wouldn't worry about her.

David's leg started bouncing. "What's wrong with you, David? God has answered our prayers." He took his eyes off the road to look at him.

"Jonathan, Faiz said she lost her memory. She won't know who I am. She won't remember she once loved me. Jon, If Anna doesn't love me..." David bowed his head.

"We'll take it one step at a time. Annie's back and safe now. That's the most important thing." David knew he was right. But the thought she wouldn't know that she had loved him since they were teenagers broke his heart.

They pulled into the parking lot behind the motel, looking for the room number. Jonathan spotted the room and pulled in a parking space right in front.

Anna ran to the door when she heard the car and opened it, as David stepped out of the vehicle. As he closed the car door, he looked up and saw her in the doorway. David's knees buckled, and he reached his hand out to the hood of the car to keep from dropping to the ground. He bowed his head, and tears made tracks down his face. He was frozen.

Anna walked over to him. "David?" When he heard her call his name, he collapsed onto her; his head fell onto her shoulder as he wept.

"Anna. You're back." His weight was more than she could support, so she slowly slid him to his knees, clinging tightly to him.

The men were in the doorway of their rooms. It was hard to turn away from the raw emotion in front of them. Jonathan finally moved away, walking into the room where he saw Faiz. The men from the other rooms all moved to the Major's room to find out what would happen to them next. They closed the door so David and Anna could have some privacy.

"Anna, do you remember me?" David asked as he leaned away from her. He put his hands on both sides of her face, not feeling the hard pavement under his knees.

"Yes, my love. God restored my memory." She kissed his lips and laid her head on his chest.

"Oh, Anna. I thought you had forgotten me." He held her close and kissed her cheek. "I was so lost without you."

"I was afraid you moved on."

"Never. I would have looked for you until my last breath." He said, pulling away from her face again so he could look in her eyes.

"How is Duke? Has he forgotten me?" He saw the anguish on her face. Fear that her son might not remember her.

"No, of course not. It was hard for Duke, your disappearance. But time allowed him to accept it. He believes you are alive somewhere. He has never stopped praying you would come home." David lifted the two of them off their knees, brushing debris off her dress and his jeans.

"Did you tell him I'm back?"

"I needed to see it for myself and make sure you were ok, first." He held her face again. "He's with CJ at the hospital."

"What? Is he injured?"

"No, CJ was, but it's a long story. I'll tell you on the ride back. Let's go inside and find out what we can do for these men." He kissed her again and took her hand.

Everyone in the motel room turned to them as they stepped in. Their red puffy eyes in stark contrast with the big smiles on David's and Anna's faces.

"David, do you have General Ozer's number?" Faiz asked after giving him a big hug. David pulled his phone from his pocket, dialed the number, and handed it to Major Jabban.

"Selam?"

"General Ozer," Major Jabban stood as if the General was in the room. "Sir, my men and I have left Syria." He went on to tell him about being put on the terrorist list. The Major listened as the

General spoke, then responded by telling the General he released those who wanted to go home. Faiz translated for David, Jonathan, and Anna.

"Major Jabban, I can have a transport pick you up in the morning. I will have papers for you that show you are assigned to my command as part of the Bilateral Exercise Detail. That way, your men can get a paycheck from the Turkish government. Then, in time, if you wish, I can arrange to have you and your men join our ranks in the Turkish Army." The General paused. "You know it is not likely your men will ever be able to go home."

"I know, sir. Thank you." The Major looked around at his men. He knew these men loved their country, but their country had turned against them. He told the General their location and hung up. He took a deep breath and addressed his men, advising them of the General's offer. The men were grateful, finally letting it sink in; they could never go home again. The Major excused everyone to their rooms. He asked the Lieutenant and Privates, Kilic and Issawi, to stay.

When the others had left, the Major stepped up to Anna and took her hand.

"I can never thank you enough for introducing me to Jesus." Aden translated what he said. The Major pointed to the Lieutenant and Privates Kilic and Issawi. "We are infants in our salvation, but we trust God will send others to help us grow."

"Major Jabban, you will always be in my prayers. I have never seen such a powerful conversion as yours and Lieutenant Arabi's. I know God has a mighty work for you to do."

David spoke up. "Major, I would like to contact you from time to time, if you are stationed close to Adana. Would that be alright with you? I want to bring you Bibles, and if you like, Jonathan and I could help guide you through the Scripture."

"Yes, we would appreciate that."

"May we pray with you?"

"Please." The group gathered close together, and David, Jonathan, and Faiz laid hands on the new converts. The power of

God fell on them, and balls of fire touched the tips of their raise hands. They prayed for over an hour.

The small group of believers stayed in the room talking about the Lord for another hour. David noticed that the rooms had a small refrigerator and a microwave. So David and Jonathan made a trip to the restaurant and ordered food for all the men for breakfast. Then they said their goodbyes.

It was 11 pm before they left Reyhanh. Faiz was in the front seat with Jonathan. David held Anna close to him in the back seat. He told her about the kidnapping and how CJ was injured.

She sat up and gasped as he was telling the story. "They are all safe and home now," he rushed to tell her. She relaxed back into his arms.

"I have so much to catch up on," she sighed. David pulled out his phone.

"I need to call Dad and Jared."

"But, love, what time is it in Texas?"

"It doesn't matter. This is news that can't wait." He dialed his father first.

"Hello?"

"Dad. Are you awake?"

"Sure, I'm up having my first cup of coffee. How are you, son?" He could hear his father take a sip of his coffee.

"I have someone here who would like to say hi." He handed Anna the phone but put it on speaker first.

"Mr. Emmett." It is how Anna has addressed him since she was a young girl. They heard something crash to the floor.

"Dad, are you alright?"

"Annie, is that you?" They could hear him pull out a chair.

"Yes, Faiz got me out of Syria a few hours ago."

"Are you hurt?"

"No, I am fine."

"We looked for you, Annie. We looked for you for a long time. We couldn't find you." Emmett's voice tightened, trying to keep back the tears.

"I know Emmett, but God had a plan, and now he has brought me home."

"Does Jared know?" Emmett asked. David spoke up.

"We are calling him next, Dad. But we need to make arrangements for Faiz. Once the Syrian President realizes he has defected, he will put a bounty on his head. Faiz was one of his confidants."

"I'll call the Pentagon. There are a couple of generals over there that owe me big time. I'll have them cut through some red tape for asylum papers. Then Jared will come to pick him up. Will he be safe with you for a few days?"

"Yes, he can stay with us."

"Ok, son, I'll start making calls..." He took a deep breath.

"Annie, I'm so glad God brought you back to us. I love you."

"I love you too. We'll do a video chat soon, ok." They said their goodbyes and then called Jared. His response was as moving as his father's. Anna was emotionally exhausted. She finally laid her head on David's chest and fell asleep. David held her tight, afraid this might be a dream and she would disappear.

It was almost one in the morning when they pulled into the hospital parking lot. David roused Anna.

"Wake up, sweetheart, we're at the hospital." She stretched a little and rubbed her eyes. They all walked into the hospital, trying to avoid nurses and receptionists. Afraid they might hinder them visiting at such a late hour.

They stepped into CJ's room. Zoey was lying on the empty hospital bed. Duke was in the recliner next to CJ.

"Do you want to wake Duke, Anna?"

"No, David, it might startle him too much. You do it. I'll wait over here." Anna moved next to the door. Jonathan moved to wake his wife, and Faiz stood close to Anna.

David moved to the recliner and whispered. "Duke, wake up, son." Duke stirred a bit and half-opened his eyes.

"Hey, Dad, where did you go?"

"I had to go pick someone up."

"Aunt Zoey said I could stay with CJ tonight."

"I know, son; I just want you to wake up for a moment." Duke pushed the foot of the recliner so the back would come up. He saw some people in his peripheral vision. He rubbed his eyes.

"Mom? Mom? Dad is that mom?" He whispered. Duke stood to his feet, still not sure if he saw clearly.

"Duke, it's me." She took a few steps toward him, not wanting to overwhelm him with her emotions. He walked closer, and she opened her arms; he ran to her.

Jonathan shook Zoey's shoulder so she would wake up. She sat up on the edge of the bed and brought her hand up to her mouth to cover her gasp as she saw Anna in the room hugging Duke. The commotion woke CJ, and he sat up. The sudden movement caused his head to hurt.

"Auntie?" Anna looked up at CJ while still having her arms wrapped around her son. "Auntie!" he got out of bed and stumbled over to hug her. Zoey got off the bed, and the three of them had their arms wrapped around Annie.

The others looked on, lost in the moment they had waited for, for so long.

TO

BE

CONTINUED

The One Who Stayed: Sophie's Story

FROM THE AUTHOR

I hope you enjoy seeing how Sophie grew up.

I wanted this book to demonstrate that everyone has hard times during their life. It is not the tragedy that defines you but how you handle it. As humans we want God to take away all of our problems. But then how would we ever grow.

If we become aware of our own failings, we can then strive to overcome them. Like the characters in this book, God will give us the power to be overcomers.

L J